FRAGMENTS

BOOK ONE OF THE SEEKERS SERIES

J. A. WEBB

FRAGMENTS (THE SEEKERS SERIES, BOOK 1), BY J. A. WEBB

Lonely Rock Press, LLC

Lonely Rock Press, LLC edition: October 2024

Copyright © 2024 by Lonely Rock Press, LLC

Print Book ISBN: 978-1-965915-02-8

eBook ISBN: 978-1-965915-00-4

Audiobook ISBN: 979-8-228315-66-2

Cover design by Jenneth Leed, InkMarker Design

Editing by Deirdre Lockhart of Brilliant Cut Editing

To learn where to buy this book or for more information about this and the author's other books visit: jawebbauthor.com

Library of Congress Cataloging-in-Publication Data:

Webb, J. A.

Fragments (The Seekers, #1) / J. A. Webb 1st ed.

Printed in the United States of America

✿ Created with Vellum

Thrilling Christian fiction . . . where the seen and unseen worlds collide.

PREFACE

It is the year 2158, and Hegemony has fallen.

But the Order, the one-world religion, remains . . . securely
ensconced as the unseen power behind all human government.

Should any desire for truth be rekindled in the hearts of men,
the Order stands ready to stamp it out. . . .

CHAPTER 1

F ather Curtis, priest of the Order of the Eternal, entered the room and faltered midstride, gagging at a sudden nausea. An unnatural chill penetrated his bones. By instinct, he searched for the source of this unseen assault, even as his conscious mind rejected the possibility.

Carved marble walls, high-coffered ceilings, and intricate tapestries framed the space, all a backdrop to the table where, at its far end, a man sat. Curtis's stomach lurched again. The bishop? Why in the Eternal would he be here?

Impossibly handsome, the bishop could've been a statue of a god.

Still, Curtis shivered to be in his presence, the man as devoid of human empathy as the cold marble from which the room had been carved.

The bishop leaned forward.

Curtis stiffened. Time slowed. His vision swam. The room elongated, and the granite table narrowed, stretching away like a highway disappearing into the distance.

Something like a spider's legs began crawling, prying at his mind. He closed his eyes and concentrated on his breathing.

Of all the overactive imaginations! Get yourself together, Curtis.

Under control now, he approached the end of the table where a footman held a chair.

He sucked in his breath. Lind, the high prosecutor, sat near the bishop. The Bloody Inquisitor was at this meeting? What could they think he'd done?

When Curtis bowed toward the two, the weakness in his legs threatened to unbalance him. He sat, eager to be off his feet, and locked hands between knees to still their tremors.

Across the massive slab, the bishop remained motionless, fingers steepled before his lips. His pinkies began to move, tapping to some unheard melody. He tightened his eyes into slits, and a veil behind those golden-brown orbs fell away, revealing something unwholesome deep within.

The vision vanished. Perhaps Curtis imagined it.

"Nob." The bishop's single word lingered.

Was that a question? Was Curtis supposed to answer?

Both the other men sat unmoving and silent. The bishop cocked his head to one side, then the other.

Curtis shivered again. Carrion birds oft moved that way, inspecting potential prey.

Prosecutor Lind spoke. "Tell us who you know in the land of Nob."

Curtis rocked backward. "I don't think I know anyone."

"Someone has been sending letters to Nob." Lind's parchment lips wrinkled in a frown. "Troubling letters. Our servants have reason to believe it is you."

"I didn't send them." Curtis stiffened his spine and squared his tall runner's frame. "I sent no letters to Nob."

The bishop remained motionless.

Heat prickled Curtis's neck, moving into his hairline. He was innocent, but who could guess what game these politicians played?

The bishop nodded toward Lind, who pulled a nearby gilt cord.

A servant appeared, flourishing a hand of invitation toward Curtis. "If you would, sir, please follow me."

Was he expected to leave with no further explanation?

Lind had focused on a sheaf of documents. The bishop examined his fingernails.

Curtis's jaw hardened, his chin rising. He didn't deserve this. He stood, his now rock-steady hands flat on the cold granite. "I've done nothing wrong. Why did you summon me?"

The two yet ignored him.

He allowed himself to be chivied from the great hall, through a maze of stone passageways, and to a set of massive wooden doors. There, the servant gestured for him to leave.

He planted himself. "What's this all about?"

He deserved an explanation. Preferably with an apology.

The servant glanced at a door guard who grasped Curtis's shoulder, eased him through, and shoved his bag into his chest.

At the force, he stumbled backward. Outside, he spun, then dodged as the doors closed.

The resounding boom echoed.

PROSECUTOR LIND ROSE and strode to the room's rear. There he slipped past a concealing tapestry and into an alcove where Maripol waited, watching through the one-way fabric.

His black hair and eyes, his diminutive, lithe frame, draped as it was in plain black robes, made him seem not to be a man at all, but another, darker shadow.

"You saw him," Lind said.

"Yes, your grace."

"Do you believe him?"

"I am uncertain."

"Do whatever is needful, but make certain."

Maripol nodded. "My men will already be on him. He'll not

reach his destination." He bowed and vanished into the secret ways of the palatial temple.

~

FATHER CURTIS STOOD where the guard had deposited him atop massive stone stairs outside the temple. He craned his neck to the inscription carved into its fascia—Order of the Eternal. He had served the Order his entire life. This was supposedly his mother temple. So why did he feel so little affinity with this building or those who dwelt within?

This unexpected summons and ill-treatment reinforced his opinion. Those who clawed to positions of power cared not for the people they swore to serve. This ostentatious edifice was a monument to misplaced priorities, a physical manifestation of everything wrong with the Order.

He blew out long and hard as if he could expel his disgust, then began the winding descent to the street. From this vantage point on the tallest hill, all the city center was visible. The government sector was nearest, a collection of squat soulless buildings. Farther down, these newer structures gave way to a sprawling jumble where old brick warehouses began their untidy march to the waterfront, the sun shimmering on the river beyond.

What a rate of change in this, the Capital of the Republic!

As a child, he'd known this city during the last days of Hegemony. But away at boarding school when the Bad Times eclipsed Hegemony's dark days, Curtis never witnessed it first-hand. He'd only journeyed back well after the Committee restored order.

Then the ruins of this once great city stood as twisted reminders of its former glory, silent testimony to the ravages of the Bad Times, the broken streets a wasteland, the buildings burned-out husks, the once thriving population nearly extinct.

Now, after over a decade of Committee rule, the Order unseen behind it, the city had transformed anew. Again the sounds of life and commerce thrived. From the market came the shouts of fishmongers announcing the morning catch, the mingled voices of the crowds haggling over wares. Somewhere a traffic cop blew his whistle, and a diesel engine roared. A baby cried.

He descended the grand stairway and eyed a nearby bike taxi, but the few lonely bills rubbing together in his wallet precluded any such luxury. So he faced the two-mile hike on foot, the new cobblestone streets making for easy walking.

He shouldered his bag and settled into a comfortable pace. Long, lean legs ate up the distance, and his muscles warmed to the effort. He resolved to enjoy the lovely fall day, the crisp air, the sun soaking into his skin, but the familiar malaise overtook him. For weeks, he'd tried and failed to shake this. Now, it seeped into his every fiber, leaching all pleasure, replacing warmth with an aching chill, well-being with jaw-clenching apprehension, bleeding all colors to gray.

Had it something to do with this summons to Capital?

Meeting with that bishop was enough to make anyone uneasy, certainly. Could the current fray over Nob, whatever it was about, be the reason for this sense of doom? If so, why did he still feel it? The sense something bad hovered over the horizon remained, not abating, but increasing like a threatening storm—like the cloud in his dream.

His dream. He shuddered.

CHAPTER 2

L ars lifted the last chair out of the freight car, the fine wood bursting aglow as it entered the daylight. The sun's rays gathered in the grain's translucent depths, so much like the internal radiance of white-hot coals in a fireplace. He ran his hands over the glossy finish, buttery silk beneath his fingers. This was a kind of magic—to take a pile of sticks and transform them into something like this, a masterwork of art.

"Hey, dreamer," his brother, Leif, interrupted. "Wake up and help me carry. The agent's waiting."

Together, they carried the stack into the new restaurant, the last of today's delivery. This load, impressive in the freight car, now looked pitiful in the large, empty dining room.

His family had fought to win this contract, their zeal borne of desperation, but today's delivery was only the first of many needed. Their millwork shop had struggled to produce quickly enough to satisfy the client.

Today, the officious little man inspected the tally sheet, his mouth twisted above sweaty double chins. "Your contract specified you would deliver by the twenty-first. I see only a quarter of the chairs and no tables. Where's my furniture?"

Leif, as usual, fielded the question. "Sir, we've promised to deliver on time, and our promise stands."

"I fail to see how at the pace you've moved so far. Do I need to find a new supplier?"

Leif's neck muscles corded, then relaxed. "No, sir. All your furniture is in the shop, being assembled as we speak. I'll be back next week with half the tables and another quarter of the chairs. You have my word."

Unlikely—even if the family worked nights and weekends. Lars kept his opinion to himself.

The little man jabbed a stubby finger into Leif's face. "I have a restaurant to open the first of the month. I'd better have all my furniture by the end of next week. If I don't, I'll exercise my rights. I *will* seek an alternate supplier, and I *will* back charge you whatever it costs."

"You can't do that." Heat flared, and Lars surged forward, his own finger pointing. "The contract says the twenty-first, not next week."

Leif pushed Lars back with one arm, holding a placating hand toward the agent. "I said you have my word. We'll deliver on time."

"I'll ruin you before I let you delay the grand opening."

The little man waddled off. Before opening the door, he paused. "Capital may seem large, but the business community is small. Word travels fast. Your failure to perform has not gone unnoticed. You should give that some serious thought." He gave a smirking double tap to the side of his nose and left.

Leif forked his fingers through his hair, tugging at the roots of the blond mat, mouth tight and eyes burning.

The unbroken expanse of shining wood floors, mirror, and glass was so very big. And so very empty. No way they'd fill it in time. Was it the fumes of fresh paint making Lars's stomach turn? "What are we gonna do?"

Leif released a frustrated growl and punched the air. "I

shouldn't let him get to me." He took a long breath and blew it out. "He can't change the deadline. We have a contract."

"What if he's telling the truth?" Lars crossed his arms. His brother may be the family salesman, but Lars wasn't buying anything.

~

MARIPOL EXITED THE SECRET WAYS, now in the deepest bowels of the temple. He stepped into a wide stone corridor and to his office, where he began to clear his desk.

An athletically built young man knocked on the frame of his open door, his tight-fitting blacks visible beneath an open acolyte's robe. "I was told to report to you immediately."

He must be one of the new men, fresh from the academy. Maripol pulled on an unadorned black traveling cloak. "Is our car ready? You brought your kit?"

"Yes, sir. Good to go."

"Button your robe. When on a mission, you are to remain in character at all times." They traversed the underground tunnels toward the carpool. Maripol held a flat electronic tablet to his ear. "Report." He listened, then said, "Keep your eyes on the target. I'm en route."

~

LARS CROSSED THE TERMINAL, his boot steps echoing off polished concrete. The next northbound wagon train, the express, was due within the hour. They'd be home by breakfast tomorrow. He licked his lips, considering Mom's hash and eggs, and the tightness in his gut eased a bit.

He strolled to the lumpers' waiting area, poured a cup of overcooked coffee from the stained pot, and gravitated toward the least filthy window booth. He sat and rested his elbows on the table, blowing steam from the acrid brew before testing a tentative sip. The stuff was as bad as it looked. He pushed it aside. He didn't need the caffeine that badly, not yet.

Beyond the window, a familiar figure strolled past, draped in the black robe of his calling. A dark look marred the man's normally friendly face, and a frown creased deep into tanned skin. Thick black eyebrows bunched above eyes narrowed in concentration. Lars knocked on the window and waved to get the priest's attention.

Recognition sparked in those dark eyes, and Father Curtis stepped closer, his face relaxing.

Lars pointed toward the passenger entrance, jumped up, and headed toward the main lobby. He gave a formal bow before they laughed and caught each other in a backslapping bear hug.

"What a shock to see you here." Lars eased back. "What brings you to Capital? Why didn't you tell me you were coming? We could have traveled together."

Again that dark look passed over Father Curtis's face. "I didn't know I was coming myself." Then his smile brightened, and his laugh lines returned. "But what a pleasant surprise. Perhaps we can enjoy the ride home together. At least, I assume you're returning?"

"Yet tonight, I hope. We delivered a load of furniture. Leif'll be here once he mops up the paperwork."

Father Curtis's face faltered. Mention of Leif often had that effect. Aside from their age difference, Lars and his older brother could be twins. They shared sun-streaked hair, broad shoulders, and devotion to the family. But Leif could be difficult.

"Wonderful. We'll have some quality time together, then, the three of us."

"Great. Can you wait here while I let Leif know where I am? If he doesn't find me, he'll get grumpy."

"No need. I'll go with you."

They entered the lumper's lounge as Leif emerged from the freight yard. He sauntered over and collapsed onto an old bench against one wall. "Surprised to see you here, Father."

Father Curtis grunted, crossed one leg over the other, and locked his hands over his knee. "Did your business go well?"

Lars winced but didn't answer, deferring to his older brother.

Leif rocked his hand in a so-so gesture. "It's a tough time. Gotta fight for every credit."

"But you passed your quarterly audit?"

"Oh no. They couldn't make it so easy." Leif raised that hand as if in surrender, then flopped it to the table. "Now they're insisting on an inspection."

"Now?" Father Curtis cocked his head. "Don't they do that at the end of the year?"

"Yeah, unless a company fails to meet goals. And we failed." Leif snorted. "The overseers gotta have their fat cut. Give it to 'em, or they make you wish you had."

The blaring air horn of an approaching engine shook the walls, dust rattling from the rough board ceiling. Father Curtis grumbled to his feet, and Lars joined him and his brother in a line of overall-clad men. A conductor stood guard at the glass door, barring the way. Outside, the great engine passed and halted. The wagon train dragged with it a cloud of dust, diesel fumes, and brake smoke, which continued to float past after the train had stopped.

When it cleared, the conductor unbarred the barricade, and the workers fanned out to intercept their respective boxcars.

Lars led the way to their freighter where faded white letters spelled "Northwoods Millworks" on weathered brown wood siding. Someone had already connected the freight car—a wooden box fifty feet long and set on rubber tires—to the rest of the train.

Their family business used the old hulk to make deliveries. For generations, they'd operated the company, and through toil and turmoil weathered even the Bad Times.

Would this proud heritage now meet its end?

He winced. To avoid disaster, something had to change soon. But what? Everyone in the family already worked day and night.

And each day brought more challenges, new problems, little progress, and less hope. He couldn't imagine life without the family business. It was inconceivable, unacceptable. And it would kill Dad.

Curtis craned toward the train's far end, dozens of cars to the rear. "I still remember seeing one of these things for the first time. As a child, I had read old stories about the pioneers crossing the prairie in covered wagons, so when I heard the Committee planned wagon trains to ship freight, that picture came to mind."

He gestured from one end of the long train to the other. "Imagine my surprise when the first one came roaring into Northwoods. We all ran out to see it, and here came this monstrosity. Over twenty of these big freight cars all hooked together like an actual train, but rolling down the road on huge rubber wheels." He chuckled. "Orange crates on roller skates."

"Yep." Lars waited for Leif to climb up and unlock the cab door. Then he grabbed a railing and swung onto the massive coupling, braced himself, and offered Father Curtis a hand up the narrow iron ladder. "I remember that day. For a little kid like me, it was a sight to see. Seemed like the world was going places back then, big and modern. Exciting."

Leif grunted. "The Committee figured a cheap way to move stuff. That it's dangerous doesn't matter. They have private vehicles, so why would they care?" He took the driver's position. "I'll take first watch, for as long as I can, anyway. You ever drive one of these things, Father?"

"No." Father Curtis surveyed the cramped space with its rudimentary instrument panel and rough wooden bench. "I've spent all of my time in the passenger compartment."

"Want to give it a try?" Lars cuffed his friend's shoulder. "Might be handy to have a spare driver."

The priest's lips pressed together, but an eagerness flashed in his eyes. Almost childlike, it eclipsed the dark brooding there earlier. "If you think I can do it?"

"Not much to it." Leif wiggled a knob with his left hand. "This is the brake control. You keep it in whatever position this light panel tells you to." He pointed at a display of lights, now unlit. He then gripped a control at his right. "This is the steering. The front wheels are steerable. A line of cars this long tends to wander back and forth. It's our job to keep 'em going straight. If you don't, the rear cars will whip, which can be a real bad thing."

Seeming careful of slivers, Curtis slid himself closer to Leif and the controls.

Lars had recently finished his own driver's training. He scooted forward. "That's the main reason each car has a cab with a driver. That and braking on downhill grades."

Father Curtis frowned. "Doesn't the engineer do that?" As they gave him uncomprehending stares, he held up both hands, palms forward. "I just assumed. That's how the trains I knew did it. Before the Bad Times, I worked summers loading cars at a grain terminal, proper trains on steel rails. Those had lines connecting the air brakes on each car. The engineer had control of everything."

Leif rolled his eyes. "All that hardware costs. Any idea what most drivers get paid?"

Father Curtis pulled a jacket from his bag and folded it to make a cushion before reclaiming his seat on the splintery bench. "I confess I don't."

"Some, like us, are hauling their own cargo. The professional drivers work for little more than food and board, and they double as lumpers when it comes time to unload. Gruel and a bunk are cheaper than hardware."

"Still, wouldn't it be safer?"

"Life's cheap too, or haven't you heard?"

The light cluster lit up and blinked. Leif released the safety catch on the brake lever and, with a series of clicks, advanced it to the neutral position. Far ahead, the murmur of the great engine increased to a beefy roar, and the line of cars jerked, bucked, and jerked again. The wagon train moved forward, accelerating. With air horns blaring, it left the terminal siding and hit the main road north.

MARIPOL WAS A SEASONED AGENT, a zealous man, and a soldier for his god. When duty called, he responded, even when it required him to do terrible things, unspeakable things . . . necessary things, all done for the greater good.

He valued other men with a similar devotion. The two now before him were of another type. Callow men of no conviction. They stood rigid, eyes forward and backs pushed against the train station's rough brick wall as if they faced a firing squad. It wasn't far from the truth.

Tonight, their lack of diligence earned them assignments guarding the cold, cold labor camps in the far north. There, failure to pay attention to detail would guarantee a slow and certain death. They would return better men for the lesson—*if* they returned.

Now, raising his voice over the roar of an incoming wagon train, he jerked his chin toward the first man. "Go over it one more time, starting at the beginning."

"He entered the station where he met someone he seemed

to know. They separated, and he went into the restroom. We took up positions in the lounge, waiting for him to return."

"We never took our focus off that washroom," the second agent cut in. "And there isn't another exit, not even a window."

Maripol adopted his customary steely coolness. It would take more than this to shatter his control. "How long before one of you went in after him?"

They glanced at each other. Then the first man leaned forward, a plea evident in his posture. "He never exited. He vanished without a trace, sir."

Maripol couldn't help it. He rolled his eyes. "You missed him when he exited."

"No, sir. I swear to you." The man's voice rose in a desperate pitch. "Inspect the surveillance cameras. No one wearing robes of office left the washroom—on my life, sir."

"Indeed, it is." Maripol glared at him, only letting up when his assistant exited the building and dashed toward him. "What did you find?"

"Cameras show him meeting a young man. They separated. The target entered the restroom, and the young man walked to the ticket window. The target exited the restroom in street clothes. The two met in the lobby and walked to the freight terminal."

The failed agents paled.

Maripol gave them a wide smile, baring his teeth. "I believe we'll have a conversation with the ticket agent."

CHAPTER 3

The wagon train had departed Capital Station in the early evening. For some time, Curtis watched Leif's use of the controls. Now, certain he understood the system, he shifted to adjust his makeshift cushion. Goodness, this bench was hard, and the vibrations were numbing his nethers.

The setting sun still glared through the side windows, but Lars had fallen into a deep, snoring slumber.

Leif pulled out a pipe and stuffed it with tobacco, the sharp smell of the leaf wafting. He lit a match and was about to touch it to the pipe, but stopped short, apparently seeing Curtis's pained expression. With a sigh, Leif blew out the match and stuffed the unlit pipe back into his shirt pocket.

They rode in silence. A rare fast transport whizzed by, moving northbound at blistering speed, breaking the monotony, and eliciting Leif's only words since the station. "Whoa, you don't see that every day. Those things haul—I mean they really haul, don't they?"

Curtis nodded, preparing first one, then another opening gambit. None seemed right. Maybe this wasn't the time?

The evening sky retreated in deepening shades of red,

chased by the indigo band of leading night. The last long tree shadows faded into the dusk. He shifted toward the side window to see the countryside since the small windscreens bracketing the front door offered only a view of the freighter ahead.

As the last of the sunset retreated, an arcing concrete overpass blocked all view, limiting the sights to the shadowed beams of the road overhead. Graffiti scrawled garish reds and yellows high on the abutment, too deep in gloom to be deciphered.

Then the night sky again filled the window, bright in comparison to the dark space, and Curtis flinched when an impact shook the boards only inches above his head.

Leif growled something unintelligible. "Jerks. They hide on the overpasses and throw rocks on the wagon trains."

What could have happened had the object come through the front windows? Curtis shuddered. "Who? And why would they do such a thing?"

Leif grimaced and opened his mouth, but something flashed in the periphery of Curtis's vision, lit momentarily by the running lights, high in the space between their car and the one ahead. He rocked forward, craning to the top of the windscreen but there was only the empty sliver of night sky, stars lost in the red glare.

"Did you see that?"

Leif squinted an eye. "See what?"

"Something out there on top of the cars."

Leif pursed his lips. "Probably the trash they threw at us blowing off."

No. Curtis had seen something. Or someone. But holding this position to watch the sky was cramping muscles. He shifted back in his seat, readjusted his cushion, and rested his head back.

Eyes closed, he drifted into somnolence with the rocking of

the car, the drone of tires. Then something like a dark cloud passed over his soul, drawing him again into the dream.

Now red desert sand, scorched and lifeless, blew in drifting tendrils across the cracked plain, the moaning of that arid wind the only sound beneath an unnaturally low ceiling of roiling yellow-gray clouds. This shattered, rocky terrain blurred to the horizon, broken only by pyramidal heaps of debris.

He stood on the summit of one, a crowd at the base—people he loved, his parishioners, his adopted family. He'd seen many of them born, watched them grow, officiated their weddings, and sat by their sickbeds. Had buried parents and even children.

Not knowing what he waited for or why, he now stood watch, focus on the far horizon, dread in his heart, vigilance rewarded when distant movement rippled.

A form appeared, like a dust storm but darker, stranger. It moved toward him, toward his charges, with unnatural speed, its surface undulating a bizarre nauseant motion.

Pulse hammered his ears. His leg muscles twitched to run, but where?

The power of the thing vibrated the earth, pulsated the air, thrummed his being. Its approach deafening.

He shook himself, breaking the paralysis. He must protect his flock. But what could one do against such?

His hand was going numb where it gripped the lantern, his fingers turning white. Of course! What does one use to fight darkness, but light? And that fast-approaching wall, rumbling ever nearer, was nothing if not darkness.

He hoisted the lantern and called for his people to draw close, to come into the light. They scrambled up the slope, desperate and afraid.

The looming darkness overwhelmed. Within the murky cloud, twisted shapes—amorphous, unwholesome things—

writhed and frolicked. They emanated an aura of rage, of insatiability, a desire to devour and destroy.

He shouted a warning and raised his light to drive back the darkness.

The churning mass closed in, the forms clawing, clutching, pulling the slowest and weakest into the unseen depths.

The wind rose to a scream. Gravel pelted him, drove him backward. His light, of little use before, was extinguished in the gale. His body lifted on the wings of the hurricane. Blown higher and higher away from his flock, he uttered a final despairing prayer.

Anguished screams rose from his people's throats as they were rended, torn, and consumed, their death throes hidden in the mists far below.

At his own soundless scream, he snapped awake, heart pounding.

Again.

The dream had come again.

Arms flailed, reaching for some hold on reality. His hands found the edge of the rough wooden seat. Right, the wagon train. Leif.

This dream was always disorienting. Always left a vague sense of foreboding which persisted and haunted his days.

But this time, there came something new. A certainty that, unless he averted the coming tragedy, the consequences wouldn't end there, in that dream world. No. Ramifications would forever change his life and those of all he loved.

Gripped by this certainty, he could no longer avoid this current matter. He rubbed damp palms on his knees. Purged his lungs, straightened his back, and held to that grip on reality. Focused on time and place. "So, Leif. We've missed you at services."

Leif gave a careless wave. "Work and kids, you know, it leaves little time."

They rocked along. Of course, such indifference was a mask, a camouflage for the deeper waters beneath. But how to get through? The inability became a physical pain. The warning of the dream afresh. But how can you help someone who refuses to engage?

Curtis groaned. He knew the answer, knew it a thousand times over. You can't. All you can do is be there, if and when. So he would be. And he would wait, not knowing if his vigil would ever produce fruit. And somehow afraid he'd never have another chance.

He moved his cushion closer to Leif, settling in shoulder to shoulder, his hands clasped as if reciting the devotions. "Leif, I care about you a great deal. If you ever need to talk about anything, absolutely anything, I'll always be here for you. No judgment, just a friend."

Leif jerked a shoulder. "Sure, thanks."

What more could be done? Searching for some kind of answer and receiving none, Curtis leaned against the rear wall, legs outstretched, the shadows sliding by the windows. Passing security lights lit the cab, then vanished.

With the darkness outside complete and no landscape visible, he again nodded off. He jerked back to awareness when a red light shone on the dash and Leif applied the brakes, hard.

Still asleep, Lars rolled off his seat. "What? What's going on?"

Leif wrestled the steering lever with one hand while bracing against the corner post with the other. "I dunno. It's the middle of nowhere."

Curtis had put out a leg to stop from sliding off his seat, nearly missing the doorframe. He gawked at that foot, barely anchored on the narrow wooden structure. Scant inches in either direction, his leg would have gone through the flimsy windscreen.

"Some express train." Lars picked himself off the floor. "Probably a breakdown. So much for breakfast at home, huh?"

In the operator's seat, Leif pointed. "Is that a lineman's light?"

Soon, the yellow light reflected off the weeds in the fence line. It bobbed and then stopped, bobbed and stopped until it came into full view along with the man carrying it. He approached the driver's side of the cab and tapped.

Leif released a catch and slid down the side window.

"Got a situation in a passenger car—couple men hurt, maybe one dyin'. Gonna be stopped until the constable sorts it out. Just hold tight and watch for commands."

"I'm a priest." Curtis leaned toward the window. "Can I offer any service to the injured?"

"If you're a priest, reckon so." The man jerked a thumb. "Second passenger car. Follow me."

Uninvited, Lars joined Curtis, and they hurried to keep up. Curtis slipped on his jacket, left partially unzipped to reveal his clerical collar.

They climbed the gangway into the narrow passage. A crowd had gathered toward the far end. The lineman led the way down a corridor between private cabins. Inside one, a uniformed constable stood over a man covered in blood. A medic provided aid, but the man appeared to be conscious.

When Curtis rushed forward, the lineman stopped him. "Father, not that one." He gestured for him to hurry. "This one up here."

Curtis pivoted to follow. Lars was tracing the number 3 stenciled on the door, his expression thoughtful. Curtis snagged his friend and followed the lineman. At the car's far end, a young man lay on the floor, handcuffed to a pipe. Blood trailed from one nostril and dribbled onto his tight-fitted black outfit. Another man knelt over him, applying chest compressions.

The unconscious man's opened shirt revealed a tattoo over

his heart, a stylized eye. Curtis grunted and clamped a hand over his own stopped heart.

Another chest compression drew the fabric higher, covering the tattoo.

Released from the shock of memory, Curtis snapped back into his role and performed last rites.

The man attempting CPR stopped, checked for a pulse, and shook his head. "I think he's gone."

"Huh." A gruff voice spoke from behind, and the constable edged in closer, worrying his uniform hat between two hands. "Guess I tapped him too hard." His hand moved, as if unconsciously, to the nightstick on his belt.

Curtis closed the dead man's eyes and covered his face with a white linen square. While doing so, he plucked up a small object near the man's palm and secreted it in his own inner pocket. Then he collected his case and stood.

The constable was far down the hall, turning into berth 3. Curtis followed. Inside, a bandaged man held a hand to his temple while speaking to the constable. "He kept asking me where the priest was. I told him and told him, there was no priest here. Thank Eternal you came along when you did."

Curtis retreated, then spun to locate Lars. The boy, so close behind, almost certainly overheard. He took Lars by the elbow and marched him to the exit while he zipped his jacket, again concealing his clerical collar.

Once on the ground, he began to fast-walk back to their freighter.

Lars tugged at his sleeve. "What in blazes was that all about? That man was looking for you. Why?"

Why, indeed? Curtis swallowed, keeping his voice conversational. "What makes you say that?"

"Are you kidding? Berth 3 was your berth. I saw your ticket when I returned it. The bad guy was looking for a priest. That's you!" Lars raised his hands skyward in appeal. "You know more than you're telling."

Curtis frowned. "Why would that be?"

"You tell me. And while you're at it, tell me about that tattoo. I saw your reaction."

The tattoo—

He shuddered. The thought of that thing made his bowels watery.

CHAPTER 4

They reboarded their freighter. While Lars, his voice high and rapid, updated Leif, Curtis shed his coat to cushion his seat and stared out the window. He wouldn't alarm his young charges, but the clenching of his guts belied his outward calm. No doubt, he'd been the target.

Lars had been right about the tattoo, as well. It was the mark of the Eye of the Eternal, the Order's secret police. Why they hunted him was a mystery, but the microinjector in the dead man's hand hinted at their intentions. The Eye used such to drug victims for kidnappings, not for assassinations. For that, they had other, more definitive means.

So they weren't trying to kill him. He hoped. At least not yet.

But why? What could he have done to cause them to pursue him? To mount a covert operation? He was no one important, had done nothing to warrant attention, but rather avoided it. So again—why?

His abrupt summons to Capital must have something to do with it, but more than that, he couldn't guess. He must get home to his friend, Administrator German. He had contacts in

Capital. This was some sort of mistake, and if anyone could get it straightened out, German could.

Meanwhile, Curtis couldn't continue his journey with these boys. He would first disentangle them from this danger, then sort the rest out after.

The boys' conversation subsided, their imaginations spent. Lars tried to snooze while Leif took the controls. Curtis rode in silence, unable to shake the feeling he'd blown the opportunity with Leif and the strange conviction it'd been his last chance. Was there something else he should have said?

Leif soon began nodding off, then shaking like a dog shakes fleas. After another such, he reached over and poked Lars. "You awake?"

Lars didn't budge, so he poked harder. "You awake?" When Lars groaned, Leif jostled him again. "Wanna take a turn driving?"

They switched positions, and Leif rolled his jacket behind his head. He soon began snoring but woke with a yelp several times. Curtis cast an inquiring gaze toward Lars, who whispered back. "He fell asleep driving once. It was a scary deal. By the time he woke up, things were pretty well out of hand, and he barely got it back under control. Now if he sleeps on the road, he wakes up like that, thinking he did it again."

These two boys, so similar, but so different . . . Lars was a member of Father Curtis's Wednesday night small group. Alike his brothers, Leif and Dane, Lars was an excellent student, but free of Leif's rebellious spirit or Dane's boldness, Eternal rest him. Leif's questions at Lars's age had seemed more challenge than inquiry, but Lars was a genuine seeker of truth.

Was that fair? That sounded judgmental. Wasn't it possible Leif might be too?

If so, his defenses made it difficult to define his motivations.

"Father?" Lars cleared his throat, then took his focus from

the instruments to meet Curtis's gaze. "You say the Writings tell us the truth about the Eternal, right?"

This was a touchy subject, and knowing Lars's bent, one Curtis would rather avoid. He squirmed on the thin cushion of his wadded coat, then gave up, and stood, head ducked, his six-two frame a poor fit for this five-six space. "The Writings themselves say that, yes."

The freighter began to swing, and he spread his arms between the back wall and doorframe, bracing against the jerking. Lars jumped to the controls and adjusted the steering lever. The car steadied, the swaying subsiding to a rocking.

Now, focus locked on his task, Lars said, "But the Writings also say not to judge others when their concept of truth conflicts with our own, that there are many truths, and all are equally valid."

"Yes, they say that." Curtis pushed down the birth pangs of some unpleasant emotion. One he didn't choose to investigate.

The car rumbled through the night, the thin wooden walls creaking and popping. Between the sound, motion, and cramped space, he could have believed they were belowdecks in a sea galley.

"Well, how can that be?" The red instrument lights bathed Lars in their glow. All outside that pool of illumination was lost to the darkness, creating the illusion they were alone, suspended in some vast unlit void. "If I say your pants are blue, either they are or they aren't. They can't be both brown and blue. There's only one truth, not lots of them."

Curtis made a noncommittal noise. Just what could he say to change the subject? He squirmed, his mind like a mouse in a maze, dashing this way and that, but finding no exit.

Lars tipped probing eyes Curtis's way, then, seeming to remember himself, snapped his attention back to his instruments. "If there can only be one truth and the Writings say they represent the only truth, then why do they also say there are many?"

The unpleasant emotion was birthed anew, and now Curtis fought back irritation, as well. Why couldn't he leave it alone? With a finger, he massaged the tense spot at the base of his skull. "When we speak of truth, it's not as simple as the color of your slacks. The truth is, well, it's so big none of us can know all of it."

"You're not answering my question."

No. He wasn't, was he? Why did this subject upset him so, make him want to avoid it? He blew out a breath, but the tightness in his chest didn't abate.

With no other recourse, he parroted the Order's rote teachings, as unsatisfying as they were. "When it comes to this kind of thing, we're incapable of understanding the truth, unable to understand the Eternal at all. You just have to have faith and know the Eternal is there, and if you have good intentions, he'll reward you."

"Is that true? If there is no singular truth, why would I trust that one?" Lars put his profile in shadow, the furrows in his brow becoming dark cuts. In the blood-red lighting, the effect was ominous, foreboding.

Slumping back to the bench, banging his head on the slat wood wall, Curtis crossed his arms and shut his mouth. No reason to step into this trap.

"See what I mean? Makes no sense." Lars's fingers massaged his forehead, but yet those furrows remained. "This all gets so confusing. When I study the Writings, things don't fit together right."

With a glance toward Leif, Lars continued in a whisper. "Besides, good intentions don't mean much in the real world. My dad and Leif both have good intentions, but the way they butt heads leads to all kinds of unpeaceability. Bad things happen. Maybe good intentions aren't enough?" He huffed. "It gets so jumbled in my head. I wish it was all clearer."

Curtis laid a hand on Lars's rumpled sleeve. "You're confused because you're taking a blessing that speaks of the eternal and applying it to the worldly realm."

"Hah!" Leif, still slumped against the sidewall as if asleep, cut in. "You're confused, little bro, because you take all that mumbo jumbo too seriously."

He yawned and sat up. "You shouldn't expect to make sense from all that 'cause there's no sense to it—just an agenda."

Lars whispered, "Sorry, don't let him offend you."

Far from offended, Curtis raised a hand of assurance and shifted position to include Leif. He'd just heard what he believed to be the first honest thing Leif had ever said about his faith.

"No reason to be sorry. This is a conversation men of good-will should be able to have." Curtis rubbed his hands together, energized. "You don't trust the Writings, Leif? Tell me—and I ask this sincerely, without judgment—what do you believe?"

Leif bit his lower lip. "When I was young, I didn't think much about it, but when I got older, it seemed like science offered cut-and-dried answers. Verifiable truth. The Writings were fluff, fairy tales, nice-sounding words you can't pin down. Slippery words. Like Lars said, somehow it doesn't all fit together."

Also unable to be pinned down, Leif hadn't answered his question. "Fair enough." Curtis edged in, hands on knees. "Every man must decide what is true for himself. May I ask, do you believe in the Eternal?"

Leif shifted toward the window, toward the darkness.

The three of them rumbled on, a universe unto themselves, the view outside the thin, rattling windows confined to the narrow circle of pavement illuminated by running lights. Beyond that, the world could have ceased to exist. With the tires' monotonous hum broken only by their freight car's creaking timbers, Curtis let the road song capture him.

Then Leif straightened and broke the spell. "Well, if you mean some anthropomorphic god"—his hand cupped air as if grasping for the right word—"some gray-haired, bearded old man sitting on a throne, no, I don't believe that. I do think there might be some universal spirit, some First Cause, or something like that."

"That's interesting." They rolled onto a stretch of broken pavement, and the humming became a tooth-shaking barrage. The sensation through his hard wooden seat too much to bear, Curtis stood again and braced against the jolts. "What makes you willing to concede the existence of some sort of universal spirit?"

"A few years back, when I was studying advanced math and such . . ."

Leif had studied nights with a local engineer who offered higher-level courses as a sideline. While Leif claimed he did so to be a better manager at the mill, Curtis suspected he harbored a desire to leverage himself into a position somewhere else, working for someone besides his dad.

"When I was studying physics, it opened my eyes. While I was in school, I hated math, but this guy made it interesting. Logical even. It all made sense, things fit together. Everything worked the exact way you could feel it should. It was just right, felt right—you know? Poetic somehow."

The tire hit a series of deep potholes, and Curtis's head impacted the rough board ceiling. Again. He massaged his scalp, probed for splinters, and lowered himself back to the bench. Still, he positioned one hand against the back wall and his feet planted on the raw wood floor, tensing to keep his weight off the jackhammering bench.

Once settled, he prompted Leif to continue. "As if designed?"

"Exactly. Behind it all, there had to be a mind that put everything in order. I can't explain—it was just something I felt. I don't get the same sense of order, of rightness when I read the Writings. So answering your question, I do believe there's some sort of higher power, but I don't believe he's in your book. Sorry."

Warmth radiated from Curtis's heart. "I'm grateful we had this conversation, Leif, and I thank you for trusting me with your thoughts."

Leif pulled a knee to his chest. "Yeah, well."

After that, Leif fell silent, and approaching Two Rivers, Lars became too busy to talk. They crested the bluffs overlooking the river valley, the entire city laid out before them. The opposite side was only visible as a dark form, the bluff tops a sharp, irregular outline against the brilliant star field.

With the valley in darkness, the residential districts rested in shadows as deep as the woods. Select neighborhoods stood out like islands of light, the powerful clustered in gated communities, the lights of those privileged environs aglow in stark contrast to the rest of the city.

As if reading his mind, Leif pointed. "How can things go on like this?"

"What's that?"

"Like *this*—the rich neighborhoods, all lit up at night. What an in-your-face insult, all that electricity burning up for nothing. They even have lights for their garden paths, yet we can't get power for the mill."

Leif's body clenched, and his lowered head swayed left and right, a bull about to charge. "Don't they know, someday, people are going to have all they can take? Come at them some night with torches and pitchforks? Those fancy lights are a beacon, leading the mob right to 'em. I feel like it myself when I think about the unfairness. Lots of people must." He thumped the side window so hard the catch failed and the glass dropped with a dull thunk.

The sound, so much like a guillotine, catapulted Curtis back to his days in the academy, back to the Temple Square in Two Rivers, where the students were required to attend public trials every month. Enemies of the Order were marched onto the platform, some stoic, some pleading, and a rare few snarling their rebellion to the last.

During his final week in seminary, a man had been dragged up those stairs, black robes torn, loose threads hanging where his badges of office had been.

Curtis nearly fainted at the sight, one of his favorite teachers, one who'd encouraged his students to think for themselves, to test accepted dogma. To seek truth. The man faced his accusers with humble strength, neither cowering from the blows nor reacting to the insults. Accused of crimes Curtis knew to be false, he'd stood resolute while Curtis waited, certain someone would come forward to exonerate him. He was innocent, after all. Justice would prevail in the end, wouldn't it?

He'd believed that even to the last. Until the dull thunk of the dropping blade proved the lie.

He closed his eyes tight against the remembered vision, hands flinching to guard his ears from the sound of blade on bone, mouth open to shout in defense of the innocent man kneeling before the basket, but too late. Always too late.

Fear for Leif constricted his lungs. That, or the thick diesel exhaust he'd been ingesting left him dizzy. How to get this young hothead to learn some caution? "Many people feel as you do, although few would take any sort of action. No matter how angry you are, knowing your children will pay the price along with you—well, *that* causes anyone to think twice."

Are you hearing me, Leif? Think, for your family if not for yourself.

With Leif's headshake, untidy blond hair tumbled into his

eyes. "Still, it takes a lot of nerve. If I robbed people daily and repeatedly, I wouldn't be advertising."

The train slowed. Then, brakes squealing, it trundled to a stop, the soot-stained siding of the terminal sliding into view. That and the dozens of uniformed peace officers waiting on the apron.

Lars pointed at them. "The engineer must have radioed ahead."

Father Curtis bit down hard on his cheek, his heart thudding and something hot rising in his throat.

Leif nudged his brother. "Go check on our connection." From his breast pocket, he removed the ticket folio. "Make sure they get us slotted. We don't wanna miss our train because someone screwed up paperwork."

"You bet." Folio under his arm, Lars slid out of the door. "You staying to get us shuttled to the spur line?"

"Yep." Leif claimed position at the controls. "Padre, you gonna ride with me, or you need to stretch your legs?"

Father Curtis knelt and fished his bag from under the seat. "I'm changing my plans. I'm exhausted and have a friend in town. I'll spend the night here, make the rest of the trip tomorrow."

Leif lit a match and puffed his pipe to life. He exhaled a cloud of aromatic blue smoke in obvious satisfaction, then gave a one-handed wave. "See you back in town."

Curtis backed down the narrow ladder and clicked the door closed behind him.

Yes. I hope to see you again too, my young friend.

CHAPTER 5

Once on the terminal apron, Father Curtis gained his bearings. Uniformed men, led by some in plain black robes, were boarding cars and preventing passengers from debarking. Some now moved toward the freighters, but he snuck around the corner and skirted the building, staying in the shadows.

At the street, he hired one of the taxi bikes. "College of the Eternal, please. You know the address?"

The cabbie grunted, pulled away from the curb, and pedaled through dark streets devoid of any traffic at this lonely hour.

The college occupied several city blocks a mile from the station. A high masonry wall topped with a spiked iron railing surrounded the campus. The centuries-old brick buildings were crumbling at the corners, and thick ivy threatened to swallow them whole. The handbrakes squeaked as the cab drew abreast of a double gate adorned with iron scrollwork.

Father Curtis paid the cabbie and approached the familiar grounds, so much like coming home, even after all these years.

Would it be locked this late in the night? He tested the latch. With whispered thanks, he gained entry and walked the worn stone path toward the far corner where a cottage nestled deep in the shadows of ancient maple trees.

His old friend and mentor, Professor Reuel, frequently traveled. Curtis prayed the man was home tonight.

As he neared the covered porch, candlelight warmed the shades. Good. He must still be awake. Curtis peered through the leaded-glass panes and rapped one knuckle on the weather-checked oak.

A crack of light appeared at the inner door, revealing the wispy white hair of the man he'd been so desperate to find.

He lit a match to hold above his face. In the dim glow, a smile touched wizened lips, and blue eyes twinkled deep in their wrinkled pockets.

The knots in Curtis's shoulders loosened.

This house was like a favorite flannel shirt, ragged perhaps, but warm and comforting. Nothing had changed in years. Stacks of books clogged every spare corner. A fire danced in the fireplace. Sweet woodsmoke evoked memories of howling winter nights spent snug in pleasurable discussion with a man as much father as teacher.

Now, he sank into one worn overstuffed chair while, in its match, the professor chewed on his unlit pipe's stem. The old man still went through the trouble of carrying the thing, even years after quitting, apparently to satisfy the craving without indulging it. Each gripped an earthen goblet of warm spiced cider.

The professor sat back in his chair and eyed Curtis over his goblet rim. After taking a deep quaff, he lowered the cup and, with an air of resolution, clicked it onto a polished stone coaster.

"You seem not to be yourself tonight. You have the bearing of a man with something on his mind." He laced his fingers and raised one bushy white eyebrow. "I know you well enough to sense you're fearful. Why do you keep glancing out the window? What brings you here without notice, on such a night, and in such a state?"

Of course, the old man would see through him. He always had. "I don't want to bring you trouble, sir, but I don't know where else to go for answers." Curtis fumbled with his goblet to cover his indecision. *If I can't trust him with this, I can't trust anyone.* "Or how to hide from my pursuers until I have those answers."

The old man wrinkled his forehead and motioned for him to continue. As Curtis told his tale, the professor's demeanor intensified, starting with encouraging nods but evolving into agitation. When Curtis finished, the professor sat for some time, studying his clasped hands.

"My boy, I owe you a great apology. Great, indeed." He made a mournful little sound. "They asked you about letters to Nob, you say?"

"Yes, but I sent no such letters."

The old man groaned. "I am so very sorry. I believe your troubles are my fault. In my caution to avoid danger for myself, I seem to have instead placed you squarely in its path. For that, I hope you can forgive me."

"Of course, I forgive you, sir." Curtis answered without thinking. "Anything, without asking, but how could you have caused this?"

The old professor collapsed back into his chair. "I sent those letters."

Curtis opened his mouth to speak, but Professor Reuel lifted one hand to stop him. "Being *clever*, I sent a servant to post each letter from locations all over the territory. Who would think there would be any way to tie them to me, much less anyone else? The method was so random."

With his head fuzzy from lack of sleep, Curtis had trouble tracking. "Why did you send them, and why would anyone tie this to me?"

"Because, my boy, by breaking the pattern, by leaving none, I created a new, false trail quite by accident." The professor massaged fingertips to temples as if nursing a headache.

"I still don't understand."

"Follow along. I shall give you the facts. You tell me if the same conclusion occurs to you as must have occurred to the authorities." He filled his goblet from the pitcher at his side.

As an afterthought, he gestured in offer to Curtis, who stood and extended his own. Resettled in his chair, he motioned for the professor to continue.

Professor Reuel took a deep breath. "I highly doubt the return letters delivered to me could be intercepted, as they come from Nob via diplomatic pouch and then to my hand by trusted messengers. At any rate, they are in code—as are those I send, seemingly harmless missives, unless you have the key." He pinched his chin between thumb and forefinger. Another line creased his already wrinkled forehead.

And now, he seemed to pale, even the ruddy firelight glow failing to impart color to his wizened old face. "Or unless one suspected their nature and had the time and ability to decode . . ." His voice grew weak. His eyes seemed to focus somewhere in the far distance.

"Coded messages? Why?"

The professor jerked as if awakened, then waved. "All in good time, all in good time, but first my story."

"Wait." Curtis shifted forward in his chair. "If the messages arrive here by diplomatic pouch, why not send your letters back in the same? Why go to all the trouble of posting them?"

"Because the pouch is sealed by the sender and not unsealed until delivery. The same goes for pouches in the opposite direction. I would need the diplomat on this end to be party to the arrangement, which he is not. The courier, on the other hand, is. On arrival, he unseals the pouch and delivers the contents. My messages, being in a special compartment, don't mix with the others, and the courier forwards them at his convenience."

"I'm still not seeing a pattern that involves me."

"Yes, yes, let me finish my tale." Reuel chewed his pipe, seemingly regathering his thoughts. "So, as I told you, my messages are posted at random locations. But by whom? This is the crux of the matter." He pointed in the air, just as he had so many times in his lecture hall. "They were posted by veiled nuns, wearing random and differing habits." He emphasized the last words as if they were some key point.

There must be more to the tale. Curtis waited, goblet double-handed at his chin, the smell of the spiced cider a balm of memory. The fire popped at his side, its radiated comfort seeping into his marrow. But wait. The old man had finished.

Curtis set aside his drink, gripped the chair's lumpy arms, and scooted forward. "Okay. What am I missing?"

Professor Reuel harrumphed and repeated. "The sisters. Each. Wore. A different habit."

"Still lost." Curtis rubbed his fingertips across the wool flannel upholstery. "That would be another random aspect of a random pattern, wouldn't it?"

"Aha." The professor pulled his pipe from his lips, scowled at it as if it were somehow at fault, then tucked it into his robe pocket. "Exactly what I thought—at least until tonight. But this pointed directly at you, or more precisely, at Northwoods and, by association, directly at you."

Father Curtis palmed his forehead. "The retreat." The retreat was a small facility in Northwoods where the sisters of the Order stayed between assignments. Nuns from every diocese in the territory came and went with frequency.

He bolted to his feet. "Surely, you didn't endanger the sisters by involving them in your schemes?"

"No, no, of course not." The professor gestured Curtis back into his chair. "It was a disguise. The point is any casual observer would remember them as nuns. Moreover, surveillance cameras would identify them as such."

Curtis sat back and sipped his cider, staring into the fire alongside his friend.

"I am truly sorry, my boy." The professor was the first to break the silence. "I did not mean to bring harm upon you. First thing tomorrow, I will contact the Order and confess my culpability and your innocence."

"Whoa, whoa, wait a minute." Curtis's feet hit the floor. A picture flashed in his mind's eye, this beloved old man imprisoned and questioned, maybe tortured? *Not if I can help it.* "Let's not get ahead of ourselves. If this is just about a few letters, I can clear this up with the authorities without involving you. What could have been in them that would be so bad?"

His mentor captured his gaze and spoke with great precision. "The letters contain heresy of the first order, a capital offense, bearing the death penalty without appeal. Not something so easily put aright, I fear."

Curtis's jaw slackened. He tried to speak but had no words.

"Oh, come now." The old man scoffed. "Don't give me that. Do not act so shocked."

Curtis sputtered, still unable to form words. Finally, he croaked out, "Heresy? *Capital* heresy? How could you? Why would you?"

Professor Reuel slapped the nearby table, jostling the cider pitch. "Do not forget to whom you are speaking." He sat back and cocked one eye. "Did you burn them as I instructed you, all those years ago?"

Curtis retreated a step. In his preseminary days, he'd studied under Professor Reuel. As a student, Curtis had been a precocious scholar and a truth seeker. He often strayed into areas of inquiry the Order frowned on, even into some forbidden outright.

He shot a glare at Professor Reuel. "Why bring that up now? You know I did."

"Yes, and you have been running scared ever since, trying to hide your true nature. Not that it did you any good."

"I've run from nothing."

"Really? Is that why you let them shuffle you off to a backwater parish in a backwater province? Why you quit research? Why you published nothing since that very day?"

Curtis stomped a foot on the thick old rug. "I do important work."

Reuel fixed him with that same quiet smile. The one he always used when a student was out of line.

The growing heat drained from Curtis's face, and at what point, exactly, had he jumped from his chair? He lowered himself to the edge of his seat.

What was it about this subject that made him want to shy away?

"Please accept my apologies, old teacher. My transgressions aren't a shock to me—but yours threw me."

"Ha!" The old man guffawed. Then he gripped liver-spotted hands on knobby knees, leaning in toward Curtis. "We have much to discuss, my boy. But sunrise comes soon, and we cannot allow them to find you here. My assistant has been scouting since you arrived, and he sees no sign you were followed. But you having visited me in the past must be known. If they did not trail you here, they will soon come looking. And this campus offers no place where you can be safely hidden."

He raised a window shade and placed a candle on the sill. "However, I have used a lodging in the past when similar needs have arisen. Phillip shall deliver you there, and we will meet again, as soon as safely possible. In the meantime, remain behind locked doors. Do not venture out for any reason. Let us ensure you are brought whatever you need."

Lost at the sudden subject change, Curtis touched cold

fingers to his temples, his pulse still thrumming hot beneath his fingertips. How had the professor communicated with any servant? Of this, he'd seen no sign.

A light knock sounded at a rear door. The professor rose and shuffled out, returning almost at once, trailing a young man on the short side of average, but with a solid muscular build. A white smile gleamed from beneath a tangle of wavy dark hair. He held out one beefy tanned paw. "Hello, Father. I am Phillip."

After the youth shook his hand, Curtis pulled his away and wiggled his fingers. "Thanks for leaving me the use of these." He looked again at those square hands. "And remind me not to anger you."

The newcomer laughed, and a thick accent, percussive and throaty, obscured his response.

Curtis tried to place that accent. It sounded familiar, somehow, but before he could ask, the professor broke in. "Time enough for that another day. Let us get you stowed in our hideaway. Phillip, show him the way."

Then he grabbed Curtis's shoulders, holding him at arm's length. "Do not jump to conclusions. Do not be rash. Do wait patiently. I will come and explain all." He shook him for emphasis. "Stay with Phillip. Wait."

CHAPTER 6

His experience as a village priest hadn't prepared Curtis for the past two days. When Phillip produced an old frock dress and a shawl and instructed him to put it on, Curtis gawked at the bundle, then at Phillip who donned a nun's habit and fastened the veil.

Phillip plucked the clothing from Curtis's hands and in one motion slipped it over his head. "Come, Father. Time very short."

He smoothed thin gloves over his fingers and motioned Curtis to do the same. Then he showed him how to wrap the shawl around his head. "This hide you good." Phillip removed one of Curtis's shoes, dropped a pebble into it, and gestured for him to put it back on. Then, after handing him a cane, Phillip stepped back and inspected. He wobbled his head from side to side. "Okay for work in dark."

He led through the campus's evergreen hedges to a gate.

"I can hardly walk." Curtis winced and reached to remove his shoe. "This pebble is killing me."

Phillip's hand clamped on his wrist, stopping him. "Is good. Fools your walk. I am nurse. Pebble help you be crippled old lady. I take arm. You lean."

Phillip cracked the gate and peeked out. He checked both ways before fully opening it, then hauled Curtis onto the dark street. Once he'd latched the gate, he shook vines back into position, concealing the opening.

"Come, hurry." He beckoned, took his arm, and hustled past the warehouse and around the corner. On an empty side street, they walked several more blocks. Often, Phillip stopped, giving Curtis's sore foot time to rest. When Phillip called these breaks, he leaned close, as if in conversation, while scanning the route they'd taken.

At a seedy apartment complex, Phillip led the way to a ground-floor flat, drew a key on a chain from around his neck, and unlocked the door. Inside, he guided Curtis to a stained easy chair. "Wait, sit. No lights, no noise."

With that, Phillip disappeared toward the rear.

Instead of sitting, Curtis trailed Phillip to a grimy kitchen and glimpsed him leaving through the back door. What was he doing? Had Curtis been abandoned here? Betrayed to the Order?

He ran back into the front room. Thoughts ajumble, he turned circles and started first toward the front, then the rear. He was still trying to choose when the door opened, and a man dressed all in black entered.

But wait—Phillip was behind the man, holding him in an armlock, his other hand clamped over his mouth. Phillip pushed through the door and kicked it closed behind himself. He tightened his hold on the arm and twisted, eliciting a muffled scream.

"Who else?" Phillip spoke, his lips in the man's ear.

The only answer was a shake of the head.

Phillip twisted harder. "Any more?"

Again a shake of the head.

"Where comms?"

The man tapped a front pocket with his free hand.

Curtis's pulse throbbed in his ears, the seriousness of his situation becoming real. Thinking of mysterious pursuers in the abstract was one thing, but now, looking into the eyes of— What? A hired killer? Another would-be kidnapper?

Phillip's gaze jerked to Curtis. "He see face?"

Curtis checked the shawl, just to be sure.

"You are certain?" At Curtis's nod, Phillip gave the man a tap on the head. "Good. You live."

Once the intruder flopped to the floor, boneless, Phillip knelt to search his pockets. He picked up an electronic tablet. When he touched it, a locked screen appeared. He pressed the unconscious man's index finger to it, then scrolled. With a satisfied grunt, he threw the unit on the ground and stomped. The thing shot sparks. Tiny glass shards tinkled across the tile floor.

Curtis hugged shaky arms across his chest, overwhelmed. Numb.

"Lucky maybe." Phillip stood and peeked through lowered blinds. "If alone is good. Last report twenty minutes, not mention us. Possible we have time. Follow. Hurry."

"Where?"

"No choice. Only one other safe place close. We go."

They made a mad, winding, hobbling dash through streets and alleys, early dawn painting the eastern horizon. Phillip kept glancing that way as if watching an approaching doom.

They stopped at an alley backing a tall building, which ran the length of the block. After checking for observers, Phillip steered Curtis to a service door. Curtis took off his offending shoe but received a low warning from Phillip. "No relax until I say."

This formerly pleasant young man had transformed into a deadly serious incarnation, proving Professor Reuel's previously undisclosed life. Curtis shivered as the reality took embodiment in this stranger.

At a service stairway, he stopped, scowled at the upwardly

winding treads, and whispered, "Oh please. Be serious, man. Let me remove the pebble."

With a flat stare and a tug on his arm, Phillip hauled him along. In considerable discomfort, Curtis negotiated the first two flights. Then, mercifully, Phillip led him through a door instead of up the next set.

They hobbled down a hallway, now recognizable as a hotel. Halfway along, Phillip removed the chain from his neck, inserted a key into the lock, and motioned Curtis into a cramped room offering a bed, chair, and desk. A cheap, faded print hung on the nearest wall, flimsy frame askew. A dusty path was worn in the burgundy floral carpet, front door to bed.

Curtis sat on the simple wooden chair and removed his shoe to dump out the pebble. How could something so small hurt so big? He held it up to Phillip. "You can have this back."

A wide grin transformed Phillip, once again the friendly young man Father Curtis met at the professor's. "You keep. Will need again. Besides, is good luck now."

"Good luck?"

"You are here. Safe. Alive. Very, very good luck. Now, shoe back on, no pebble. We stay not here."

Curtis groaned. "No? Then where?"

"Follow." Phillip opened the closet door and stooped. He fished along the carpet before lifting a trapdoor. Ladder rungs disappeared into the darkness. He returned to the desk, removed a candle from a drawer, lit it, and handed it to Curtis. Then he pointed at the ladder. "Down."

Curtis descended. As his feet searched for the rungs, the odor of old books and beeswax surrounded him. His feet found a solid floor.

Phillip closed the trapdoor and followed, then took the candle, and motioned Curtis along. "Come." He walked to a table hosting a candelabra. One by one, he lit the tapers' stubby remains. The circle of light expanded to encompass a long room.

Wall, floors, even the ceiling were unfinished concrete. Pipes ran overhead, disappearing into a dark hole high in the far wall. Papers and stacks of books littered a table, surrounded on three sides by bookshelves overflowing with tomes, more rows of towering shelves marching into the gloom beyond.

A counter, sink, and cot nestled against the opposite wall. A corner fireplace completed the arrangement. That and a door next to the sink that surely led to a washroom. Curtis ran a hand through hair stiff with the oily grit of the wagon train. He needed it.

"What is this place?"

Phillip waved an arm. "Home for you for now. Professor comes, soon maybe."

He padded toward the ladder and pointed a thick finger at Curtis's chest. "Stay. Door stay shut. I am here maybe tomorrow. Food there." He jerked his chin toward a cupboard above the counter. "Stay. Hide. Be safe."

And he was gone, closing the trapdoor behind him.

Curtis climbed the ladder to investigate. When he pushed, the door didn't budge, and there was no latch on this side. So Phillip had meant to ensure Curtis would, in fact, stay.

Off the ladder, he walked about his new prison. The lack of windows gave the cement space a subterranean feel. He sensed the weight of the building above him. Trapped here, buried, he swayed, stumbled, and reached to catch the back of a straight chair. He heaved great, gasping breaths, the air too thick to breathe. He was suffocating.

No! He shook himself. "Get a grip."

He'd heard of claustrophobia. Had never before felt it himself.

He rested there, consciously relaxing until his breathing

steadied. He scowled at that cursed door, there above the ladder, and muttered, "I could break out if I needed to."

That thought made him feel better. A little.

He wasn't a prisoner, not really. He trusted the professor, so by association, he trusted Phillip. All was being done in his best interests—unless proven otherwise.

Body growing heavy as the adrenaline left his system, he dragged his aching self toward the apartment area, slipped off his shoes, and lay full length on the bed, not bothering to remove his clothes. He'd only rest his eyes for a bit, then investigate if that little door did, indeed, lead to a washroom.

CHAPTER 7

L eif fumed. No reason to hide his foul mood. As much as he hated drudgery and repetition, he hated it even more when bureaucrats and drones wasted his time.

He earned a glare from Dad across the wide rosewood conference table. With a last frown of disapproval, Dad repeated his previous sentence to the auditors. "We're glad to show the Committee our work at the mill here. We got all the paperwork you asked for. We can account for every credit spent, and we're dead-on with all the rules."

Daylight streamed from windows beyond his shoulder, casting his face in shadows, forming a halo over his graying blond head as he paused and gathered himself. "A bigger deal is our request to get us signed up for the plant's electrification. We were hoping you could ramrod this thing through the Committee. With electricity, we can make more furniture for you."

The auditors began rolling eyes, shaking heads.

Dad's fist thumped the table. "Working without lights or power tools is crazy. How are we going to keep this place running like that?"

One of the auditors flipped open a ledger and tapped it. "If you can't do better than this with the resources you've been given, why would the Committee waste more of the public's treasure on you?"

Pointing a shaky finger at the ledger, Dad stood. "Our workers don't even make an effort anymore, and it doesn't matter how hard you drive 'em. They know we can't fire 'em, and they get paid the same whether they work hard or not."

He stepped back, held up a palm, and foisted a smile. "Okay, look. The point is, folks, you want more profit, and we gotta have power to make that happen."

He was half right. Restoring electric power to the plant would increase productivity, perhaps even stop the plant's slow decline into penury. Good luck getting it.

Power generation was expensive, and the Committee controlled it with a miserly fist, doling out the utility to the well connected.

Unlike their chances of getting the electrical power, some of Leif's ideas *could* be implemented to help the bottom line. His most ambitious idea would require more time and resources, but even it had a better chance of gaining Committee approval. If he could get someone to listen.

Dad identified the problem but mistook the solution. Productivity was down and getting worse—that much was true. But Dad's management style left the workers alienated and resentful, destroying all motivation.

If you put positive energy out into the universe, positive energy in the form of good things would always come back to you. Right? If the employees felt respected and valued, they'd want to be more productive.

Imagine a team working together, achieving a common mission with zeal. He could see it, and it was his fervent desire. But would Dad listen? Or the auditors?

Advisor Haman, their case handler from Capital, spoke up in a bored, flat voice. "Very well. Once we finish the inspection,

I'll review your proposals. If they are correctly completed, we'll submit them."

Haman, a severe-looking man of late middle age, made it clear he had no intention of taking the proposals seriously. His thin shoulders poked out of his robes of office. With dark hair receding in a widow's peak and sallow pockmarked skin, he evoked images of that old Bela Lugosi movie poster Leif had once seen in a museum. Maybe it was the subconscious association, but the man made Leif's skin crawl.

The auditors filtered off to begin their work. Eager to escape Dad and Advisor Haman, Leif nodded to a pair. "I'll take you to the shop floor."

They followed close as he lit his steps with a raised candle to avoid a fall on the interior stairway. The descent ended at the north wall where glass enclosed the entry vestibule. Alongside it, he opened the door to the first-floor working offices.

The younger of the two halted in the doorway. "Well, this is quite nice."

Leif sheltered the candle. "The drafting tables are some of Dad's scavenging finds. Back during the Hegemony, the local college evicted the tables to storage. Dad resurrected them to their current second life after the Bad Times."

Leif drew in a slow breath, taking in the familiar scent of ink and paper. Here, a squadron of managers created, first in the mind and then on vellum, designs for furniture and other wood products. These were then born into physical existence in the mill, shaped by woodworkers' gnarled hands.

"Shall we continue?" From the office, they moved into the semidark shop, an open metal building, the roof lost in the gloom two stories above. "The space was once windowless, but again, Dad foraged, and workers cut his scavenged windows into the south exterior wall."

Light from those openings now bathed simple, sturdy workbenches with racks housing esoteric implements. He waved toward them. "After the Bad Times, Dad and the men scrounged hand woodworking tools, some modern, some antique, many contrived or repurposed. Amazing what a skilled hand can do with so little. Imagine what they could do with electric tools."

The Bad Times . . . Funny how someone had named it something generic. It was always thus, wasn't it? The World Wars. The Great Collapse. The Bad Times. Didn't matter what you called it, the mill had shut down, as had every industry. When the Committee began restoring civil order in Northwoods, with it came communication with the outside world. Word came that populated areas had restarted basic utilities, had resumed the beginnings of a trade economy.

In those times, he'd known belly-gnawing days of hunger. They all had. At that time, everyone in Northwoods lived a hardscrabble life, squeezing the barest subsistence from the land. At least, the lucky ones did.

Even in his desperation, Dad looked for the big picture. He reasoned that specialization of skills, efficient manufacturing of needed items, and trade would offer a higher standard of living. So he began to rebuild the old family business, offering mill-workers a place to practice their craft.

Men desperate for work fought each other for the chance. At first, Northwoods Millworks made only the crudest and most needed items for people struggling to survive in this new, nearly preindustrial reality.

A functional society resulted, limping along without modern conveniences, so Dad's gamble paid off. By the time the rich—or more precisely the Committee adjacent—began placing orders for handcrafted wood furniture, the family had the only operating factory in the territory, and Dad was inundated with requests, some even from outside the Republic.

But, while Dad was a visionary, who were these committeemen? They'd built nothing with their blood and sweat, but presumed to lord it over those who had.

They passed by the workbenches and moved further into the building, deeper into the gloom, their footfalls echoing in the cavernous space. Here, the smell of wood shavings and sawdust gave way to the tang of iron and old oil.

Looming shapes appeared one by one in the flickering candle's light, only to disappear into the shadows as the candle moved on. Abandoned to the perpetual darkness, they remained observed only by rows of fluorescent lights as dark and lifeless as the machines themselves.

Leif slapped one. "These babies are the engines of industry Dad wants to give new life. They can cut, plane, shape, or sand wood with a speed and efficiency no human hands could ever achieve." He set down the candle, braced a hip against one dormant machine, and crossed his arms. "I remember visiting the mill as a child. How the roar and the raw power frightened me."

The younger man clucked his tongue. "Not anymore, eh?"

"No, not anymore." Leif's shoulders slumped. He looked down the line of silent hulks. Now they sat in metal limbo, waiting for either rebirth or burial. So which would be their fate—and the fate of the mill? Of his family?

What if he could save this company? These machines? The idea—his best one—teased him yet again. He'd sanded, smoothed, and polished it so often, refined it over many sleepless nights. He'd intended to pitch this proposal to the advisor. Had even requested a private meeting today, but with no response.

Dad would never support him. Whenever he suggested an idea, Dad rejected it. No matter how many times Leif promised himself he wouldn't, he automatically reacted by shrinking back in his chair, arms crossed, heart thudding, face heating, emotions roiling. And ultimately, his anger taking his words and good sense.

He grabbed the candle and pushed off, just as he pushed these thoughts from his mind. Now's not the time. He led the way past the bulkhead separating the shop from the warehouse and presented the inky space with a sweep of his arm. "This is it. Do you want to check inventory stack by stack, or do you have some order we need to follow?"

"No particular order." The lead inspector, the older one, slid a set of clipboards from under his arm and passed one to his companion. "Let's start at one end and move our way through."

The first row was rough-sawn lumber, palletized in towering stacks. Leif found the inventory tag stapled to one end and read the count.

The lead inspector interrupted. "The point of an audit is not to read your totals. We're here to verify them. Please pull the pallet into the aisle. We'll do a manual count."

Molten lead broiled in his belly. "Okay. So you're going to do some random counts. Fine, I guess. But I can tell you they'll all match up." He shrugged, willing the muscles between his shoulders to unbunch. Probably better not to pose the question. Still, it burst out. "How many stacks you gonna check?"

The inspector gave him a look to indicate he, Leif, was a bit slow. "We'll be counting everything."

The burn was moving fast, already into his chest, showing no sign of stopping. He exhaled, blowing through pursed lips as if he could cool his temper. "Everything? That'll take all morning. Maybe longer, and it's a waste of time. I already counted all of this—*all* of it."

"Why would we trust your counts?"

Raised hands fisted, he gave up all effort at control. "Because we're honest hardworking people, because our reports have always been spot-on, and because we have real work to do. We have to produce products to make a living. We don't get paid for wasting other people's time, unlike some bureaucrats."

The inspector thrust his clipboard aside and stomped up, nose to nose with Leif. "You stewards really think you're something. You act like you own this place. Everything here belongs to the people, not you. We're here to make sure you don't cheat them. Now pull out that pallet before I forget I'm a public servant."

He squandered the rest of the morning identifying, counting, and measuring materials, proving his painstaking inventory. Once they reached the end of the warehouse, he led them back toward the offices, sighing silently as he did. His work never failed to pass audit, but it was always a gut-tightening thing until it was over. Especially when the inspectors were jerks.

Near the conference room, Dad's agitated voice drifted out. "You've got to get this pushed through. It's the only way."

As they entered, Advisor Haman was scowling over his wire-rimmed reading glasses. "Sit down, sir."

Dad didn't sit. "Mister, the people of this town rely on the mill for their livelihood, and we won't make it unless we get electrical power."

The advisor tapped a thin file folder on the table's edge. "You have bigger problems than your desire for electricity."

Dad spluttered, but Haman slapped the flat of his palm on the file and stood, his face darkening with blood—so maybe the man wasn't a vampire. Just another bloodsucking predator.

He snapped the folder up and shook it. "These numbers are down fifteen percent since last quarter. If you don't get your productivity back on target by year-end, I must consider whether we need to seek a new steward for this mill. Can you explain why performance is so abysmal and how, exactly, you will be correcting the situation—immediately?"

Dad's face seemed undecided whether it was going to

remain red or turn white. In the end, a sickly green tint won. "I told you. That's why we need the power. These workers you saddle us with don't give a rip about the mill, the work, or anything else. Everything we do to squeeze production out of them is as worthless as they are."

"That is your job!" Haman whacked the folder against the desk. "If you cannot do it, we can find someone who will."

"You c–can't do that." Dad's words strained past his throat. He seemed to be having trouble getting enough air. "This mill has been in the family for generations. We've kept it going with our own blood."

Haman sat down, leaned back, and crossed his arms. "You appear to be under some sort of misapprehension. This mill belongs to the people, to the stakeholders, not your family. You are a steward for them, and I am to see to it the people's interests are served. I shall do exactly that. You have until the close of business on December thirty-first to show me why I should allow you to remain steward here."

Dad stuttered as if looking for a point to argue. Apparently finding none, he sat rigid and fumbled a cigarette to his lips.

Haman stood and began packing his files into his open briefcase, mouth in a tight line.

This was not a great time to bring up his proposals. Leif deflated into a slouch. His requested meeting with the advisor hadn't yet happened, and now it was too late.

He kept his position at the side of the door, calling no attention to himself. As the crew filed out, he slipped away with them. He and Diana had agreed to have dinner with Mom and Dad tonight, and that would be painful enough. Better not to get in Dad's way now.

He ran into Mom on the stairs. He arched a brow. "Done already?"

"Done with the accounts. Those extra inspectors are still poking around records storage, but they're running out of stacks to look at. They should be done soon. Strange that. They've never checked the old accounts before. There's nothing there they don't already have in their archives."

Leif let the comment pass, barely hearing her. "Dad and Advisor Haman didn't do well. They're giving us until year-end to bring up the numbers."

She screwed her face into the funny half-serious frown she used over bad news. Or mud on her clean floor. "I'll go up. What time are you coming over?"

"Six, unless you want to give Dad a day or so to calm down first?"

She let out a long sigh. "No. I've had the roast in the oven all afternoon, so you might as well come. It'll be fine."

One could always hope she was right.

CHAPTER 8

L ars looked out over the farm, sighing with the satisfaction of a productive day's work. The verdant green hillsides, shone bright in the late summer sun. The clean air filled his lungs, his heart swelling along with his chest.

He loved coming here, loved the peace and the wide-open space, loved spending the day with his grandparents. Not much he could do at the mill, shut down for inspection as it was.

He stood over Grandpa's garden beds, just about to pick the reddest, juiciest tomato when a convulsion, something like a shiver, but deeper and more disturbing, shook him. A shadow passed over the sun. Shading his eyes, he tilted his face upward, but the sky spread out as bright as ever, no cloud in sight. Not even a bird.

He rubbed the shivers from his bare arms before the bark of tires on pavement intruded. Beyond the eastern fence, a line of three official vehicles sped bullet-like toward the farm.

He sprinted toward the house and slammed through the front door, almost colliding with Grandpa pulling the straps of his pinstriped overalls onto his shoulder. Spinning around at the intrusion, Grandma, in her gingham-checked dress, dried her hands on a flowered apron.

They were always thus, except in Sunday dress or for funerals. He expected, without thinking about it, that they'd never change, like the granite boulder in the middle of the meadow, battered by the years, but standing stolid while all around came and went.

At a crook of his finger, they joined him under the porch overhang as the three cars turned onto the gravel drive.

The cars, armored fast transports, low and sleek with windows tinted so dark the occupants remained unseen, halted in unison as if operated by a single hand.

The dust stirred by their passage rolled over the farmyard, soiling the bold Committee emblems stamped on each car's rear doors. The proud eagle, its sharp beak open in an unheard scream, spread its wings while its talons clutched a sheaf of wheat, the stylized scroll below reading "For the Greater Good."

Hot metal pinged, and the first car's front passenger door opened. A security officer's helmeted head emerged. He marched to the middle car, joining others like him. The men, armed with stubby submachine guns, fanned into a semicircle while the second car's driver opened the rear door and bowed. The occupant stood from behind the tinted glass.

Lars's tensed shoulders relaxed. He cracked a smile and moved toward the short man. Sunlight glinted on his gold wire-rimmed glasses, the bows of which disappeared into tufts of unruly white hair, framing an otherwise bald head. Those glasses and his anachronistic tweeds, complete with silk cravat tucked into vest, gave him a presentation like no other.

But when Lars reached a hand of greeting toward his friend, something put him on alert—the lack of recognition in German's cool gaze, the unspoken warning in his rigid posture.

An officious little man next exited the transport and

offered a hand to someone inside. This last arrival could've been chiseled from a block of marble, a vision of otherworldly perfection. Multitoned thick golden hair skimmed a golden tanned face, from which shone brown eyes so light and so variegated even they could more truthfully be called gold than brown.

This man stood, then stopped, head high and swiveling, eyes slitted. And strangest of all, nostrils flared and lips slightly parted, tongue on teeth. He took long shallow breaths, pulling the air through nostrils and over tongue. How bizarre. Lars had seen Frank, the old farmyard cat, do the same, trolling about for a hidden mouse nest.

Then his gaze fell upon Lars.

That focused attention hit with an almost physical impact. Time stopped. No, it was more like it expanded. He and the man seemed caught in some sort of bubble, the rest of the world frozen in place, while the man—Did what? It felt like an interrogation, but no words were spoken. No, that wasn't right, either. It was more like being searched for stolen candy at the grocer's or having your hair inspected for lice by the county nurse. Intimidating. Embarrassing. An invasion.

And then the world was moving again, and Lars wondered if it had happened at all. He scoffed at his foolishness. He was just jumpy, dizzy from working in the heat. That's all.

German cleared his throat. "I would like you to meet our bishop and his assistant, Nicollo." With a flourish toward the visitors, German continued. "The bishop is making his first tour of our district."

Lars shook himself and bowed, then remembered to make the sign of the Eternal over his heart, acknowledging the bishop's station.

The bishop smiled, then swept his gaze over the group.

German straightened his stance, rocking on his heels as he locked his hands behind his back. The gesture thrust out his portly chest. "The bishop has requested a short tour of your property."

At the last car, two more men disembarked, dressed in martial uniforms.

Lars froze, not daring to look at Grandpa. An inspection by interior men was any steward's worst nightmare. These guys specialized in finding problems where none existed.

As if reading his mind, German made calming motions. "No need for concern. This is not an official inspection."

Lars shifted to keep Grandpa in his line of sight, to take his cues from the old man.

Grandpa cleared his throat with a deep rumbling *hrmm.* Then he hooked his thumbs in his overall straps. "Can we offer you or your men something to drink, Bishop?"

"Oh, thank you, no." German waved him off. "As you might imagine, we have a lot of ground to cover today. Perhaps the tour now?"

Grandpa made a stiff-legged turn toward the center of the farm, hand to chin. "Well, not a lot to see. We've not been a working farm since the reorganization." He raised a big open palm. "We spend our time growing flowers and keeping up the property. The barns are storage for the county now. We can walk the place over. You just yell if something catches your interest."

Grandpa led the group east toward the barns. He glanced at Lars and made a quick flick of his eyes.

Lars allowed himself to fall back, then stepped behind a lilac. Keeping the thick foliage between himself and the others, he sidled south toward the gardens. He passed rows of nut and fruit bushes, organized and pruned into decorative lawn plantings, on his way to waist-high wooden structures overflowing with lush green growth. Beyond these, grape vines curled along decorative arches, creating what appeared to be nothing more than a garden walk.

A casual observer would see a well-manicured flower garden, likely not guessing every plant was edible. Tucked behind a wire-mesh door below each planter, rabbits grazed on fresh-cut greens.

Lars dashed from structure to structure, fitting wooden covers over each opening. Once done, the planters gave no hint of their furry secret.

He then made a low sprint across the grounds and into a wooded grove. There, he dragged branches, many with leaves still attached, over a metal grate covering a dugout cut into a steep hillside, where a flock of chickens resided, only the top and south side open. Now, the construct looked like nothing but a brush pile. In the gloom below, the chickens quieted for what they took to be the sudden onset of night.

Back on the hill, he caught up with the group. Grandpa ushered the visitors inside the old poultry barn. The air was heavy with the scent of oil, dust motes danced in the few rays of light penetrating the grimy windowpanes, and underlying all was the sharp tang of old chicken manure. Scant light scarcely illuminated the jumble of machines and metal racks choked with small parts. Their boots cut new trails in the undisturbed blanket of gray dust.

The bishop remained near the entry while the Bureau men did their inspection. When they shook their heads, he exited the building.

Grandpa ambled double-time to catch up and pointed toward a lower field. "Down here, I can show you how we restored part of the pasture into a wetland—"

The group wasn't following, and he wound down.

When the bishop shaded his eyes and faced the machine shed, his assistant nodded toward it. "Show us the rest of the buildings, if you would."

They made the circuit of the other structures, the uniformed men searching them, not even pretending to tour them now. At last, the route brought them back to the vehicles.

As the group prepared to depart, Grandpa caught German by the elbow. "At least stay a bit. I think Mom has whipped up some protein flour brownies."

"That is so kind." Nicollo, the assistant, opened the car door and ushered the bishop inside. "But we're far behind schedule. Another time?"

With half-hearted invitations to return, the official visitors boarded their transport. As they were about to reembark, Nicollo stopped in front of Lars. "By the way, we are concerned about Father Curtis. He was to meet us today, but we cannot locate him." He studied Lars's face. "The last trace we have of him was on his ride from Capital to Two Rivers late on Monday. He didn't complete his journey to Northwoods. I understand you made that trip in his company?"

Lars's mouth had gone dry, and he had to swallow several times before he could speak. "Yes, he did ride with us. He told us he'd be coming later the next day."

Nicollo waved a long-fingered white hand. "I'm sure it's a simple miscommunication. He may even be at the parish as we speak. Did he say why he didn't continue on with you?"

"No, just that he needed sleep. He went to visit a friend."

"Hmm. But did he name the friend?"

"No, sir?" Lars shifted his feet, beginning to think he wouldn't tell if Curtis had. That incident on the train . . .

"Ah." For a moment, the thin man studied him, acting as if he expected Lars to say more. Then he stooped to enter the vehicle. The door closed with the muffled *thwunk* of sound-proofed armor.

As the vehicles crunched down the gravel, Lars clamped a hand on Grandpa's shoulder. "I thought they were gonna haul us all off. I can't believe they left without any trouble."

Grandpa frowned, watching the retreating cars.

CHAPTER 9

Leif arrived home with the sun low to the horizon. He braced himself as a pair of towheads streaked toward him. They met his legs in a squealing collision, each child struggling to gain purchase on his torso. "Daddy," they chimed in clear, high voices. He wrapped both in a bear hug, squeezing their little bodies into him, and basked in love received and love returned.

Then he scooped them up and rounded the living room corner. His wife, Diana, sat on the old overstuffed couch, highball glass raised to her mouth. She looked at him, green eyes nonchalant as the man beside her retracted his hand from her knee.

Leif's heart wilted.

She pushed a lock of dark hair from her eyes. "Hey, honey."

The man's wide gray eyes met Leif's, his smile not reaching their depths. "Leif." He hoisted a drink in greeting. "We were wondering if you'd ever join the party."

A rush of unpleasant emotion churned him, a confusing mix. He stuffed the feeling and averted his eyes. "Rough day at work." Under his breath, he muttered, "And apparently, I wasn't invited."

After setting down the toddlers, he poured himself a generous whiskey. The bottle clinked on glass, and the fumes of distilled grain wafted to his nose.

Diana moved to separate herself from her visitor by getting up to check their youngest's diaper, the tyke lying on his belly at the foot of the couch, gnawing on a wooden block.

Leif gulped his drink, the warmth of it moving down throat, spreading through chest to belly, but failing to loosen the knotted cords there. "What brings you here, Adrian? I thought the wagon trains had you away this month?"

"Oh yeah. We were all set, and then the mechanics found a fault. Parts needed to be ordered." Adrian was the lead engineer on one of the new transcontinental wagon trains. The coast-to-coast circuit took a month to make the round trip. He smirked at Diana.

With a secret smile, she lowered her gaze to her drink.

Once, Leif had enjoyed this man's fantastical tales. That was then. Now, his half-concealed flirtation with Diana, often right in front of Leif, had worn thin. Lately, Adrian arrived unannounced, and as if by happenstance, these visits coincided with Leif's business trips. Leif steeled himself to remain polite, out of respect for the friendship between their parents, but couldn't this guy just leave? Preferably never to return.

"Diana, I told you we were to be at Mom's for dinner. The kids aren't even clean."

She rolled her eyes, her gaze toward Adrian. "Always complaining. It gets so old." She scooped up the baby and marched toward the stairs. "Suz is dressed. Get the twins ready. I'll change the baby."

Leif set aside his empty glass and picked up the toddlers. "Adrian, were you planning to join us?"

"No, I have to do a last inspection. I may have time later for a nightcap." He drained his beer, used the empty to salute Leif, and stood to leave.

Not bothering to show him out, Leif headed upstairs. While he'd been stressing all day, Diana had been lounging around, drinking and flirting. She hadn't even fulfilled her one responsibility.

He found her in the bathroom, adjusting her makeup, the baby on the floor—unchanged. "I thought you were getting him ready?"

She scoffed and continued to reapply lipstick.

The tight band of control snapped. He set the toddlers down and stormed across the room to stand behind her. "I told you to quit hanging with that guy."

Their gazes met in the mirror.

"Oh, don't you trust me?"

He didn't, but he had enough sense not to say so. "I don't trust him. Get rid of him."

"How can I help it he wants to visit? We're just friends, anyway." She toyed her hair with a brush. "I've always had more guy friends than girl friends. I don't know why."

"It might have something to do with what guys want from you, and you need to quit egging 'em on."

She gave herself a smug smile in the mirror.

His gut churned. He gripped her shoulders. "Get rid of him, or I will."

She slapped her brush on the counter. "You have no respect for me. You just want me here, waiting to serve you. Well, I'm sick of sitting home alone. At least Adrian is a friend. Maybe you should try that instead of working all hours of the day and night."

"Oh, really? You have a new plan for how we'll pay the bills?"

She grabbed the baby and shouldered Leif out of her way. "Jerk."

He forked his fingers through his hair, fisting clumps. Why

did he work so hard? Why was he the only one trying to do the right things?

Then his little son tugged at his pant leg, and Leif scooped him up and herded the boy's sister toward their room. "Time to get changed, guys. Ready to see Grandpa and Grandma?"

But the upbeat tone couldn't ease the ache in his chest, and twenty minutes later on the two-block walk to Dad's house, neither of them tried to thaw the stiff silence.

Leif knocked and entered without waiting. The kitchen smelled wonderful, the air warm and moist, redolent with the aroma of baking bread. Mom pulled the roast out of the oven, its juices bubbling.

That chunk of meat was at least a month's ration, even for people of their status. The average family would be lucky to have this meal twice a year, if that.

He relieved the kids of their light jackets, and Lars entered from the living room. Newly named stakeholder, Lars still lived with Mom and Dad. He'd requested several house assignments, but competition was stiff, especially for the choice dwellings. Being single and with no immediate prospects for a mate, he had time to be picky, and when his seniority level improved, he could snag a nicer home, instead of settling for the leaking hulks he qualified for now.

Leif caught Lars in a backslapping bear hug. "Headed to small group later, little bro?"

"Stopped by. There's a note on the door. Said all activities canceled for the week." With a meaningful look, he whispered, "Later, outside."

Leif maneuvered past the milling kids and wrapped Mom in a smothering hug, then kissed her forehead. "Smells delicious. You shouldn't waste such luxury on us. The kids are just as happy with rice and beans."

"They need proper food if they're going to grow up healthy."

She patted his cheek. "I wish we could feed them fresh food every day."

Thanks to Grandpa and Grandma, the kids ate a diet high in farm-raised eggs, meat, and vegetables. They got much more than most, but Mom wanted only the best for her family and fretted about the mass-produced industrial food. People seemed content, but an educated woman, she warned against the toll such toxic food exacted.

She asked for someone to say grace, and they linked hands around the mahogany table. Its high polish reflected their images as well as those of the many overflowing dishes, the little pink roses of the china the same as in his first memory of this table. Good memories. Mostly.

Lars intoned, "Eternal One, we thank thee for the bounty with which you have blessed us, for the hands which have prepared it, and for the health which it brings to our bodies. We ask that you be with us today and all days, that we improve our walk to better embody the truths of your teaching. In the name of the Eternal, amen."

They echoed his amen, took seats, and passed the food, including a salad of fresh greens Lars had harvested today. The roasted vegetables also came from the farm. For dessert, there was peach pie. The peaches, too, were from the farm, and the sugar was from the stash Grandpa put aside before the Bad Times. How he'd known to prepare remained a mystery.

Diana dished plates for the kids, and Lars helped her, Leif too distracted to think to help until it was too late. Since his arrival, he'd been working to determine Dad's mood. Surprisingly, given the day, Dad seemed pleasant. So Leif took a deep breath and cleared his throat. "I don't think we're getting electrical service anytime soon. We need to find another way."

"There is no other way." Dad scowled. "Besides, we deserve it. I've seen the invoices for our deliveries. The advisor is making a huge markup on everything we send. They need to give some of it back."

Old gripes. They needed new plans. Leif tensed, choosing his words. "I know, Dad, but they won't give it to us. We need—"

"Don't start with your schemes." Dad pointed a rigid finger at Leif, lips tight. "And don't you dare think of whispering them to the advisor. I know you tried to set up a private meeting."

The lightheadedness of fear fled as hot blood warmed his cheeks. "And you blocked it?"

"Darn right, I did."

Leif threw down his fork, quivering now with an unspent adrenaline surge. "Why?"

Lars was vying for Leif's attention, making cool-it motions. Mom plucked at Dad's sleeve, but he jerked free and pounded a fist on the table, finger still aimed at Leif. Diana scrunched down in her chair as if she thought she could disappear.

"We can't afford your crazy ideas." Dad's face blotched a purplish red, and the tendons in his forearms popped, spit flying with his words. He whipped his arm as if casting Leif and his ideas out the floor-to-ceiling windows. "Get your head out of the clouds and do your job."

Leif tamped down the instinctive reaction to return insult for insult, making an almost physical effort to force his body, now fully primed for a fight, to remain still, his mind to focus. How to make him see?

"They're not crazy ideas, and what you're doing isn't working." He leaned in, hands open in the posture of a penitent, pleading with his whole being. "How do you expect different results if you keep doing the same old thing? It's time to change before we're sunk." *Please, you can't be this blind. You've got to see this!*

"It's my home and my business at stake here." Dad pointed toward the door. His extended arm, his whole body shook. "If you want to try your harebrained ideas, go start your own business and try 'em there."

Diana had stood to gather the kids and shepherd them from the room. Part of Leif's consciousness noted them as they went, Diana pulling them by their little arms while they turned, stumbling, to stare at him with wide eyes. But the part of him now in control, the bullish part, ignored the damage being done.

He thumped the table, rattling Mom's good china. "My life's work is on the line too, not just yours. You keep telling me I'm paid less than the other men because I'm working for equity. What equity? When?" He slammed his chair back. "I'm only twenty years younger than you. Will I have that equity in time to be rolled into the county home?"

He threw down his napkin and stalked from the house.

FATHER CURTIS SPRINTED over the rocky ground, dodging craggy pyramids, seeking a safe hiding place. Finding none, he pumped his legs but made no headway.

He looked for his pursuer but couldn't see them, could only feel a presence behind, somewhere in the black swirling mist. Spurring him to greater speed was what emanated from that darkness: an unnatural hunger, a need to devour and destroy.

Then he sensed something else. New hunters had joined the chase, moving fast. They broke from the curtaining fog, the lunging shapes closing in. Wolves, huge black things, bigger than any in the zoo, their opened maws full of fangs, snapping at him.

Just ahead, another form separated from the darkness—a lion, crouched to spring. It launched itself before he could react.

He fell to the ground and rolled into a ball, arms wrapped to protect his head.

No attack came.

He peeked out from between his elbows.

In a furious blur, its movements too fast to track, the lion tore into the black beasts' throats. Tufts of fur and foamy slather sprayed. Then the wolves broke contact, turned tail, and fled, yelping into the darkness.

In their place, a larger, darker form coalesced deep in the mist, undulating closer, every movement a threat. Hunger still pulsated at its core, but now, it radiated something else, an intense anger, an unreasoning hatred of . . . *him*.

He froze in place. The assault of that hatred struck as if a physical thing, as if a smothering weight had settled on his chest. He fought to breathe. He could not.

Rising high on its haunches, the lion lifted its head and roared. The ground shook. The form in the mist hesitated, then withdrew, leaving him alone with the animal.

He sucked gasping breaths, fearing his lungs could never be satisfied.

The cat sauntered toward him, head down and eyes slit. Oh, Eternal! It had only been chasing away the competition, and he was again the prey.

He whispered a prayer and prepared for the inevitable.

The beast stalked about him in a tightening circle. A deep sound rumbled from the magnificent chest. It drew near, and the big square head shot toward his throat.

A rough tongue licked his face. Then the great cat settled next to him, head up as if guarding him. A bass purr offered settling comfort.

Curtis lay where he had fallen, arms still rigid around his head. Should he trust that comfort? What now?

But there was something else. This other was like a whisper, a susurration woven into the air, into the purr, not coming from the cat, but from everywhere and from nowhere, from inside his mind, and yet still part of the cat's throaty purr. And now . . . yes! Concentrating, he made out words repeating over and over, saying, "Seek the Truth."

"Seek what Truth?"

The lion went silent and looked down at him as if to answer. Then it licked his face and purred anew.

The words resumed, felt as much as heard.

The lion again lifted its head, watchful, guarding Curtis as if he were a cub.

CHAPTER 10

His parents ate in silence, as did Lars. He barely tasted it. Finished, he excused himself and found his brother sitting under the porch overhang, whiskey in one hand and pipe in the other. Lars leaned up against a pole.

The acrid smell of pipe tobacco tickled his nose. He scowled at his brother, drinking and smoking. The priests said these things done in moderation weren't sins, but what, exactly, was the definition of moderation? It seemed to be one of those words people used when they want to sound like they were answering a question while doing nothing of the sort.

Lars crossed his arms and tipped his face to the sky. A few stars poked through drifting gray wisps of cloud. "Did the bishop show up at the mill?"

"No, why?"

"He was at the farm with interior men."

Leif jerked the pipe from his mouth. "What?"

"Said he was touring the territory, but they were looking for something. Father Curtis didn't show up for a meeting. They asked if we knew where he was."

"Nope, wasn't at the mill, but goons poked around more

than usual. You say they canceled your small group. Was Father Curtis around?"

"Couldn't find him, there or at the rectory." That train incident niggled him anew. "Everything's dark and locked up tight."

"He's probably still visiting that friend of his, or his train was delayed. He'll show up."

"Yeah." Lars rubbed the back of his neck and scuffed a shoe across the worn porch planks. Leif hadn't seen what he had on the train. But Leif was sinking into one of his brooding moods.

"You let him get to you again." Lars settled into the wide planked deck chair next to Leif's, the joints creaking as they took his weight.

"Every time, I prepare myself to stay calm, but every single time, he riles me up. The next thing you know, I'm out of control, arguing." He puffed on his pipe. Jaw muscles clenched, and teeth ground the stem. "Like anything I say would make a difference. He's not listening. Why do I bother?"

Lars locked his hands in his lap. The calluses grated each other. "I don't know." He blew out a breath. "You guys can't seem to connect. Mom says it's because you're so alike."

"We're anything but."

But Mom was right, and this was their problem. Not knowing what to say, Lars sat without speaking, simply keeping company with his agitated brother.

LEIF DRIFTED DEEPER into his thoughts and puffed on his pipe. He took another sip of his whiskey, and the warmth of it flowed down his throat, the only medicine he'd found to loosen the chafing bands around his heart. He'd begun self-medicating this way over these last years. Lately, he started as soon as he arrived home from work, sitting on the deck, brooding, and drinking alone.

He knocked out his pipe. "The men resent the way Dad treats them. We're not gonna beat them into producing higher numbers. A great man once said you can't push a string around a desk—you can only pull it. We're trying to push the men when we should be pulling, leading them, giving them a reason to care. You know this."

Lars stretched back, locked his hands behind his head, and crossed his ankles. "Yeah, I know, but what are you going to do about it? Fighting with Dad will get you nowhere—worse than nowhere."

Leif filled his pipe, fumbled for a match, and sheltered the flame from the night breeze. He puffed, watching the ember glow. "Yeah, well? You got a better idea? Someone has to lead us out of this, has to convince him." He locked the pipe stem between his teeth and drew deeply, the sweet draft warming his mouth. "You gotta do what's right."

He blew a smoke ring. If only all his hurt and frustration could drift away like that fading torus, dissipating, rising toward the stars until they were no more. "You can throw a cat over a volleyball net, but only once. We need to make the men feel valued, part of a team, make them *want* to excel."

Lars gripped Leif's knee and leaned into his space. "The same you say of them is true of Dad. The more you beat on him, the more he'll dig in."

Leif coughed, the smoke going down the wrong way. They sat then, silent, sharing the night sounds, a chorus of crickets in the front lawn, the croaking of frogs echoing from the lake a few blocks distant. Nearby, a cicada began its whirring song. Inside the house, the kids laughed.

Then the door opened, and Diana stepped out, keeping hold of the doorframe. "Help me get them ready. It's bedtime."

With a light groan, he levered himself out of the chair and slapped Lars's shoulder. "See you in the morning, little bro."

"Yeah, bright and early, right? You know how Dad gets."

"What, it gets worse than this?"

FATHER CURTIS WOKE with a body-snapping jerk. Sweat soaked through his clothes. He cast about but couldn't tell where he was. Such profound darkness added to his disorientation. He waved in front of his face and saw nothing.

Had he somehow lost his sight? His chest constricted. Something cold squeezed the air from his lungs. But, no.

He must have fallen asleep. And the candles burned out in this strange reading room.

Hands shaking, he fumbled for the book of matches stowed in his inner pocket. But his groping fingers touched traveling clothes, not his robe. He reoriented and dug the matches from his trousers.

After lighting one, he stood, fumbled for a candle, and placed the match's dwindling flame to the wick. Then he searched until he located a fresh supply of tapers in a cupboard. He replaced the candles around the room and added a single brass candleholder and a book of matches next to the bed, ready for the next time he woke to utter darkness.

Was there no clock? In his daily routine, plenty stood in ready view, so he never gained the habit of wearing a watch. Would he now be guessing at the passage of time? Was it yet morning, or had he slept through the day?

The vivid dream flooded back, and he shook himself to dispel the lingering images. Given recent events, little wonder he dreamed of being hunted. But that cat? Where had that come from? How strange.

His growling stomach provided a much better thing to focus on than lunging wolves, churning darkness, and purring lions. He made his way to the kitchen, mumbling to himself. "Food there. Stay, Curtis. Good dog."

He opened the wooden cupboard door, its hinges creaking. Inside, stacked in neat rows, were an assortment of canned goods, cheeses, sausages, and crackers. No gourmet feast, but he wouldn't starve.

With a handily provided can opener, he opened some pork and beans, then shoveled them into his mouth cold as he walked to the table where loose papers formed haphazard pyramids. He sorted through a random collection of old literature, poetry, songs, and other texts.

No, not random. Something wove them together, an element in common. Several contained verses from the Writings, but the text varied from those he knew.

A verse caught his eye, akin to one from the collected writings of the Great Teacher. The verse he knew read:

Rulers are appointed by the Eternal. They are not a terror to good conduct, but to bad. Would you have no fear of the one who is in authority? Then do what he says and you will have his approval, for he is the Eternal's servant for the greater good.

In contrast, this verse ended differently:

Then do what is good and you will receive his approval, for he is God's servant for your good.

Using the word *God* in place of the *Eternal* smacked of the old religions with their varying deities. The order taught that the Eternal was the only true god while it forbade invoking the old gods. The Order's rational religion had replaced all others, and much for the better, if the stories of the religious wars of history were any indication. Calling on this "God" caused Curtis to shiver at the thought of those violent times.

Added to that, changes to the words altered the core meaning.

Doing "what is good"? How would you apply such teaching to your life? Who got to define what good means? Every man for himself? Such anarchy!

And what about the phrase "for your good"? A perfect

prescription for a selfish attitude. How did that protect the interests of the collective?

He stood, too agitated to sit, and paced the room, examining the contents on row after row of heavy metal bookshelves, their thick rivets and truss-like braces, the deep patina on metallic green paint testimony to great age.

And all of these shelves were filled end-to-end with massive tomes, bound in heavy leather, their spines cracked with age. Some were books with recognizable titles. Most were not. Many matching volumes bore only digits corresponding to an unfamiliar numbering system.

He took one off the shelf, opened it, and thumbed through handwritten sheets. Like those on the table, this volume also displayed verses from the Great Teacher's time. Each disturbingly varied from the Writings he knew, twisting meanings, subverting the teachings.

With a dawning queasiness, he opened more volumes. Each contained similar collections. The more he read, the more the small muscles at the back of his neck clenched.

Why collect such noncanonical writings? Heresy and blasphemy were capital offenses, and this was high heresy, without a doubt. Why take such a risk? What was the point?

Father Curtis thumped the book closed, dust wafting into his face, and sat staring into the candlelight.

He wasn't against studying the Writings. He was even willing to debate the proper interpretation. Of course, age and wisdom had tempered these debates. His rash seminary forays into heresy were a short-lived juvenile phase, an old memory he preferred to forget.

This was not an interpretation, but an outright corruption.

He loved the Order, and he loved the Writings. They were his touchstone, the foundation upon which he had built his life.

His only other solid rock was Professor Reuel, his most

trusted mentor, the one man who'd been there for him. Being an orphan, Curtis cherished this friendship and the father he'd never had.

But now, surrounded by these damnable volumes, he thrashed about in his mind, searching for some solid ground. Yet the once firm footing of a world in order slipped into the void.

Reuel wasn't who he claimed to be. And never had been, apparently. Curtis imagined the feeling akin to a child who overhears a whispered conversation between beloved parents, only to learn they despised him. Or was this worse? The professor was involved in high crimes against the Order! He was a destroyer of everything Curtis held dear. Further, he'd kept his duplicity hidden over decades of friendship—or *supposed* friendship. What kind of friend did that?

The man he'd most trusted was a fake, a heretic, and a liar.

Pincers gripped his chest, a chill vise around his heart.

He would not be involved in this treason.

He sprang to his feet, needing to move, but unable to take more than a handful of steps in any direction before another featureless concrete wall stopped him.

His path brought him back to a spot opposite the table. There, in a room fit for human habitation, would be a window. He stood, back to the room with all its terrible secrets, hands braced against the cold concrete. Then with an oath, he slapped the wall, feeling the impossible weight of the structure, its immovability.

What to do? He was trapped, locked in, having been made easy prey by those he'd trusted. The Order might be on their way now, coming to capture him. If they found him, all the evidence to convict him lay on the table. He must escape right away, must distance himself from this madness.

Breaths ragged, he climbed the ladder and searched for an exit, pounding and clawing at the hatch. It didn't budge. He scrambled back down, grabbed a candle, and holding it in jittering hands, climbed back up the smooth, time-polished rungs.

Above his head, flickering yellow light danced on wooden door slats. A dark patch, lustrous with the oil of a thousand handprints, showed where others had pushed it open. He placed his hand on the spot and shoved. Nothing.

He ran the candle around the perimeter, and there, something glinted. A wire loop. He inserted one finger and pulled.

The door clicked open. He raised the lid a crack and peered into the empty room.

Night draped the window. But who could guess the time?

He put out the candle and eased open the door. In the dark corridor, no movement was visible. He slipped out of the room and stole down the hall on the balls of his feet, expecting a shout of discovery.

In the dark street, with no way to tell where he was, he picked a direction and set off to find a recognizable landmark.

The gentle night breeze, still warm with the last memory of summer, caressed his brow, but he took no comfort. He'd find no comfort again until he was home, the nightmare behind him. Jaw clenched, hands jittery, he darted glances up and down empty streets.

He paused at the first intersection. He was halfway up a hill, the river at the bottom on his left. On a whim, he turned downslope, a thin crescent of moon breaking through feathery clouds to light the way.

Once he cleared the tall building, he overlooked a sweeping view of the valley. Nearby, the wagon-train terminal lit up the night, a beacon set in a dark neighborhood.

He'd escaped with no plan and no destination. Now he had both.

Curtis passed through empty streets without seeing another

soul. He searched but found no sign of dawn. He should be miles away before it came.

Approaching the terminal grounds, he slowed to cautious steps. He stayed across the street, ducking behind the shoulder-high hedge lining the road. He hunched low and peeked through the foliage. Now, how to enter the freight yard unseen?

The night perfume of the remaining honeysuckle blossoms drifted into his awareness, tickling his nostrils, carrying fond memories of the years he enjoyed with his grandmother. Such a hedge bordered her backyard next to the rusty swing set where he'd once played. He and the neighborhood kids gathered there regularly. Many summer afternoons passed in the shade with his friends, crushing the delicate pink and yellow blossoms to smell the deep, sweet scent, squeezing the berries to shoot a stream of red juice toward each other in mock battle. How he ached to be back in those simple days, a time with no worries of heresy and no thought of black-clad hunters!

A tug parked by the curb across the street, blocking the terminal entrance. He used this opportunity to dash—unseen?—into the dense willow thatch at the freight yard's nearest end.

He hadn't forgotten Professor Reuel's warnings. If he was going to enlist Administrator German's aid, he must avoid arrest between here and home.

Curtis squared his shoulders. Yes, that old codger would know which strings to pull. He'd have this mess cleared up and Curtis back where he belonged, with his flock, the people who needed him most.

He stayed deep inside the thick stand of saplings. The screen of green interwoven leaves concealed his movements as he crept toward the property's working side.

A wagon train was assembling on the apron, some freighters familiar, regularly working out of Northwoods. *Please let them be traveling home.*

He slipped from the thicket into the lighted yard, keeping

his gait casual, just another bored freight hauler. He'd drawn abreast of the train's rear when voices rang out from the terminal. A man was speaking into a radio, shouting to someone out of view, pointing at Curtis.

Back into the willows he dove, whiplike branches slapping his face. Shots rang out. Bullets clipped nearby limbs. Were they *shooting* at him? Why?

He sprinted through the thicket and onto the street, making a beeline away from the industrial district.

At a residential block, he stopped in a patch of evergreen shrubs. He rested, hands on knees, and snuck a look over his shoulder.

While there were no immediate pursuers, the sound of a chase echoed from the terminal. But more troubling—shouts came from the opposite direction, from the center of town. They'd radioed for backup and trapped him between two forces.

He changed direction, taking a lateral course to outrun the pincers. At a full sprint now, he made only minimal efforts to keep under cover, seeking speed as his best chance of escape.

He broke onto a street, bowling over a uniformed officer. Curtis didn't stop but put on a greater burst of speed, blessing the Eternal he had kept up his daily workouts.

The pursuers weren't in the condition he was, and their footsteps were receding. He was gaining a lead.

Then more men intercepted from ahead, moving to block his path. He was surrounded, and the wolves were closing fast.

Physically fit or not, he couldn't keep up this pace. His legs were burning, beginning to falter, and a stitch stabbed his side.

He rounded a corner, moving away from the sounds of pursuit.

Out of the dark loomed a garden gate guarded by a stone lion, like a proud desert king on a low pedestal. He dove behind the statue to allow the pursuit to pass him by. Had the dream prompted him?

Soles slapped cobbles, and heavy breathing grew nearer from his left. More running footsteps closed from the right. He lay on his belly, stifling his gasping breaths, and peered between fern fronds.

In the dim moonlight, uniformed officers stopped directly opposite.

They conferred in murmured words, too muffled for him to hear. One gestured in his direction. Curtis recited a silent prayer as the pair moved toward his hiding place.

The weight of some unseen evil closed in like the dark presence of his dreams, reaching for him.

The eagerness of the thing palpable.

CHAPTER 11

After dinner with Mom and Dad, Leif put the kids to bed. Diana did her makeup and dressed to, "Have a nightcap with the girls."

She left him in what felt like an empty house. It just wasn't the same when she wasn't there, for all they fought when she was. He spent the hours slaving away on office work. When his eyes gave out, dry and burning, he went to bed. He lay sleepless, tossing and turning. The press of his body heated the sheets beyond comfort, and each toss further disheartened him.

At three a.m., the gut punch struck. "A nightcap with the girls" had been another lie. He flung himself from the bed and walked to the window, drawing back the filmy curtain Mom had made. Moonlight slipped over his bare legs as his breath fogged the glass. How many nights had he lain there waiting for Diana? He didn't know who she was with this time, but he knew what she was doing. Again.

He wiped the fog from the window but couldn't wipe it from his mind. Why'd he make himself such a patsy? Why keep taking these soul wounds? Why not end this charade?

He closed his eyes, listening to the light breathing escaping from the little mouths in the adjacent rooms, those sweet sounds his answer. He couldn't lose them, wouldn't upend their world.

Diana's high heels clicked on the sidewalk, and the entry hinges squeaked. He padded barefoot down the stairs and sat in a living room chair. Furtive movements approached through the dark kitchen, the only light a candle burning in the dining room. She came around the corner into that pool of flickering light, high-heeled sandals held by the straps as she tiptoed into view.

When she saw him, she started, then giggled. "Oh, isssh you."

He crossed his arms. "Who was it this time?"

"Whadya mean?" She hiccuped and shrugged. "I tol' you I was with the girlssh."

Something about her body language—maybe the ducked head hiding defiant eyes—confirmed it. He struggled to keep his voice even. "You were with Adrian." Once spoken, he knew it was true.

She cringed like a child caught in a lie, despite her protest.

Leif sat motionless, his vision becoming distant. A tightness pinched his forehead, the lines surely deepening between his brows. Diana said these were his involuntary tell. They appeared when he clamped down emotions, attempting to project stony calm.

She strode into the room, sat on his armrest, and lowered her hands to his face. Her shoes dropped to the floor. She smoothed those lines with soft fingers. "I'm sorry." She seemed suddenly sober. "I didn't mean it. It just happened."

A confusion of competing passions warred within his soul. In an invisible inner battle, he jammed that bundle of emotions into a mental closet, locking them in, never intending to open that door again.

He jerked away. "'Just happened'? What? You slipped and

accidentally fell on the rug, and—*oops!*—there he was?" He mimicked coquettish surprise, hands clamped to his cheeks. "Don't take me for a fool. We both know this is hardly the first time."

"Oh, it was." Again, she ducked her head, dark hair slipping over her face as her voice dipped. "And he feels even worse than I do. He loves you like a brother. He hates himself for this." She looked at him with cow eyes and reached for his hand.

He sprang to his feet and paced, arms animating his speech. "I doubt he's capable of hating himself. He thinks it's a miracle anyone turned out as wonderful as he is."

She glided toward him, satin dress whispering against her thighs, and put her hand on his cheek. He began to pull away, but her other hand held him by the back of his neck. "It was nothing, and it wasn't even that great." Her tone wheedling now, she continued. "You're the only man I'll ever love. You know that."

She peered into his eyes. "But I have told you this before—you will not be the only man in my life."

As she moved her face closer, he pushed her away. "And I told you we're married. That means you and I don't do these things."

She moved close to kiss him again. When he growled and turned away, she recaptured him, holding his face with both hands. "It's not a big deal. It's only a little harmless fun."

After planting a light kiss on his cheek, she stooped to gather her shoes, lifted the hem of her slit skirt, and tiptoed up the stairs.

He flopped onto the couch, staring at nothing, and searched his soul for a reason to keep going on—any reason. He fell into a nightmare-ridden sleep before he found one.

LARS WAS in the habit of arriving at the office before dawn, partly to make time for trips to Grandpa's farm and partly because Dad was such an early riser. The smell of his eggs and coffee inevitably roused Lars.

Today, he woke to the absence of that smell. He checked the time. It was after four. He wandered into the kitchen, rubbing his eyes. He poured a cup of coffee and lifted it to his lips, then spit it back. Cold. He shot a glance at the cast-iron skillet. Still in the washrack where Mom had placed it last night, and Dad's lunch bag was gone.

He must've left early, forgoing their breakfast custom. Why did that send a chill down his spine?

At the office, Lars peeked in on Dad, already at his desk, but something was wrong. He was sitting head down, face in his hands, elbows planted on a thick drawing.

Lars rapped on the doorframe, and when Dad looked up, his face was gray, his eyes red. "Whoa." Lars whistled. "What's wrong?"

Dad's head dropped, and his body began to jerk in silent sobs. "I can't do this anymore."

Lars hurried across the room and laid a hand on his shoulder. "Can't do what?"

Waving at the drawing, Dad said, "This thing bids next week. There's no way I can get it done."

The drawing was for the Capital Event Center. Lars frowned. "We decided not to bid that job. It's too big."

"We have no choice but bid it."

"Why? No way can we do a job that size, especially on top of our other contracts."

When Dad averted his eyes, Lars's gut dropped. He tightened his grip on the shoulder. "What aren't you telling me?"

"We need this job."

"What's going on?"

Dad's mouth tightened into a thin line. His gaze slid to a

pile of envelopes on the floor. They bore certified mail stamps. Lars picked them up. One by one, he slipped out the contents. Now, he held a stack of contracts, all stamped with large red letters—C-A-N-C-E-L-E-D. He dropped into the nearby chair, legs now too weak to hold him. "When did this happen? How many did we lose?"

"All of them that mattered, thanks to that restaurant jerk. We're done for." Dad tapped the drawing before him. "This is our only hope."

Lars whistled again. "How can I help?"

"No one else knows. Want to keep it that way. Was hoping not to put this on you guys."

"What do you need me to do?"

Dad nodded, his back straightened. "Okay. Here's what I'm thinking. . . ."

MARIPOL MARCHED through the main doors of the Two Rivers Bureau of Peace headquarters. The guard at the security station looked up at his approach, manner bored until he spotted Maripol. His eyes widened, and he nearly tripped over his feet rushing to unlatch the inner door, where he escorted Maripol through, body rigid and movements jerky.

Maripol never broke stride, not taking conscious notice of the man nor of the barrier that so nearly stopped his forward motion.

The problem he'd been analyzing all these many days consumed his attention. What was he missing? He must've overlooked something, failed to interrogate a witness with the necessary ruthlessness, failed to pull a string somewhere.

The slippery priest hadn't stayed on the train. He couldn't prove where the man had gone, as the terminal security cameras provided inadequate coverage. Plus, only one train departed that night, the spur line to Northwoods. Watchers riding it surveilled all movements. Agents also remained at Northwoods but found no sign of the priest there either. So where could he be?

Was it really Father Curtis who the Bureau men had chased this past night? Or a misidentification? And what a debacle that had turned out to be. Three Bureau men on medical leave as a result, supposedly assaulted and incapacitated by the fugitive. And the man had escaped. Into thin air if the Bureau men were to be believed.

He cursed. How was he to produce results, with incompetents like these?

He slowed the torrent of undirected memory, then took an imaginary step backward. He breathed deeply, in and out, forcing his sleep-deprived mind to clarity.

Time to work the investigation through a second time, starting at the beginning. Failure in his business was not a forgivable offense.

He entered the closed office at the end of the hall without knocking. The burly mustachioed man behind the desk glanced up, his obvious irritation quickly replaced with an obsequious welcome.

Maripol sat in an ancient wheeled armchair, the wooden joints so loose he perched on the edge, his feet on the floor, ready for it to betray him.

The chair matched well this decrepit office with its stained mint-green paint, scarred dark-olive woodwork, and frosted wire glass windows. No wonder the Bureau men here seemed so demoralized, dwelling in this sooty sewage lagoon of a city, living out pointless lives in a soul-leeching building.

He laced fingers under his chin. Chief Cawley and his local goons had served their purpose. He'd need a more sophisticated approach. "The Order has appreciated your assistance." He held up a palm to stop Cawley's stammered response. "I've read your report. You are correct. We've done all that can be done here, and I understand your forces are already overburdened. We need not continue to overload them with this affair."

Cawley's face crept into a glad, open-mouthed smile before he snapped his back straight to give a sober nod. "As always, the Bureau is at your service, but yes, you are correct. My men have a full slate, much to do, quite too much."

Maripol held up a finger. "I would, however, request your men keep an eye open for our target, should he stick his head out of cover again?"

"Yeah, yeah, of course." Cawley rubbed his hands together, then gripped his armrests, and shoved himself from the chair. Almost laughing, he strode to his door to open it for Maripol. "Anything for the Order."

What an idiot. The man was giddy with relief. Well, so be it. Better to leave the locals feeling cooperative.

"Right, then." Maripol stood and arranged his robes. "I'll be in contact should we need anything else, and thank you again for your invaluable aid. It will not go unnoticed." He spun and strode down the corridor.

When he exited Bureau headquarters, a figure shadowed him, keeping a discreet distance.

Once certain he wouldn't be overheard, he motioned the man to his side and bent his head to the operative's ear.

As the sun broke the horizon, Leif was cycling his two-mile commute to the mill. He passed other men and women, the wealthy riding bikes, and the average person walking.

He should have been enjoying the fine air peculiar to early fall. Refreshing, invigorating. The wind in his face smelling of new-mown hay and ripening grain. The sun warm on his neck, still so low on the horizon that his shadow stretched impossibly far ahead, wobbling in time with the revolution of the pedals. But he enjoyed none of it, noticed little, too deeply sunk in the morass of ruminations.

He'd started working with Dad young, even before the Bad Times had begun. Back then, public schools were still in operation, but after classes, on weekends, and on summer holidays, he'd worked in the mill. By age fourteen, in his drive to earn Dad's approval, he'd become a journeyman woodworker and often exceeded the skills of the grown men.

Those had been the times when he'd bounced out of bed, arriving at the mill, early and eager. Now he dreaded mornings. Work started at seven sharp, but judging by the angle of the sun, he'd be late again.

He sighed as he forced himself to keep pedaling, even when every fiber of his being wanted to go somewhere else. Anywhere else. He muttered to himself his morning litany. "It could be worse."

Sparse motivation as that was, in this world, he was lucky to have the position. Few got a job of their choice, most forced into a Committee-mandated work assignment. All was owned by the collective, and all was decided from on high "for the greater good."

Was this all there would ever be? What did a guy have to look forward to? The blessed unawareness of death? That this soul-killing existence was the best things could ever get was an irresistible weight, dragging him deeper into the gray fog of the wall-less prison he called his life. What was the point?

He guided his bike into the rack and clicked the locks in place to secure the invaluable transport. He then untied his backpack and shouldered it, heavy with drawings and work orders.

For years, he'd taken projects home in hopes a burst of extra effort could get him caught up on the backlog. He'd promised Diana it was a temporary solution.

Now, it was an inescapable necessity.

As he passed through the worktables, he mumbled hellos to early arrivals. He entered his office and set the briefcase on the low desk next to his drafting table, then slid out last night's work.

The draftsmen would take his original drawings to trace for the shop and outside vendors.

More than the big machines in the shop would roar to life should the Committee bless them with electricity. Drafting, job tracking, accounting, communication, and other functions would also soar to new levels of productivity. But, short of highly placed allies in Capital, this would never happen.

As he carried a stack of paperwork upstairs, he passed Dad's office and peeked in.

Dad looked up, checked his watch, and twisted his lips in a disapproving frown. He bent his head back to his work.

That wordless rebuff bit hard, and Leif stayed in the doorway, waiting to be acknowledged, waiting for his dad to soften, to look up again, this time with a smile. Eventually, Leif gave up and walked on, head down, now wearing a matching frown.

CHAPTER 12

Curtis was in the rocky plain again, atop a pyramid. Inky darkness swirled below, other pyramids poking from it like icebergs in a dark sea. People crowded the tips, jostled toward the peaks, fled the surging black shoals.

Forms darted from the dark, writhing, amorphous things, reaching and grasping, occasionally plucking an unlucky person from their perch to fall and be swallowed by the churning mass.

On the nearest pyramid, two babes—toddlers, cherubic figures—stood hand in hand, their backs to him. Dark things surged at them from below, the attackers coming closer with each charge. They backed away, being driven up the slope. With one more step, they'd be at the peak's sharp summit, in danger of falling backward with any further movement. Behind them, another dark shape crouched, ready to spring when they fell.

He shouted a warning, his words ripped out of his mouth by the wind. They couldn't hear him. He screamed and hollered, to no avail. He picked up a stone and threw it with such force his shoulder threatened to dislocate.

It fell far short.

The two backed the final, fatal step. Finding no footing, they teetered, arms flailing.

The crouching figure leaped for the kill—

Curtis woke to his own shouted warning.

He slowed his breathing as he pushed from the cot. How many nights must he wake this way, disoriented and terrified, only to trade a bad dream for the real nightmare, this one of unjust persecution, of panicked flight from a very real pursuer?

He rubbed his goose-pimpled arms again, still feeling the icy dream wind, compounded by the dank gloom of this prison. The massive concrete walls seeming to suck all heat, all life from his limbs. He moved to a rocker by the fire and held shaky hands toward the still-glowing coals.

Who'd have imagined he'd be a hunted criminal—him, a simple priest! That he'd need to be hidden like this? That his most trusted friend would prove to be a liar and a traitor?

He again searched for the nonexistent clock. Was it evening yet? Would Reuel come soon? Early the previous morning, he'd allowed Phillip to lead him back to the hideout, too frightened, too weary to resist.

While they slinked through back alleys, Phillip said he'd been sound asleep when a great wind awakened him. He'd opened his eyes to see a vision standing over his bed, a glowing figure who said "fear not" and told him to find Father Curtis in the "garden of the lion."

Knowing of only one garden with a lion in it, Phillip had risen and arrived just in time.

Curtis had been crouched in the bushes, the policemen closing on him when a hand clamped over his mouth. Seeing Phillip's face inches from his own, Curtis barely choked off an involuntary shout.

Then they'd slithered into a culvert alongside the garden. The officers searched the area, but no lights had penetrated their hiding place.

A hand now touched his shoulder. "Your sleep bad, not rest well."

Curtis waved off the comment, not ready to speak of his dreams when his friend's night vision had led him to mount a rescue. "I owe you my life, Phillip."

"Is small thing."

"It's not a small thing, and I won't forget it." Curtis ran a hand through his tangled hair. His throat tightened. "I'm sorry I endangered you. It's just . . . I feel as if I'm living in a nightmare. No, more accurately, as if my life until now has been a pleasant dream and I now wake to this nightmare of a reality." He tipped his face to the ceiling and groaned. "Eternal One, what am I to do?"

"Oh, my boy," another voice answered. "It pains me to see you in such distress, and more so to know I am the cause."

Startled, Curtis spun.

Professor Reuel stood at the ladder's base, blinking at him with rheumy, remorseful eyes.

"You!" Curtis launched himself from his chair. "All these years you've been lying to me. You pretended to serve the Eternal, to be my brother in ministry. You gave your oath to the Order, and yet you have this secret life? This?" He flailed an arm toward the rows of books, a mute testimony, a menacing presence, terrifying in what they represented. "What kind of man can do that? How can I ever again believe anything you say?"

The old man weathered the tirade, his face a mask, his eyes betraying gentle sadness.

Father Curtis wound down. His hands hung idle at his sides. His shoulders slumped. No answer was forthcoming. "Well? What do you have to say for yourself?"

"I have no answer to satisfy the wound I caused you." The professor seemed to grow smaller, more wizened, aging in real time. "What is done in this place is done in secrecy, out of necessity. Only those involved are aware of it. This is not by my choice, but is as it must be."

Only their unmatched breathing disturbed the silence. Then Reuel took a tentative step toward him, arm out as if to take him by the hand. When Curtis crossed his arms and stepped back, Reuel dropped the hand and hung his head, shaking it side to side. "Moreover, I kept this from you not only for the protection of those involved but also to protect you, my boy." He dabbed his eyes with his shirtsleeve. "You, above all others, I wanted to keep from this, to insulate from this danger."

His voice breaking, he sank into a chair.

The sight was so pathetic all heat went out of Curtis. He slumped, elbows on table and fingers buried in his mop of dark hair. "Well, do you deny this is treason to the Order? A dishonor to the Writings? Why would you do it?"

"Is it treason to the Order?" Head cocked, the old man fixed bright eyes on the fire as if seeing something in its flames. "I wonder. If our Order values truth as we claim, how can it be treasonous to seek it? Truth is only an offense to those loyal to a lie."

The professor had always been able to turn Curtis's thoughts into a pretzel, and he was trying to do it again. Not this time. "That's sophistry."

"Is it?"

"Of course it is." Curtis gave another violent arm gesture, bumping his elbow on the wooden table, nearly as heavy and immovable as those gray walls that now caged him in. "We rely on the Writings. I've seen lives helped by them and lives ruined when people stray from them. You attack that, you attack the foundations of our faith, our civilization." Rubbing the elbow, he shoved his chair back and stood to pace.

"As I recently reminded you . . ." Reuel settled back in his chair. His head swiveled to track Curtis's movements. "A young man once wrote a number of papers. These came perilously close to challenging the Writings where they conflicted with what he called 'evident truth.'"

Curtis grunted and turned away. "I was young and arrogant. I grew up and realized there are things I can't understand."

"So you have given up?" Reuel stood, braced his palms on the table, and bent over them. "Given in?"

Curtis spun, his finger pointed, a flashing heat rising from his core. "I battle every day for the good of my people. How is that giving in?"

"Yes, indeed. I understand this about you, perhaps better than you do yourself. Let us examine. You say you've seen lives destroyed because people strayed from the Writings. You claim that, by teaching the Writings, you have helped those people. Please elaborate."

"You're deflecting." He flattened his hands on the table, matching Reuel's stance, leaning in to bring himself face-to-face with the old man. "This conversation is about you, not me."

Phillip tapped Professor Reuel's shoulder and whispered in his ear. Reuel patted his back, sending him off. Then Phillip waved to Curtis and climbed the ladder to the exit.

"Hear me out, my boy." Reuel puffed a breath through his lips and sank back into his chair. He nodded Curtis to his own. "I stand accused, so allow me to mount my defense. Now, an example, please. How have the Writings helped your flock?"

"You know all this already."

"Humor me."

Curtis scowled at the pipes running along the otherwise bare concrete ceiling. "You know Northwoods was a mess when I began my apprenticeship there. It took me a while to get to the root of the problem."

"And that was?"

"That complicated, dysfunctional mess of a congregation

flummoxed me, but then I realized it was thus. People are self-ish. They do destructive things, chase temporary happiness, and hurt everyone around them. I often compared those bad choices to a grain of sand that started an avalanche, a cascade of bad consequences."

He stood, went to the dying fire, and added a new log to the embers. It'd been so long since he'd thought of those early days, now a lifetime ago. He remained on his haunches before the fireplace, speaking as if to the fading coals. "I went to Father Angelo, but he wasn't open to new ways. So I did what I was able with the youth groups."

His chest warmed, both from the memory and from the coals that bloomed to life as he fanned them. Those early years, seeing the seedlings sprouting changes, so much like the growing flames now licking up the side of the log.

"A year later, Father Angelo died, and I became the senior pastor. I then implemented my ideas in the church as a whole." Leveraging himself against the concrete hearth, he pushed to his feet, then spread his hands. "You already know this history. You know when I was allowed to teach the Writings properly, it made a difference."

He reclaimed his chair, sliding into the smooth wooden seat. Across the table, Reuel's face was side lit by the dancing flames, deepening the shadowed wrinkles. So old, so bone brittle. How could Curtis stay angry with this fragile, precious little man?

Reuel laced his hands over his chest, the perfect pose of a seasoned lecturer. "Give me an example of the destructive things people stopped doing because of the Writings."

That conversation he never got to have with Leif... "One of the biggest problems is alcoholism. It drags down the family and, therefore, the entire community. I've made it my mission to change that. Slowly, over time, it's gotten better."

Reuel nodded his encouragement. "And you made this change by teaching the Writings?"

"That's my point. The Writings make lives better."

"What verses did you find most helpful when teaching about drunkenness? Can you name any offhand?"

"Of course." Curtis rattled off several from memory.

Head tilted to one side, Reuel gave him a confused look. "The verses you reference are general teachings about living an exemplary life. None specifically address alcohol. Can you offer me any which do?"

Good point. Heart thudding, Curtis floundered. "I'm sure I can, but not offhand."

Reuel slid a copy of the Writings toward him. "Here, perhaps you have simply forgotten. Can you find one for me?"

Curtis's hands began to jitter as he searched the table of contents and then the index. Then he stopped. Why did he feel the need to prove this, to justify himself to his old teacher? He slid the book away and slumped against his hard wooden seat. "The argument might be derivative of more general teachings, but it's still valid. The proof is in happier families and healthier communities."

"Of that, I have no doubt, my boy. But this is the problem with the Writings. They are majestic enough to seem authoritative, yet vague enough one may read into them anything one is predisposed to find." He raised gnarled hands in a plea. "Can't you see, my boy, they are designed to give comfort without offense. In the end, there is no true substance in them."

Curtis recoiled from those reaching hands. Blasphemy!

And not true. He could prove it.

The Writings had helped him teach against so many things —gossip, greed, marital infidelity, and vengeance. He'd used them to extol brotherly love, charity, kindness, and more.

He could defend all of these teachings by the evidence of improved lives, but where were these written as direct teaching in the Writings? He snatched up the book and flipped page after onionskin page, each time thinking this next reference would prove that Reuel was wrong. Was lying. But each passage fell short of the remembered specificity.

He threw the volume down with a ruffling of flyleaves. "What's the point of this exercise? I shouldn't be the one defending myself." He spread his arms as if to encompass the offending collection of books. "*You're* the criminal. How're you going to fix my reputation? That's what I want to know."

Reuel reached across the table and caught Curtis's forearm with one hand, patting his hand with the other. "The point is this. You accuse me of attacking the foundations of your faith. You're angry because of that. I am trying to help you see the Writings aren't the foundation you believed them to be. They're not as pivotal to your ministry as you think."

"Ridiculous."

Reuel slapped the table, his sleeve jostling empty cider cups. "Think about it, man. You spent your life convincing yourself you served the Order when you were really serving your people, as you should. The Writings had little to do with it. You know as well as I do, many of your teachings run contrary to the traditions of the Order."

"I've been a loyal priest."

"Really? I remember one of your first actions was to eliminate the holy day wine festivals. Those parties are a staple in most churches and encouraged by the Order. Nothing in the Writings contravenes such observances. You suffered great controversy over that." His gaze lanced Curtis from beneath those shaggy white brows. "Given the trouble it caused you, why did you embark on such a campaign?"

Being led into a trap, but uncertain what Reuel was leading at, Curtis exhaled his caged breath. "I didn't do that out of disloyalty. I did it out of concern. Alcoholism was rampant in my church. How could I, in good conscience, promote more drinking?"

"I take no issue with your position—no, I applaud it! But my point is this: you served your people and ministered to them based upon truths you observed in the world around you. You did not find those truths in the Writings. You say you built your life and ministry on the Writings. I say poppycock. You built it on truth and then ascribed that truth to the Writings—*after the fact.*"

Curtis braced against the table, his understanding of himself, of his world crumbling again. He scrambled to regain his footing and, half rising from his chair, opened his mouth to protest.

Reuel waved a placating hand. "Please understand this. My aim is not to attack the Writings. I seek truth, just as you have, even if you knew it not."

A whisper drifted through Curtis's head, an echo from a dream. "Seek the truth," he murmured, dropping back into his chair.

"What? I did not hear you, my boy."

One of the candles guttered, and a thread of sooty smoke coiled to the ceiling. That swirling, inky pool grew, high above his head, but he wasn't thinking about the candles, or even about this room. He was back in that dark, cold place. Back with the lion.

Something in his mind clicked, almost audibly, like tumblers falling home in a lock. "In my dream, the lion told me to seek the truth."

Reuel's eyes widened, then glowed. He grabbed Curtis's arm, shaking it as if to wake him. "And you have always done so, even when you deceived yourself into thinking you followed the Writings. You could not help yourself. It is your nature. You and I, my boy, have always sought truth, each in our way. Always. How can you fault me for doing so now?"

Curtis took in the rows of books on the shelf. The weight of their consequent presence pressed on him, the unseen mass of their significance creating a kind of psychic gravity. Now, instead of being wholly terrified by their pull, a part of him reached, ever so tentative, toward them. *Is there something there? Something I should learn?*

No! He snatched his hand back from Reuel as if snatching back that imaginary reaching hand. "If we can't trust the Writings, then what?"

"Ah." Reuel smiled. "Now we come to *the* question. What can we trust, or more to the point, what is truth? What if I were to prove, beyond a shadow of a doubt, the Writings have, indeed, been targeted, but not by me? They have been under assault for a long time, have been altered. What if I were to prove our efforts here are an attempt to rescue them from that very attack, to recover that lost truth?"

CHAPTER 13

After entering Dad's office, Lars spread a drawing on the desk. The furnishings plan for the event center.

Dad set aside his pen, rolled his chair a few inches from his desk, and rubbed his eyes. "What's up, bud?"

"I started the counts on this job. This thing is huge. The first phase is supposed to deliver by the end of the year." Lars wrapped his arms around his legal pad, hugging it to himself as if for comfort, hoping the pressure would relieve the growing pain in his belly. "I'm not sure we can make this much product by then, even taking in to account the canceled jobs. Even if we could, we don't have the capital to do it."

That wasn't the worst of it. Once they purchased materials, it'd take time for the product to make its way through the mill, then came acceptance of delivery, final inspection, closeout documents, and a two-to-three-month wait for payment. "Dad, even if we somehow survived the production costs, we'll be bankrupt while we wait for our money."

Dad's jaw flexed, his posture rigid. "We've got no choice."

You need to listen for once, you stubborn old coot. "Look at the numbers!" Lars swallowed hard against his rising voice, then braced his hands on the desk, and pushed into Dad's space to force his focus. "We can't finance something this big, this fast, even if the shop could perform, which it can't."

"Leave that to me. I have some ideas. You just get the counts done."

He had to be kidding! Lars shoved away from the desk and strode back to his office. He slapped the notebook onto his desk, picked it up, and slammed it down again, harder. The counts alone were going to take him every hour he had, even working the weekend. Then he'd still need to do material and labor breakdowns. Good thing there were only a few dozen elements in the furniture package, albeit in dizzying quantities.

Hours later, Mom called him into the lunch meeting, and he was surprised at the time. He'd forced himself into a Zen-like groove, ignoring his indigestion. Were those boiled eggs he'd eaten too old? When he entered the conference room, Leif, Mom, and Dad were already there, as were their lawyer, insurance man, and County Administrator German.

They unwrapped sandwiches and released the sharp bite of onion, the smooth tartness of cucumber.

The lawyer got down to business. "We're meeting to review where we are with the succession issues." He drank from his tea and pulled out a sheaf of paperwork, sheets rustling as he passed copies around the table. "Your parents have put in place a last-to-die insurance policy to help pay Stewardship transfer fees, should either or both of you wish to pursue assignment of the stewardship at the time of their deaths."

Lars frowned. Just *what* was going on here?

Beside him, Leif sat upright, suddenly alert. "What do you mean 'at the time of their deaths'? What does that have to do with anything? We plan to transfer the stewardship when Mom and Dad retire, right?"

Mom focused on her sandwich. Dad stared at the wall.

Leif glared toward German. "What is this?"

German spread his hands, palms down in a calming

gesture. "Just a formality to protect the family's interests. If you have other plans, this won't affect—"

"Actually . . ." Dad cleared his throat. "It will be best for the mill if we hold off on transferring stewardship. We can't afford the fees right now, and your mom and I feel you need more time and experience before taking the responsibility."

Leif's whole body jerked, his temper obviously kindled.

Lars gripped his brother's shoulder, squeezing to get his attention. "It doesn't matter, does it? We're all a team, no matter who holds the official stewardship, right?"

Leif snorted. "Let me tell you a story. Last month, I was at the Hollander plant for meetings about the new lacquer formulation. As ancient as old man Hollander is, he's not *the* old man Hollander. During one conference, an older guy burst in and began berating him about how the sidewalks hadn't been properly swept."

Eyes narrowing, hands flattening on the table, Leif leaned toward Dad. "Sound familiar?"

While Dad shifted in his chair and Mom touched Dad's arm, Lars picked cucumber slices from his tomato and chickpea sandwich. Where was the meat? And Mom knew he hated cucumber. They curdled his stomach. He suppressed a grunt. Who was he kidding? He knew what was making his gut clench.

"I mean," Leif continued. "He let him have it, right there in front of everyone. Old man Hollander sat and took it, never uttered a word. Just hung his head and nodded. Later on, I asked the chief engineer about it. He said Hollander's dad does that kind of thing all the time and Hollander can't do a thing about it because the old guy, not Hollander, holds the stewardship."

Lars sank back in his chair and eyed the space under the table. Years ago, he'd have crawled under it for a place to hide. Maybe this would be a good time to see if he could still fit.

Mom shrunk into herself, her slim shoulders folding over her chest. Dad had turned deeper and deeper shades of red, eyes stony.

Leif pushed to his feet, hands still pressed on the table as his shadow loomed over it. "He says Hollander may even lose the stewardship when his dad passes because he's grown the company to be so big and profitable, the succession fees will be ruinous. So I ask you—Why would I work until I'm old enough to retire and never see the stewardship, never have any authority?"

His stomped footsteps thudded away. The door slammed before Lars dared raise his gaze from its hiding place under the table.

Mom addressed the visitors after Leif marched out. "I'm sorry. This was very embarrassing."

German drummed his fingers on the table. "We blindsided the poor boy. Grant him patience. He'll see this is the only option."

German and the lawyer packed their briefcases and left.

Mom patted Dad's arm. "Give him time to adjust, honey."

"Time?" Dad jerked even further from her. His jaw was locked, and veins pulsed in his temples. "That boy has gotten too big for his britches. Someone needs to cut him down to size."

Lars shrugged at Mom and retired to his office to scale the work mountain awaiting him. But the undercurrent of tension in the air, like a building lightning storm, made the burning tightness in the pit of his stomach grow.

No. It wasn't the cucumbers, and it wasn't the eggs.

The staff felt it too. They moved about, heads down, unusually intent on their paperwork, not stopping to converse at the coffee dispenser. He munched another bismuth tablet.

~

Professor Reuel climbed, sliding the smooth leather of his sole until his heel was set on the rung. Then, joints creaking, he lifted the next foot. As his head cleared the hatch, the bed came into view. On it lay a man wearing the robes of the Order. Reuel jerked back, nearly slipping from the ladder.

Something creaked.

He wrenched his gaze to Phillip sitting in a straight chair near the closet.

He slowed his breathing, hand to heart. "What in the Eternal?"

The chair scraped. Phillip stood and walked to the bedside, looking down at the sleeping man. "Is man follow you. I find picking lock to room."

Apparently having heard the commotion, Curtis popped his head out of the closet. "Everything okay?" When he saw the robed man, he flinched.

After limping to the bed, Reuel pressed the man's jaw for a pulse. "You did not kill him?"

"No, he sleep the forget-me sleep." Phillip lifted the man's hand in which nestled a microinjector, then pointed to the red dot on the man's neck. "Amnesynth."

Curtis studied the injector. "Amnesia-inducing drug?"

At Phillip's nod, Curtis screwed up his face. "If he had the injector, why is he the one asleep?"

"When he try to inject me, missed. Inject self."

Heavy black brows shooting up, Curtis asked. "How'd he manage that?"

Phillip shrugged. "I help, little bit."

This shouldn't be happening. Reuel peeled back one of the man's eyelids, the dilated pupils gone black. "How long will he be out and what will he remember?"

"Sleep six, maybe eight, hour. Not remember me. Not remember room, maybe. Does remember was follow you."

Curtis puffed his lips and blew out air. "So now what? They'll come arrest the professor?"

Would they? Reuel crossed his arms and put a thumb to his chin, trying to see it from the enemy's perspective. "No. At least not yet. They hope I'll lead them to a bigger prize."

Curtis pointed at his chest. "Me?"

"Yes, you, or more importantly the group sending all those letters to Nob." *Meaning me.*

Like a trapped animal, Curtis jerked his gaze about the room. "We need to find a place to go. Fast."

Ah, poor boy. Reuel patted his most promising pupil's shoulder and steered him toward the hatch. Time to calm him before he did something rash. Again.

"Don't you worry, my boy. You are quite safe. They do not know you are here, else they would have broken in rather than sneaking about. What we need is a convincing and final end to their interest in me. I remember a trick Butterman and I used, back in the old days. It ought to work nicely here."

One foot on top of the ladder, Curtis paused. "Did it work, the trick, back in the day?"

Reuel, mind spinning web upon complicated web, had to tear himself away. What had Curtis just said? "Hmm? Did it work? Oh, never you mind that. It will have improved with age."

He hoped.

A quiet voice deep inside whispered, *Why would it? Nothing else has.*

LARS CLOSED a file and leaned against his chair back, stretching stiff muscles. He'd worked through the week, but was still behind schedule. He might be facing a task beyond himself.

Leif shuffled past his office, his complexion sallow, his eyes fixed, his face locked in a grimace. He'd been like this before, but never this bad. What might be done to shake him out of it?

Needing a break, Lars pushed back his chair for a stroll around the shop floor. Maybe he'd stop by Leif's office, cheer him up.

He'd just made his way downstairs when Dad approached, his taut stride and narrowed brows warning he was in a mood and best avoided. About to reverse course, Lars pretended to study a stack of work orders, but Dad marched unseeing toward Leif's office, stopping in the doorway. "Where are the Hansen work orders? They need to be in the shop now if the job's going to make schedule."

Leif jerked his head up, his eyes flaring. "Where are they?" He waved toward his already overflowing inbox. "They're right there, waiting for someone to do them."

"Why aren't they done already?" The heel of Dad's hand thumped the doorframe. "They're overdue."

"And everything on top of them is even more overdue. Maybe you'd like to tell me which order we can miss delivery on, so I can move your pet job up in the queue."

"You're supposed to get them *all* done on time. That's *your* job, so do it." Without waiting for a response, Dad stomped away.

Leif gaped. Then, in a burst of movement, he stood and gathered the pile of backlogged work. He marched through the office after Dad.

Lars followed. He caught him just as Dad reached his office chair.

Leif plunked the pile in the center of the desk and leaned in, face-to-face with Dad. "Guess what? It's your job now. I'm not doing this anymore."

Spreading his arms in a gesture of finality, Leif spun on his heels and strode away.

Dad sat motionless, his face stony. He fumbled in his shirt

pocket and fished out a pack of cigarettes. With hands trembling, he shook one out, lit it, and drew hard. He exhaled a stream of smoke, purging it from his lungs as if into the face of some unseen enemy.

OUTSIDE THE OFFICE, Leif unlocked his bike and secured his pack. A rush of soft, familiar footsteps padded across the cracked cement. Then Mom's hand landed on his shoulder. "Leif, stop for a minute."

He jerked away, trying to see her through burning eyes. "I can't take it anymore."

"What are you going to do?"

Her gentle question stole the anger he needed. He took a deep shuddering breath. "I don't know. I've had offers. I need to think."

Pain flickered in her eyes. "Don't make any final decisions until we talk. Let me speak to your dad."

"Talk?" Leif snorted and yanked his bike from the rack, rattling the chain. As if there'd ever been a way to talk to Dad! Besides . . . "Talking won't change this. I'm not going to come crawling back for more abuse."

He turned, pushed off, and swung into the seat. He used his entire weight to propel it forward in a single surge.

But he could feel her behind him. Could still see her eyes full of tears she refused to shed. Could feel the building too, a place housing the dreams of generations, both dreams fulfilled and dreams shattered.

CHAPTER 14

Curtis's heart boomed in his chest, thudded in his ears. He drew a shaky breath, then another. But calm wouldn't come.

By now, he was used to waking like this, still in the terror of the dream.

But this was different.

The dream hadn't woken him.

Something else had.

He lay unmoving on the cot, his tangled blanket wound around his legs. Fear sweat rank in his nostrils, the clammy fabric of his nightshirt chilled where he'd soaked the underarms.

Slow, silent breaths, in and out. In and out.

He focused on the darkness, listened for the sound that wakened him. Had it been a sound? Or a sense of some presence there, somewhere in the dark stone prison?

And that sense was strong now, growing stronger. Had the Order found him? Was one of their dark assassins even now creeping his way? Ready to slip a dagger between his defenseless ribs? An ice pick into his temple?

There it was again. A rustle, almost inaudible. Then a scrabbling, this time even closer.

The dark was complete. Even the coals in the fireplace dormant, only glowed the dullest red.

Then a shadow passed before that spot of light, blocking it before it winked back into view. And whoever it was, they were coming his way.

He sprang from the bed, hands raised. Little good such defense would do against anyone trained by the Eye. But he'd not die a coward. He'd leave his mark on the man, even with his dying strength.

The blankets knotted about his legs, and he went down hard. His right knee slammed concrete. The point of his shoulder crunched, and his head struck like a hammer on wood. Bright yellow flashed inside his closed eyelids, fading to red, and he lay stunned. Helpless.

But no attack came.

All was still.

As he was falling, hadn't he heard that scrabbling again, edging away? What kind of killer would miss such a chance? And what kind of murderer would flee?

He disentangled himself, then levered himself to his knees, to his feet. With his first step, he staggered against the bed frame, disoriented as much by the complete dark as the knock on the head.

His knee whacked the nightstand, the same he'd landed on in the fall. Another yellow flash lit his inner eye, and he stood, braced against the tabletop until the wooziness departed.

He then fumbled, bumped the candleholder to the floor, but trapped the matchbox. He slid it open while waiting for a blow between his shoulder blades. Muscles twitched in anticipation.

The match popped and sputtered, taking fire. Light flared

along with the sweet sulfur smell. Match above his head, he turned a circle, his other hand ready to ward off a blow.

None came.

No one was there.

He stooped, his head still cottony, his balance unsteady. The candle had fallen from the brass holder and rolled beneath the bed. He scooped it up and lit it as the heat of the shortening matchstick burned his fingertips.

Now, his every motion sent long shadows across the far wall. He needed a weapon, but what? This bare room housed naught but books.

Ah. There, on the table. The large brass candelabra, the only suitable weapon in sight.

He'd have to cross the room to it.

What he wanted to do was huddle in a corner and hope whoever had snuck in would go away. What he did was step forward, stoop to check under the table before getting too close.

With a lunge, he snatched up the candelabra and, wielding it like a pitchfork, backpedaled into that corner.

Nothing moved. No sound. No sign of the intruder.

No. Not true.

Past the table, past the bookshelves, in the darkest reaches, a shadow stirred.

He thrust his candle higher, angling it toward that dark space.

A cat. The shadow was a cat.

It fled the light and scurried beneath the bookshelf.

Curtis's back pressed to the wall. He slid down it to sit, hard concrete cold beneath his rear, thin nightshirt still damp from his somnolent exertions.

He blew out long and hard. Stilled his jittering and chuckled.

A cat. It was just a cat.

And by the glance he'd had at its bony ribs, it was hungry.

Never a pet lover, he still couldn't let the poor thing starve. Not something trapped here, as he was. Prisoners must care for one another. Who else would?

From the cupboard, he pulled out a hard sausage. He pinched a morsel onto a saucer and, crooning to the cat, set it before the bookshelf. The soft clink of china rang like a dinner bell.

It poked its nose out, head lifted, sniffing the air. Then slinked on haunches toward the prize, its glossy black fur nearly invisible in the shadows.

It snapped up the meat, blurred beneath the shelf, and crouched, growling as it tore at the offering. Meal devoured, it backed into the darkness, only glowing green eyes remained, staring.

Curtis rekindled the fire. Heat now warmed his sodden clothing.

He added two new saucers to the concrete hearth, one with more sausage, another with a dollop of the cold tea he'd forgotten last night. When his eyes had given out from his frenzied search of the writings.

He'd been determined to prove Reuel wrong. Had been sure that, without Reuel's badgering, he'd succeed.

His life had not been a sham or a waste. No matter how much Reuel tried to convince him otherwise.

But he was still unable to make his case that the Writings were internally valid, internally consistent. He pushed that aside. Along with the gut-clenching panic it threatened to reawaken.

The cat darted out, muscles bunched, legs like springs, ready to bolt. It crouched there until hunger apparently won out. It flowed low to the ground, slitted eyes watching Curtis.

He leaned back in the rocker, the cushions soft, moving further from the hearth, from the cat. Less of a threat.

The creature leapt, its padded feet silent before the saucer.

It worried at the meat, not growling this time, then lapped at the tea.

He'd name the cat Dantes, his fellow prisoner, victim of cruel fortune. Perhaps they could plot their escape? The recovery of their good names? Exact the justice the original Dantes yearned for.

Curtis broke another chunk from the sausage. Firelight played over his extended offering.

The cat stepped closer, froze. Then took another step, then another. Until it landed in his lap, feeding from his fingers.

It perched on his thighs, so unnaturally light. The poor thing must have been starved near death. How had it gotten in here? How long had it been trapped?

Meal complete, it curled into his midriff, green eyes looking up at his. Not slitted this time, but open. Expressing a mute thanks? He cupped a hand near its head, a cautious invitation, and it butted his palm.

It felt good, to hold this creature. To give comfort, to receive the same.

It brought to mind another cat, the one of his dreams. The otherworldly comfort, the love, he'd felt then. So much more. So much greater, beyond measure, beyond imagining or explanation.

A sob racked his chest. A tear trickled and splashed onto his skin, hot as it ran to his fingertips.

Oh, if only one could find such love in the real world, not only in a dream. If only he could bask forever in that joy. If only he could fill this hollow, empty space that had always existed, deep inside. This terrible aching void.

If only.

CHAPTER 15

Leif pedaled faster, sweat popping on his brow, spreading a dark stain from the armpits of his shirt. His fists clenched the handlebars, worrying them until his knuckles went white. Would he finally get relief from this tight ball in his guts? And he did feel it, didn't he? "Yes," he insisted, hoping to speak it into being. He did feel relief. Relief and freedom, leaving Northwoods Millworks behind. For the last time?

Free, but numb. His chest constricted, his throat tightened, and he fought to breathe past a sense of doom, of somehow having—What? Sinned? Even having rejected the double-talk of the Order, he could still think of no other word.

No. He wasn't the one in the wrong here. He was the victim.

But work at the mill had been his life. What now?

He pedaled around the abandoned sandpits, the wind of his passage blowing his blond hair back from his forehead. He loved to be out in the wild places. Today, the scenery passed him by unseen, the honking of the geese unheard. He whizzed by a thicket of wild plums, the fruit plump and dewy red. A doe stood beneath the trees, interrupted in her feast, tensed and muscles shivering, ready to bolt. He passed within ten feet of her hiding place, but couldn't appreciate even this.

His wanderings brought him to the church, and he found himself opening the sanctuary doors. In the shadowy interior, a priest was arranging altar hangings. "Father Curtis, you're back."

The priest turned—a stranger.

Leif stepped back and looked around the room, searching. "Is Father Curtis here?"

"He's been delayed in his travels. May I help you?"

"Nah, was just dropping in," Leif muttered, turning to go, unsure why he'd come, other than some vague notion of having a friend to talk to.

"May I have your name? I can let him know you stopped in."

"No need." He spun back. "Have you heard from him? Do you know when he will be back?"

The man smoothed a velvety altarpiece. "I only know he's been delayed."

Leif left the sanctuary. Having no other destination, he rode home, to the solace of wife and children.

THROUGH A SANCTUARY WINDOW, the substitute priest watched Leif pedal away. He slid an electronic tablet from a pocket and tapped a note. After he finished arranging the altar clothes, he left the main church building and walked to the rectory.

There, he completed his other assigned tasks. When done, he entered the bathroom and shed his robe. He lowered his head to douse it beneath the faucet. Sputtering, he stood, grabbed a thick towel, and dried his face. Each movement of his chest muscles caused his tattoo of the Eye of the Eternal to dance in the mirror.

LEIF STEPPED INSIDE to Diana napping on the couch, the baby in a playpen next to her, the toddlers nowhere to be seen. He shook her awake, smelling sour wine. As she opened bleary eyes and regarded him, he sank onto the cushion beside her. "Where are the other kids?"

"Marylin took them to her house so I could rest. What are you doing home?"

"I quit my job."

She jerked upright. "You did *what*?"

"Quit. Not taking it anymore."

"Seriously?" Her voice rose several octaves. "What are we going to do now? I can't work. I have to take care of the kids."

She didn't appear to be doing either, but he bit his tongue. They'd been fighting enough lately as it was. "We'll figure it out. I've had offers from folks down south. Maybe we should move there."

"Move? No way, Leif. I'm not leaving my mom alone. You know how fragile she is."

That pried his grip on his temper loose. "Oh, so we're going to make all our decisions based on what your mom wants? What about *our* needs? Your mom's not going to decide anything for us."

Fragile. That woman was about as fragile as a blacksmith's anvil.

Her narrowed eyes couldn't hide the flames, just focused them. On him. "If you want to go, then go. Get out. I don't need you or any man."

"Good. You start paying the bills."

"Let me tell you something." All bleariness gone, she poked his chest. "You are no great provider. You think I can't do this without you? Think again. Everyone says I'm stupid to keep putting up with your nasty self, and you're darn lucky I do."

He stood and backed away from her sharp finger, but she pursued him, a berserker pixie. He left the room in no mood for this. She chased him. "Where do you think you're going? You get back here. We're going to work this out."

He kept walking, which would further anger her. But so what?

"No wonder your dad can't stand you!" She padded after him, her bare feet slapping the linoleum. "You're a jerk."

She cornered him on tiptoes to face him, her breath hot on his lips. "Do you wonder why every girl you were ever with cheated on you?" She thumped his chest and stomped off to reclaim the crying baby, calling over her shoulder as she did. "It's you, buddy."

Once on a roll, she'd go on for hours. Before she could trap him again, he left. Forgoing the bicycle, he walked toward Medium Lake.

LARS FOUND Leif on the big rock, staring out over the lake. Lars had to squint against the late afternoon sun bouncing off the glassy ripples. He sat next to his brother in silence, listening to waves wash the shoreline, running his hand over the weather-smoothed granite. He wrinkled his nose as a breeze came off the water, heavy with rotting fish and seaweed.

Leif threw a pebble. It sailed into the brownish-green depths where it disappeared with a sucking gulp. "I guess you think I blew it."

"Blew it?"

"Yeah, lost my cool. Let my anger goad me to something I regret. But I don't, you know? Don't regret it. I don't know what the right thing is, but keeping on like we were, isn't it."

"I get it." Lars hooked a hand on his brother's shoulder. "So what'cha gonna do?"

Leif exhaled so long and hard his whole body deflated. He braced his hands on his knees. "I'd like to get far away from here. But . . . Diana refuses to move."

He shook his head, the mussy hair moving like wheat in the wind. "I don't want to either. Not really." He drew another long breath, then slumped again. "Maybe freelancing. Rich folk at Capital are looking for custom-designed stuff and willing to pay for quality, not that crap Artisans passes off."

"Mm-hmm?"

A painted turtle surfaced near shore, paddling stubby legs as it made for the rocks. It hauled itself onto a flat boulder just out of the reach of the lapping waves. Leif picked up another pebble and wrenched back his arm to throw it. Until now laconic, the turtle pulled into its shell in a burst of lightning reflex.

What a terrible instinct. Wouldn't it be better to flee back to the water? Now it just lay there on the rock, blind and helpless, an easy mark for any passing opportunist.

"Yeah. I could market directly to clients like that. Offer a full package, from design through installation." Leif's face, drawn and morose, began to brighten, a first gleam of hopeful speculation in his eyes. "The mill would get the work, but I could run my show, my way. Win-win."

Better than watching his brother drift away, maybe far away. Maybe for good. "I can see that working. Do you have any prospects?"

"Actually, yes." Leif's mouth twisted, and he threw another rock at the water, grunting with the effort. "I had approached Dad with some. He always shot them down—out of spite, I think. I'll head to Capital and meet with people, see if they're still looking. One way or another, I'll shake something loose."

Lars bumped his brother's shoulder with his own. "I need to deliver a bid next week. Maybe I can get Dad to let you ride with. You could start working on it."

"Maybe I'll hammer an agreement out with Dad. Not looking forward to that. Assuming I can, then yeah, that sounds good."

"Well, that's partly why I'm here. Mom wants to see you at the house."

Leif pulled his shoulder away, going rigid. "Nope, not dealing with Dad right now."

"He's at a meeting." Lars moved his shoulder to Leif's, bumping him again. "C'mon, Leif. It's just Mom. I'll go with you."

At the house, Lars grabbed the cookie jar and absconded with a handful of molasses cookies, his favorite. He tossed one to Leif. "Want one?"

"You take a fistful and offer me one. Nice."

Mom walked to Leif and hugged him, then pulled back, holding him in place as she searched his eyes.

Lars broke the silence. "Leif has an idea. He wants to work with us as a freelancer, get himself a little elbow room."

Leif claimed the cookie jar and sat at the kitchen island, the dwindling cookies spread before him. "I can bring in work for the mill. Profitable work, negotiated contracts we don't have to bid."

"Okay." Mom climbed on a barstool, her sandaled feet dangling. "That would be helpful, but who'll replace you in project management?"

"Dad seems to think he can do a better job." He bit off a large chunk—like he obviously thought Dad had bitten off more than he could chew this time—then swallowed it down fast. "Let him prove it. That's his problem now."

She puckered her mouth and shot Leif a look.

"Sorry." Leif winced, ducked his head, and used a thumb to scoop up crumbs he'd spread on the butcher-block. "But he'll have to handle that. I'm done."

"So, how do you propose we do this?"

He gestured with the rest of the cookie. "I could draw the same salary I have, but against commissions. I'll do everything —sales, engineering, and project management. I'll even handle installation and client satisfaction. I can do it for a fifteen percent commission. All the mill has to do is produce the product."

Lars shifted. If his brother was right, a commission at that level represented a major windfall for Leif but was still a profitable proposition for the company.

"I'll talk to your dad."

"So it's a plan, then?" Leif made those same puppy-dog eyes they so often used on her.

"Okay." She laughed and ruffled his hair.

While his brother jumped up and hugged her, Lars broke into a grin and slapped Leif's shoulder. "Glad we won't be losing you."

Lars sat, slipping the last cookie from the jar. He was about to toss it in his mouth and then stopped. He handed it to Leif, who took it without acknowledgment and ate it in one bite, his eyes far away with his plans.

Lars's grin faded along with the momentary glee, replaced by a sense of having forgotten something or, more accurately, of having overlooked something. It nagged at him. He pushed the feeling aside, refusing to lose the joy of this moment.

SOMEONE WAS BANGING on the door, knocking the cheap motel print from its nail. Leda swung feet out of bed, fumbling in the dark for slippers, then snatching up the candle from the nightstand. Where were those matches?

Candle lit, she grabbed her robe and wrapped it tightly, then tucked the covers around the man-shaped bundle of sheets she'd placed next to her in the bed, adjusting the frayed white wig on the pillow. Did that look like a sleeping man? She certainly hoped so. Her life may depend on it.

The pounding came again, louder, the windows now rattling with the force. "Bureau of Peace. Open, or we'll knock it down!"

She unlatched the dead bolt but left the safety chain in place, peering out. "What is the meaning of this? Waking a respectable woman in her lodgings, and at such an hour?"

A man in Bureau uniform stuck his thick red face into the crack, trying to peek through. "I'm here to search the room."

"You most certainly will not. How do I know you're an officer?"

The face turned a deeper shade of red. With a growl, the man stepped back a pace and stuck his chest toward the door. A brass shield glinted in the candlelight. "Here's my badge. Now open up. Last chance, or I'll kick it down."

"I believe you need a warrant for that, don't you?"

Another voice, this one calm, smooth, and unhurried. "You were looking for this?" A black-gloved hand appeared, unfurling a warrant. Behind it stood a young man in the robes of the Order.

Leda's stomach clenched—not only over the robes but also the tiny red welt on his neck. Her fingers fumbled with the chain, and it took three tries to release it. She stepped back and stumbled when her legs hit a chair. She pulled the robe tighter against a sudden shiver, but it didn't help. The shiver wasn't from the cold.

The beat cop barged into the room and straight to the bed. "And what's this?" He grabbed the covers and ripped them from the mattress.

Professor Reuel sat up in bed and snatched the sheet back from the cop's hand, placing it over his legs like a carriage blanket, bare feet sticking from nightshirt. "What, exactly, do you think you are doing, Officer? The effrontery. Give me your badge number."

The uniformed cop ignored him and stomped around the room. He emptied briefcase and bag, dumping the contents on the floor.

The black-robed man glided into the room. "He is doing as he has been instructed, Professor, under the authority of the Order. It is you who will answer the questions. And don't attempt prevarication. You've been under surveillance, and we are aware of your movements. All I need from you is the answer why? For what purpose have you repeatedly snuck here, and at such an hour?"

Professor Reuel looked at the man from beneath lowered brows. "If your parents failed to explain such things to you at an appropriate age, I believe it to be outside my purview to do so."

Now the face above the collar of the robes reddened, matching that of his sidekick. He pointed to the bed. "Sit. Be still while I collect the evidence."

Reuel grasped Leda's hand as she scampered to sit beside him, furthest from the men. She did her best to feign helpless female hysteria. It wasn't easy, never having experienced it herself, but years of studying coeds at the academy had given her ample time to observe those who did. Her performance must've been acceptable, as the two men ignored her and focused instead on Reuel.

The robed man snatched up the papers the uniformed cop had kicked around the floor, assembling them in an untidy stack and moving to the desk. He pointed at the drawers. "Check them. Look for hidden compartments. Look underneath every stick of furniture."

The cop drew himself up. "I know how to toss a room." And began to disassemble the furniture.

The Order man spread the papers on the desktop and

flipped through them before slapping them down. The ancient wooden desk creaked as if ready to collapse. "What is this? Code?" He moved to stand before Reuel, papers wadded in his fist. "What does this mean?"

Reuel enunciated every syllable as if to the dullest of students. "It means I failed to grade my papers last night. Distractions, you know." He gave Leda a wink.

She reached behind him and poked his rib with a pointed thumbnail, a warning hiss under her breath. He was going to pay for that one. A mission was a mission, but there were limits.

The black-gloved hand snatched up the papers. "We'll be taking these, and when our crypto guys get done with them, you'll wish you were more cooperative."

"My students will be disappointed. Please hurry back with them?"

The cop had finished breaking the desk. He now moved to the bed and backhanded him. "Have some respect. Where you're going, you'll need to watch your mouth."

Reuel touched his lip and pulled away a bloodied finger, which he regarded with mild surprise.

She had been controlling the slow burn in her gizzard, but at this last, it boiled over. She snapped erect, toe to toe with the cop, hand on one hip and lecturing finger in his face. "He'll be going nowhere, and you'd know this if you were competent. You have no evidence upon which to arrest him."

The cop pushed her back onto the bed, stepping in close, looming over her. "Who says we need any? Lot of people disappear. You can be next."

She struggled to stand. But he kept a knee on her thigh, unbalancing her. The helplessness of her position brought another hot rush, so intense she imagined she might burn him down with the heat of her narrowed eyes. She started to give him a swift kick, but somehow stopped the impulse. "Young man, if you think you can disappear a luminary of the academy, you are sadly mistaken. We aren't the helpless day laborers you're accustomed to bullying."

The robed man put a hand before the cop's chest and used it like a spatula to separate him from Leda. "Plenty of time for all this later, Officer. For now, we take the evidence and process it." His scowl found Leda. "Then we'll be back with the leg irons."

He pointed the roll of papers at Reuel. "Don't even think of running. I'll know where you are within minutes."

Reuel blinked. "Run, why? I need to wait here so you know where to return my papers."

The cop curled his lip, but let the Order man herd him from the room.

Reuel followed, watching through the cracked door before closing and double-locking it. He then propped a straight chair against the handle for good measure.

When he turned, she glared.

"What?" He raised hands in innocence.

"You know very well what. Bad enough I should destroy my reputation on your behalf. You needn't take advantage."

His little boy grin faded. "I am sorry, Leda. I admit I let myself go a bit, but how to resist? That was so much fun. It so reminds me of the good old days."

"Fun? And a night on the rack is what to you? A jolly time? Perhaps you forget our companions who sacrificed all in those glorious old days of yours?"

Now his grin was gone, an abashed look taking over. "No, Leda. You know I have not. Pardon me."

She focused on the tight muscles of her neck. Breathing out slowly as she forced them to unwind, she massaged that spot at the base of her skull. It seemed to flare up anytime she got involved with this crazy old fool. She caught his unguarded remorse and sighed. "At least you got up here in time."

"Only thanks to you, my dear. You were magnificent."

A light knock came from the closet, and Reuel leaned down to open the hatch.

The dark below outlined Phillip's broad face. "Is all good now?"

Behind him, Curtis was barely visible in the wash of light from the candle, brows furrowed, body tense.

Reuel offered a hand to Phillip, who clambered from the hole. "For now, yes, but it was the same Order man you neutralized before. He is on a mission to exact his revenge."

"So will be back. We have plan to end this thing?"

Reuel patted Phillip's shoulder, crinkled his eyes, and nodded.

She'd seen that nod so very many times. She was not reassured.

CHAPTER 16

The tension in the muscles of Diana's forehead eased as she entered her mom's little house. Something cozy about the cluttered old place, a connection to childhood memories, soothed her. The healing crystals dangling in the windows, incense in bronze icons, statues of protector angels in every corner—none of it ever changed.

Mother poured an oversized wineglass nearly to the brim and handed it over, wine slopping onto the cheap, stained wood table as she did. "What a nice surprise. Where did you say the kids were again?"

"A friend's watching them." Diana took a healthy swallow of sweet wine. It warmed her all the way down, a comforting, happy feeling. Her edginess melted under that heat. Then she caught her mother studying her over her wineglass. "What?"

"Oh, nothing. How is Leif?"

Diana tossed dark hair over her shoulder. "Fine."

"I take that to mean working too much, making too little, and ignoring the best thing in his life. Am I right?"

She narrowed her eyes in her don't-go-there look. The sandalwood incense failed to lift her confidence or create harmony, among the other things her mother claimed she burned it for.

"Fine. I won't tell you I told you so. But you know I did. That boy's a dead weight dragging you down. We all see it. You used to be such a bubbly, beautiful girl." Mother tsked. "Now look at what he's done to you. Drab, dreary, and depressed—even your aura."

At Diana's eye roll, her mother threw up her hands. "What? You deserve better. That's all."

"Stop. I didn't come here for a lecture."

"Fine, let's change the subject. You never listen anyway."

Mother leaned her head back and drained her wineglass, then reached for the bottle and poured. Thick pink wine sloshed up the side of the glass, rising toward the lipstick mark on the rim.

Alcohol fumes, overlaid with the cheap, fruity notes of artificial raspberry wafted to Diana's side of the table.

Mother thunked the cork into the neck of the bottle and then froze, eyes widening, seeming to have remembered something. Her index finger jabbed skyward, the bed of the pointed nail showing white against the chipped red polish.

"I have something for you." She stood and rummaged in her writing desk. "Ah, here it is." She drew out a purple velvet pouch stamped with the symbol of the Eternal, handed it over, and sat again. "The new priest is such a nice young man and making some very positive changes. Here, put this on."

Diana opened the drawstring and poured its contents onto the table—an elaborate chain carrying a pendant, a gem-inlaid golden heart inscribed with an intricate three-sided knot.

"Put it on." Mother twitched her fingers in her hurry-up gesture before reaching for her wine. "I want to see it on you."

Why was her heart rate rising? Diana swallowed hard. "Where did you get this?"

"From the church." Mother flicked her fingers again. "From the new priest, like I said."

"You didn't say." Diana turned the charm over on the table, candlelight licking like fire along the gold. "It's pretty, but . . ." She traced the knot with her pinkie. "I'm not sure. It's a charm, isn't it?"

"It will help your love life."

She hugged herself, rubbing goose bumps. When Diana had been a child, Mother's charms and power talismans hadn't bothered her, but ever since she'd learned of the dangers . . . "Father Curtis says using charms is magical thinking, useless at best and dangerous at worst."

"Don't talk to me about that man." Mother slammed her wineglass down with such force, wine shot toward the smoke-stained ceiling. "He's a heretic. Why, they've all but found him guilty. I always knew it, ever since the day he came."

"I think he's . . . nice."

"Nice?" Mother snorted. "He was an uptight puritan who made the Church of the Eternal into some sort of fun-hating prudes' club. Father Angelo must have been rolling over in his grave." A distant smile stretched thin, pallid lips toward sagging porcelain cheeks. "Now there was a man who knew how to have a good time. He said fun was a blessing from the Eternal. The world needs more men like Angelo."

"I still think—"

Mother made a chopping motion, causing the runed crystals of her bracelet to clack together. "You only think what Curtis taught you to think. All those rules of his aren't from the Writings. I know. I've talked to the new priest about this. The Eternal just wants us to be happy. Father Curtis never understood that."

Mother took a deep breath, waving a hand before her face. "I'm sorry. That man raises my blood pressure." Then she picked up the charm, unclasped it, and held the ends toward

Diana. "Now, please, put it on. I only want to help you. Doesn't your love life need improvement?"

"I don't know." Diana let it dangle from her grip. The charm spun to catch the light. It was pretty.

Mother plucked it from Diana's hand and fastened it on her neck. "Oh, that is beautiful, and the gems highlight those gorgeous eyes of yours. Go look."

Diana stood before the mirror. The green tourmaline did bring out her eyes, made them seem brighter. And she had felt so drab, lately. Besides, what could it hurt? It was blessed by a priest, after all.

Coming up behind her, Mother patted her shoulder. "Better already, isn't it? You'll be fine. You just need some help from the spirits. Have a little fun."

Diana looked at herself in the mirror again. Mom was right, if Leif didn't want to be fun, that was his choice, but he didn't get to choose for her. She deserved some happiness.

She'd keep the charm. And she'd see where the spirits would lead.

THAT NIGHT, Curtis reentered the nightmare landscape. He hadn't previously, but this time, he realized he was dreaming. Even with that knowledge, he couldn't wake, couldn't extricate himself. As always, this place was somehow more real than the waking world.

He was again in the broken land, was again atop the steep pinnacle. People were still clinging to other peaks, attempting to avoid the doom below. The cherubs still stood atop their perch. Hadn't they fallen? No, they'd only begun to slip before he'd woken himself.

From another nearby pyramid shone a blinding white light, too bright to focus on, to see from where it emanated. The dark forms at its base were agitated, moving more violently than those on the rest of the plain. Groups of the beings occasionally dashed up the slope in an attempt to reach the light but were driven back, screaming in unholy rage.

By squinting his eyes, protecting them with cupped hands opened enough to create a slit, he just barely made out the shape at the center. Was it . . . a sword? Yes, yes! A double-edged short sword shone with otherworldly light.

And he stood there, his body drinking in the glow like a plant does the sun, welcoming it like a babe welcomes its mother's milk. He somehow knew this sword was that for which he'd so long sought. If he could only reach it, all things would be made right. He sobbed as he woke, wanting to return to the dream and the comfort of the light.

MARIPOL MARCHED through the main doors of the Two Rivers Bureau of Peace headquarters. This time, the guard at the security station was watching for him and opened the barricade when Maripol was still several strides away. With one look at his face, the guard's open mouth of greeting snapped closed, and he found something interesting to study on the far wall.

Maripol's boots rapped out a hollow cadence on the worn wood floors, his palm rattling the frosted wire glass of the conference room door as he stiff-armed it midstride. It banged against the wall and rebounded, then slammed shut in an even more violent rattle of glass with some last-minute assistance from his boot heel.

"Out," he said to the thick beat cop who sat, red-faced next to Maripol's black-robed investigator. The cop glanced across the table at Chief Cawley, who jerked his head in assent. He stood and slapped his hat against his thigh as if about to object, then seemed to think the better of it and left.

Maripol made the hint of a bow toward Cawley. "Your assistance, as before, is appreciated. I am sorry my investigator troubled you with this matter. We'll take it from here."

Cawley rapped knuckles on the wooden table, then levered himself to his feet. "Anything for the Order, as always." If the cop had been reluctant to leave, Cawley made up for it with his obvious desire to be far away from this Order business, and quickly.

Maripol stood across the table from his man, arms crossed behind his back, studying him like a butcher studies a side of beef before swinging the cleaver. He pointed at the red dot on the man's neck. "Explain that."

The man rubbed the welt. "It'll all be in my report."

"Report now."

The man's jaw set, then with a visible effort loosened again. "I assigned a team to tail Reuel as you ordered. They reported he had made multiple excursions to a particular hotel. I followed him, identified the room he occupied, and intended to make my entry by stealth, to catch him in the act."

"In the act of what?"

"I'm still in the process of determining that."

"So did you? Catch him in the act?"

The man's features remained blank, but the petulance hiding behind that practiced exterior was visible, if one knew what to look for. "My next memory was of waking beside a dumpster in an alley near the wagon-train station."

Maripol walked once to the end of the table, face to the ceiling. "So someone jumped you. Drugged you?"

"Yes."

"With what?"

"With Amnesynth."

Maripol slapped his gloves on the table's edge. "You had blood work done? By an outside lab? And without my authorization?"

"No, it wasn't necessary."

"Then how do you know it was Amnesynth?"

"It was taken from me, sir. When I woke, the injector was still in my hand."

"Aside from the fact you have jumped to that conclusion without sufficient evidence, can you explain how someone used your injector on you?"

The blank facade was cracking under the strain. "I don't remember, sir?"

Maripol blew out a great huff. He pivoted to the dirt-streaked windows overlooking a nearby blank brick wall. The drizzle matched his mood.

"So let us summarize. You moved in on a primary target—without permission, without an approved attack plan, without backup—and you let someone disable you with your own weapons."

He spun on a heel, planted his palms on the table. "I wish that was all you'd done, but to top that, you commandeered a beat cop and a local judge and served a warrant on that primary target, again without permission." This time, his gloves hit the table inside his curled fist. The man jolted. Pathetic. In his day, any fieldman unable to face painful death without flinching would have been drummed out of training. Another symptom of the unraveling of society. No principles, no foundation, no backbone.

"Well, is that correct?"

The investigator sat rigid, eyes focused at a point over Maripol's shoulder. "Yes, sir."

"And what did your investigation yield?"

"Some papers, sir. I'm certain they are code. The crypto guys are on them now."

Maripol pulled a folded sheet from his breast pocket and tipped it into the man's hands, who opened it, his pallor going white. Maripol lowered his voice, tone warm and friendly. "And were they code?"

The man gulped. "Apparently not, sir."

Voice like a whip, Maripol shot a forefinger toward the man's face. "You have nearly destroyed the entire investigation. Do you understand this?"

The man's jaw worked, and the paper shook in his grip. "But I was trying to nail the traitor, sir."

"No excuses. Never. No matter what." Maripol leaned across the table. "Correct execution is its own witness, failure, its own testimony."

Then he folded hands to his mouth and paced the room. This kid was ambitious, a hard charger. And not stupid, just inexperienced. Could he channel that energy? "Many would cut you loose now, consign you to your punishment. You realize this?"

The man nodded, eyelids drooping.

Something in that contrite gesture decided it. "I will suspend judgment for one reason only—because your error was predicated on excessive zeal. Learn from this, and you may yet survive this posting. From this point forward, you do nothing of your own initiative, nothing without my explicit approval. Do you understand?" Maripol stopped opposite the man, hands on table, looming over the investigator.

The agent's eyes lit. "Anything, sir."

Maripol drew another envelope from his breast pocket. "Very well. Here are your first instructions."

CHAPTER 17

Father Curtis finished a round of morning exercises. He remained prone on the pleasantly cool concrete floor until the flush of exertion faded and the chill became uncomfortable.

In the kitchenette, he rummaged in the wooden cupboard and prepared a platter of bread, cheese, and meat. Light washed the room from the opening hatch before Phillip descended the ladder. Curtis heaped more slices on the platter. "Phillip, I was preparing a meal. Are you hungry?"

"I am, little." The young man handed over a pack and sat. "Brought more food."

"I'd like to visit the professor when he's safe to come. Can you relay word to him?"

"He comes." Phillip pinched a slab of meat, which he dropped straight into his mouth. He followed the meat with a generous slice of cheese. "Soon."

As if he'd been summoned, the hatch opened to reveal Professor Reuel's smiling face. Back in the kitchenette, Curtis reloaded the platter for a third mouth. Phillip, claiming to be "little hungry," had already emptied wide swathes of meat.

As they sat and picked from the platter, Phillip slid an envelope across the table to Professor Reuel. Its passage across the ink-stained surface hissed a soft whisper. "Is message you ask for."

"Ah, good." Professor Reuel wiped his fingertips on a cloth, then slit the envelope, and slipped out a typed note. As he read, his face darkened.

Curtis tossed a morsel toward the bookcases for Dantes. "What is it?"

Professor Reuel handed the note to Phillip, who read without expression before handing it back.

Curtis gripped his friend's hand. "Is this about my case? Can I go home?"

The professor drew a deep breath and let it out, his expression pinched. "That is not an option, I am sorry to say. My boy, I do not know how to break this to you. All law-enforcement agencies in the Republic have been charged to find you and bring you in, by any means necessary."

He pushed the paper across the table face up. Bold letters stamped the words *wanted, dead or alive* above a recent photo of Curtis. More particulars followed in smaller print.

Curtis shot out of his chair. "Why, for heaven's sake? How could this have been blown so out of proportion?" He charged for the hatch. "I've got to get this straightened out."

The professor stepped to intercept him. He gripped Curtis's biceps, looked him in the eye, and intoned gravely. "You cannot go out there. It would mean your life to be seen. You have been convicted of murder by a tribunal, in absentia, and sentenced to death."

Father Curtis slumped into a chair, rocking it with the force of his collapse, not seeing the room, his mind numb. Murder? Sentenced to death? How could this be?

"This is some mistake. We need to correct the record. Immediately. I'm innocent." He palmed his face, rubbed at his head as if he could wake from this nightmare. "I've got to get back to my people. They need me."

A tsking exited Professor Reuel's lips. "My boy, listen very carefully. The ruling was passed down from Capital, from the highest levels. This was no mistake. It is an intentional political assassination—*your* assassination."

"But *why?*" Curtis wailed out the final word.

Professor Reuel ran a hand over his wispy white hair. "As I explained, you have been accidentally implicated in our work. We are engaged in one of the most important cases I have ever dealt with. The Order wants our project stopped. They believe that, by eliminating you, they can prevail."

"But I'm not involved." Was he beginning to sound like a child insisting his brother, not he, spilled the milk? No one was listening. Or maybe no one cared.

Dantes snatched up the crumb and darted off.

"That matters not." Reuel gestured to the ceiling as if offering a supplication for patience. "They think you are. If found, you'll not live long enough to make your case, or if you did, you wouldn't be believed." He dropped that hand onto Curtis's shoulder, his touch, his look, tender. Loving. "You must navigate this new reality. Your old life is gone. A new course lies before you."

His old life was over? The life he loved? *I don't accept that. I won't.* "So, I'm to . . . what? Hide here—forever, without purpose, no one but a feral cat for company?"

"Not necessarily without purpose. You might have a great purpose, indeed. Join our effort. Assist me in my research."

"I can't abandon my flock. They need me."

Reuel slapped the table, then exhaled, and spoke as if to soothe the child he must think Curtis was. "You must forget the restoration of your name or your old life. This is not a misunderstanding to be set straight. Even if some official learns you are innocent, it will solve nothing. Those in power will silence you, permanently, guilty or no." He spread his hands. The gesture encompassed the cement cave. "Stay here. Work with me."

If only he could crawl away with Dantes. Ignore these realities and care about naught but food. "And be part of the conspiracy?"

"Well, by virtue of your presence here, you are an accessory already. But no one but the three of us knows this. Well, and Leda, of course, but your secret is safe with her. You need not be an active participant if you don't wish to be, although I do hope to convince you to help with the research."

Curtis put his head down on the cool wooden tabletop and covered it with his arms, releasing all his frustration and anger in a wordless howl. The chair clattered backward as he spun to his feet. Steps hard, he paced, table to cot and back, the musty confines squeezing in on him, constricting, a coffin.

He stopped, hands to wall, forehead on the cold rough concrete. He'd been buried here as if already dead, forced to accept the end of the only life he'd ever known, the life and the people he loved with every fiber of his being. But what could he do against the faceless powers aligned against him? Was what Reuel had suggested true? Was it possible to fight back? To claw a new life from the ashes of the one the tyrants had taken from him?

Curtis returned to the table, clapped hands onto the back of a chair, and faced the other two.

Phillip watched, his face a mask, while Professor Reuel's expression spoke of love and heartbreak.

Curtis's fingers whitened in their grip on heavy oak. "I want you to explain what you are doing here and why. Now."

Professor Reuel spread his hands. "Seeking."

Phillip gave a start and eyed the professor.

Curtis stomped. "Seeking *what*?"

"As I've told you, we seek the truth, my boy, the truth. Truth is preeminent. Without it, we wander in darkness. Without it, all we do is in vain."

He rolled his eyes. "Again I ask, what truth and why?"

"I can best answer with a brief story. May I?"

Now Curtis spread his own hands in acquiescence.

"Many years ago, at the inception of the Hegemony, and the Order and the Writings with it, these structures of power we are all too familiar with were built on the ashes of an earlier civilization.

"What you do not know is before the Writings, there was a text which held the keys to the truth of our world, about Creator God. About the nature of Truth. About ourselves." Reuel stood and spread his arms, his gesture encompassing the room. "This entire operation, all you see here, is an effort to reclaim that truth. We are working to find, to uncover, to recreate what was once the true text of the Word of Creator God."

Curtis rolled his eyes. "The true text? Which one? It's common knowledge the old religions disagreed amongst themselves. Not one of them grasped the truth any more than the others. Why bother?"

"Ah, but your premise is flawed." Reuel clapped, almost giddily, his eyes aglow. "One of them did hold the truth."

Phillip had been leaning in, following the conversation, his intensity palpable, his eyes bright with an inner fire. What did he know?

Curtis refocused on Reuel. "How can you know that, if this supposed true text was lost?"

"A great deal of what I claimed must be accepted by faith. I do because it was handed down to me as a true telling from my father, as he received it from his own, upon pain of death. You have, however, come to the heart of the matter, to the point of our efforts. We work to recover the True Text in order to have the documents, the evidence, for these claims."

Curtis sucked in a breath and reached to touch one of the handwritten pages nearby.

"Yes, my boy." Reuel laid a hand atop Curtis's. "We have recovered many of what we believe to be portions of the text. I hope you'll study our work and decide to join our effort."

He patted Curtis's hand, then rose, and shooed Dantes away, who'd been eyeing the meat platter. "You'd think the fellow thought he was an invited guest."

Curtis smirked. "Or a pet."

"Pet?" Reuel cocked his head, wisps of white feathering onto his high forehead. "I seem to remember you are the one who coined the phrase house pests."

"Dantes and I are cellmates." Curtis waved away the looks of incomprehension. "You'd have to have been falsely imprisoned yourself to understand."

"My boy, I hate to see you losing it when you've only been in here a few—days? Weeks? I lose track." Reuel sat back down. "And speaking of losing track, where was I? Oh yes. Once, all we had were the stories handed down from generation to generation. The destruction of the written record was nearly absolute. However, some did hide the old writings in the hopes, one day, those like us, those who love the truth, would look to find them."

He adjusted in his chair, smoothed his slacks, and unbuttoned his collar. "No complete copy of the writings has yet come to my knowledge, but I once studied a portion from one of the books of the true text." He and Phillip shared a knowing look. "You must understand the true text was not a single book like our Writings, but was many books in a single volume. A very large volume."

Reuel's gaze rose to the shadowed concrete ceiling. But he seemed to see something far beyond, and his blue eyes shone. "My heart burned as I read the words of the true God of

Creation. My very being recognized them as the voice of the creator of my soul."

Sighing loudly, Curtis rubbed his forehead. "Professor. You know how much I respect you, but the fact that a book gave you heartburn doesn't constitute the kind of proof I'm—how did you word it?—*seeking*."

"I know, I know. My experience is subjective. But we were able to find objective verification, as well." Reuel pointed a lecturing finger into the air. "The text was about a time in the remote past, many thousands of years ago, and contained a great deal of prophesy. We also found archaeological references to this same book, all of them dating prior to the events foretold in the fragment, proving the book predated those occurrences. Do you understand what I am saying? We uncovered historical proof the predictions of this book were accurate, predictions of then-future events."

He shot forward, grabbing Curtis's knee and shaking it. "My boy, the book foretold the future, something only Creator God can do. It also spoke of the Creator God we now seek."

"Who is this Creator God?" Curtis jerked upright and gripped the table's smooth wood edge. "Why are you saying Creator God instead of the Eternal?"

"That is a subject we will discuss another day, or not. For the sake of this argument, let us define Creator God as the Supreme Being, the creator of the universe. The Eternal is the god presented by the Writings, which I believe we both agree are flawed. I am differentiating the two to avoid confusing the Eternal with the concept of a true God, fair enough?"

The wood edge cut into his palms as his grip tightened. "Talking about the Eternal that way makes me shiver."

"It will pass."

"Still, I don't understand," began Curtis. A part of him, that part wanting to believe what Reuel was saying, warred with the part afraid to be betrayed by a lie. Again. "If they destroyed all traces of these writings, then how did you find this evidence?"

"Not all traces. Let's be clear. The fragment I read was one of those traces, after all, but I digress. The Order did a remarkable job in their pogrom to wipe out all extant copies of the true text, much more complete than one would expect. Remarkable, but not perfect. They did not and could not destroy all related historical texts. Because so much of the work done in other academic disciplines relates to the historical events referenced in the True Text, we are not without such resources to draw upon."

Curtis stood and turned his back to the room. He studied the cooling embers of the fire while processing so many new concepts. His heart yearned for this to be true, burned with a desire, a fervent need to touch the miraculous, the sublime, to see past the clouded understanding of this corporeal life and into the bright, clear air of some unseen world, some eternal truth. And that settled it. He wanted it too much. He must guard his heart. "This is flimsy evidence. Too flimsy to overturn my theology, and for sure, not enough for me to accept a new one. I need proof."

Phillip spoke for the first time. "Some truths can only be seen if eyes have been opened to see them."

That was too mystical. Curtis was seeking objective truth after all, but he held his tongue.

The professor reclined in his chair, arms crossed and fist to chin. He studied both men. "The two of you had a recent experience, a brush with the unexplained, the unexplainable."

Curtis gave a wide, emphatic shake of his head. "I've said this before. Experiences can lie, are subjective. Our perceptions can be distorted."

"True, but by the testimony of two witnesses, can the experience be trusted? Why do you brush aside such evidence of supernatural intervention? Intervention that saved your life? Saved all of us? Phillip, most importantly."

Curtis said nothing, but his question must have been apparent because Professor Reuel raised a finger and said, "Phillip has more bearing on the matter than you might believe." He smiled. "I met Phillip when he was but a young child. I was on sabbatical, vacationing on the Great Salt Sea. You know of it?"

Curtis nodded. "I've never visited. They don't send a parish priest on exotic world travels."

"Yes, yes, just so. At any rate, a local family invited me to dine with them, and there, I met Phillip."

Phillip sat up taller, much like a little boy wishing to please.

"It was there, also, that I received my first experience with the True Text, the very same of which I just told you. The area is a rocky desert with many caves in the bluffs, largely unexplored. A local boy had found a rusty tin in one of them. Inside was a sheaf of papers, quite old and heavily burned at the edges, some burned nearly through. But there remained enough to study, more text in one fragment than we had ever seen before. I had the good fortune to examine it before it was once again lost. That is to say, good fortune for me, at first, but bad fortune for Phillip and his family." The professor bowed his head and lapsed into silence.

"Not your fault, Professor." Phillip spoke in his thick accent. "Murdered for having book. Glad I am you saw before taken." He seemed to be having trouble with his breathing. "Else they die for nothing."

The professor gripped the young man's shoulder.

"Perhaps that is enough for one day. We have all been through a great deal, and you, my friend"—he winked at Curtis —"have quite enough to process. In the meantime, please do review our work here. Decide for yourself if what we do is truly anathema. All I ask is you study the evidence with an open mind. Can you agree to that?"

"We'll see." At Professor Reuel's insistent look, Curtis huffed. "Okay. I'll study your work. I'll let you know when I decide. In return, allow me one favor?"

"Name it."

"I'd like to send for some of my things. I feel lost here without them. And I want word of my people."

"So you have decided to stay?"

"What choice, until I'm cleared?"

"Of course, tell Phillip what you desire. If it can be done, we will see to it."

As Reuel and Phillip rose, the cat darted back into his hole. Curtis could relate to a creature afraid to stick its nose out for more than brief intervals. Would he ever again feel otherwise?

CHAPTER 18

Lars made the sign of the Eternal over his heart and sat in his usual pew, the rearmost one. Voices joined in worship filled the tall sanctuary. His voice rose with the chorus. There was such a power to it he fought back tears, the weight of it like a physical force pressing on his chest, choking off the words. He told himself he sat in the rear to encourage those in front with his voice, which was decent, but he knew the truth. He hated to feel watched when it became necessary to wipe his eyes.

He scanned the bulletin for any announcement regarding Father Curtis. Perhaps he'd see his friend officiating services today. When the choir finished the opening hymns, another man stepped behind the lectern. Lars's heart sank. Seeing the unfamiliar priest in Father Curtis's spot felt almost indecent, not to mention disappointing.

The priest opened the service with announcements and prayer requests. No mention of Father Curtis.

How strange. In the past, when the father was unable to serve on a Sunday, there'd always been an explanation. Why not this time?

After the service, Lars held back, making small talk with

acquaintances to ensure he was the last to file past the priest. Then he asked, "Where is Father Curtis today?"

The priest offered a banal smile. "Of truth, I don't know. I was sent here to fill in. The only word I have is the good father has been detained in his travels. What is your name, if I may ask? Is there a message you'd like me to pass on?"

"Lars. And no, I was just hoping he'd made it back. We were supposed to start a book study."

"Ah, what book?"

Lars shook his head and turned away. Walking home, he spotted old German toddling along in his tweeds. Lars ran to catch up. "Hey, German!"

"Ah, Lars!" German pivoted, one effete hand moving to fix his ascot. "How are your parents?"

"Working hard, as always. You know we just finished a special audit?"

"I heard something about that. Troubling, indeed. I hope you can satisfy Advisor Haman. He's a hard man."

Lars shrugged. "Dad's working on a big contract that bids next week. If we land that thing, the advisor would have to be pleased, right?"

They'd reached the lake, swallows skimming its surface near to shore. A handful of nearly grown ducklings, following their mother, plucked at something among a patch of water lilies. A larger flock paddled further out in the bay.

German pointed to a park bench. When they sat, he peered at Lars over his wire frames. "You know, of course, whoever the advisor chooses will win that bid, don't you?"

"Not so," protested Lars. "This is a formal opening with sealed proposals. The lowest qualified bidder will land the contract. Dad nailed down all the qualifications, so if we have the lowest price, they have to give it to us."

German ducked his head, rubbed the back of his squat neck, and mumbled something to the yellow bobbing dandelion heads at his feet before raising his chin. "Things in Committee business are seldom as they appear and never go in a way contrary to the Committee's desires."

"How can they mess with sealed bids? They have to follow their own rules!"

"Oh, they will most certainly appear to." German tugged at his ascot again and wiggled in his seat. "You have been to lettings before? So you are aware of the process. You know all bids must be received thirty minutes prior to opening? Received by a clerk who logs them in, correct?" When Lars nodded, German continued. "Why, pray tell, couldn't you hand them over to the head table at the time for bid opening?"

Lars reached down and plucked a dandelion, the sunny yellow blossom in its full prime, awash with hope and cheer. He could use some of that. "I guess it's so they have time to print the forms?" He clung to that hope, even while he tore tiny yellow petals from the innocent flower. "They hand out blank tabs so all present can record the bids as they are opened. That way, everyone has a record, and there can be no chicanery later."

"Ah yes, chicanery. That doesn't happen later, at least usually not. The chicanery occurs *prior to* the bid opening."

That spot between his shoulder blades was starting to cramp. A mosquito buzzed his ear—or was that noise in his head? "How can they cheat before the bid is opened? They're in sealed envelopes, sealed with glue on the flap and those metal tab things. You can't see the interior through the dark-brown envelope. Besides, if someone changed my bid, I'd know and raise a stink."

"What makes you think yours would be modified? Have you noticed how the clerk opens sealed bids?"

Where was German going with this? Lars released the dandelion remnants, bright hope dropping to his feet. "They slit the envelope with a letter opener and slide the paperwork out right there. The others at the head table pass it around to verify signatures and bonds and such, and then the administrator reads it."

"Have you ever looked at the flap as they are opened?"

He slapped the mosquito as it landed on his arm. Good, he hadn't imagined the buzz. "I can't think that I ever noticed."

"Well, I have. The envelopes are all placed on the stack face up, the flaps on the bottom. When the clerk picks one up, they turn the face toward the room, showing the bidder's Certificate of Qualification. They then slit the top, as you have said. The flap is never visible during the process."

Lars jolted. "Are you saying they have opened all the bids beforehand?"

"Oh no, not necessarily, but important ones have been, shall we say, perused?"

Now that buzzing was in his ears. Lars's fingers twitched to clamp over them, but he couldn't block out the sound coming from inside his head, couldn't block out what he'd just heard. Dad had told him only Northwoods and their major competitor, Artisans, had qualified for the big job this week. If the Committee wanted to hand the job to their pets . . . Well, how easily that could be done? Artisans always seemed to have lucky bids, just undercutting Northwoods on the choicest jobs. Now, perhaps, he knew how they managed this.

German puffed his cheeks. "I'm taking a risk telling you this. I work for these people. I trust you'll keep this between us?"

Lars braced both hands on the bench, needing the keep his balance. That cramp between his shoulder blades now burned, spreading toward his stomach. "Of course."

"Especially your dad, not a word. When he gets his dander up, he makes a scene. That could be dangerous for everyone."

"You have my word. I'd never jeopardize you."

German pushed to his feet and reached a hand to shake

Lars's. "You and your dad should find another way to satisfy the Committee. Just in case."

How were they going to do that? This was their only chance. "Thanks again. Would you like to come to Mom's for lunch? I'm sure she'd love to have you."

"Oh, thank you, but no. Pris is waiting, and I've promised to host the substitute priest for lunch. I should step briskly, or he may beat me home." With that, the old man limped away, accompanied by the staccato beats of his carved cane.

A crescendo of splashing, flapping wings and the caterwauling of waterbirds drowned out German's retreating footsteps, something having frightened off the ducks. They skimmed the waves, feet trailing as they gained speed.

The mother and her babies, too, churned the air with their wings. They lifted off, flying far behind the main flock, beating the air with all their might. At such a disadvantage, would they ever catch up? Lars remained as the trees' reflections danced on the lake's glassy surface until the lengthening shadows alerted him he, too, was going to be late for lunch.

FATHER CURTIS WAS AGAIN in the frightening, surreal world of broken rock and darkness. Across the way, the two cherubs stood hand in hand alone on their pyramid, watching a new form emerge from the darkness. A large shaggy pup. Unlike the other twisted figures, it seemed wholly made of light. The two embattled children giggled in happy wonder. It stopped short of their position and laid its head on its paws, tail wagging a joyful greeting, a friendly invitation.

The two, their fears apparently assuaged, scampered to the animal, petting it, wrapping their arms around its wide neck, rejoicing in the light. But the aura around the animal appeared to be off, not quite right, not like the light of the Sword.

He pivoted toward the Sword again, studied its radiance, its essence, then the animal. The afterimage of the Sword still occupied his field of view. Seen through it, the creature was revealed to be an abomination identical to the others. Then the Sword's afterimage faded, and his natural vision again reported the puppy to be the harmless being of light.

This dark entity had taken on a disguise, appearing as a creature of light to lure the two children in.

He jumped up, shouting into the wind. "Look at the Sword! Look at the True light."

He was still shouting as he woke, sitting up in his bed, limbs quivering with pent-up stress.

LARS PLANNED to catch the early train tomorrow, so after Sunday dinner, he and Dad met in the home study to review the bid. They reverified the totals on the handwritten takeoffs before penning the bid amounts onto the proposal forms. Lars then arranged a row of documents for Dad to sign, and he and Mom to witness.

Dad scooted forward in his desk chair and readied his pen, but then stopped short. "Why are there extra copies?"

"I'm going to take a separate set of signed blanks. We ran these numbers so fast it makes me nervous. While I'm making the trip, you'll have two more days to recheck everything. German has a landline telephone. Be there at six p.m. Tuesday night, and I'll call from the hotel. If you find any errors, I'll use the spare set."

Dad sat back, capping his pen with a soft click. "You'll be traveling with the equivalent of a blank check. If someone got ahold of them—"

"You have my word. I'll guard them with my life. If I don't have the blanks and you realize we missed something, there'll be no way to correct it." When Dad didn't budge, his skeptical expression unchanged, Lars looked to the ceiling, hands spread. "Come on. When have I ever let you down?"

Dad rocked his head from side to side. He finally pulled the papers close and began scrawling signatures, the scratching of his pen the only sound in the room. Lars remained frozen, afraid to twitch, until all six forms were signed, then swept them up before Dad could change his mind. He tucked the blank proposals in a separate envelope and slipped it into his inner breast pocket. He patted them. "They'll burn Tuesday night if you find no errors."

That night, he slept fitfully, waking often in vague unquiet, but once woke sweating, heart pounding, still in the grips of a vivid dream. He'd stepped on a road only to find it wasn't a ribbon of asphalt at all, but a dark serpent, coiling and writhing, speeding off across the wilderness with him clinging to its back.

He let his breathing, heavy and gasping, calm, then whispered. "Dreams don't scare me."

He forced himself back to sleep, but soon he woke. Someone—no, some*thing*—was in the room with him. He opened one eye a slit, afraid to move, but at the same time, afraid not to turn and face the enemy he could feel behind him, crouched in the shadows at the far corner. He shot upright, fist clenched and ready to battle.

The whipping blanket stirred the curtains, allowing the moon to send a shaft of light into the corner in question. No one was there. He hopped out of bed, hands still raised, checking every corner, then under the bed. Empty.

He lay back down, punching his pillow, curling as if against a blow. He did his best to deny the unseen presence sharing his room. After all, his eyes told him nothing was there.

Another part of him knew something quite different.

CHAPTER 19

Professor Reuel tossed onto one side, then another, trying to force some measure of drowsiness upon himself, but it was no use. Who'd have guessed the lovely Leda snored so loudly? He reached behind his head and curled the pillow around his ears, but he could still hear it. Hard enough to sleep, sharing a room with someone else, without this. He sighed and thought of his own bed, where no one stole the covers the second he drifted off. How did married folk get any sleep at all?

The windows on either side of the bed disintegrated in a spray of moonlit shards, followed by the dark menace of hobnailed boots. The bed bucked as the wearers of those boots landed, knees in his belly, and Leda's too by the sound of the air whooshing from her lungs. One way to stop the snoring.

Somewhere behind him, a door splintered and crashed open, more booted footfalls clomped toward them on the thinly carpeted concrete. Bright lights blinded him. Then he was lifted from the bed and spun, face to the wall, hands jerked behind him. His wrists were wrenched, restraints bit flesh, and he was spun again, the bright headlamps in his face.

"What, what is the meaning of this?" He winced, ashamed

at the quivering of his voice. Better that way, though. Play the part.

From the doorway, a voice answered. "This time, you'll be answering our questions, Professor. And there'll be no hiding the truth. Give it to him."

A wasp stung his neck, and he began to weave on his feet, the world spinning. Across the room came a rustling struggle and Leda's sharp cry. "Leave him alone. Stop it!"

Hands guided him to the bed where he was slammed into a seat. Leda was thrown to the mattress beside him, but having trouble focusing, he couldn't see her clearly, couldn't tell if she was injured.

"We'll give that a minute to take effect, then the questions." That voice again. Was this the same man Phillip intercepted?

Behind the wall of lights, boots paced left to right, left to right. Then they stopped. "Professor Reuel, where is Father Curtis?"

Here it was, the moment of truth. The moment of truth serum. He giggled. What a great product name. It said what it did and did what it said. He could help them market that. He giggled some more. This was just too sublime. He needed to get the formula from this nice young man when this was all over. His mind had never been so sharp, so bright.

"Where, Professor? Answer. Where is Father Curtis?"

He wanted to answer. Wanted to help. Without any volition on his part, the words flowed out like a stream of cool water. The thought made him thirsty. "I couldn't tell you where he is, even if it was to save my own life." He giggled again. It was true, wasn't it? He really could not. To tell them where Curtis was would be at the cost of his soul, much more precious than his life. What an elegant solution to such a difficult question. Phillip was a genius. He must hug the boy when next he saw him.

He was about to tell the nice young man about Phillip,

about what a genius he was, but this one had a real problem with patience and started asking more questions. Professor Reuel's vision blurred, and time slipped. He heard himself responding, regurgitating answers. They came so smoothly, his mouth making the words as if operated by someone else, but he couldn't seem to focus on their meaning. He hoped the nice young man could understand, hoped his answers were helpful.

And then he was regurgitating in fact, all over a set of shiny black boots. The man in front of him swore. Someone behind the lights spoke. He had such a pleasant voice. Professor Reuel hoped he would keep talking, hoped he would tell a story. He was in the mood for a bedtime tale. One with a happy ending. He hoped he could stay awake long enough. Would Leda tuck him in? He would like that, wouldn't he?

"Give him the antidote. The old fool is wasting our time."

A different voice now. A familiar voice, but he couldn't place it. A rough hand grabbed his nape and then came an explosive pain, another wasp sting. A fireball bloomed behind his eyes, and someone drove a freight train through his skull. The restraints loosed, his arms falling free, and he doubled over. This time, the boots were quick enough. He missed them, splattering the carpet instead.

Beyond the rushing in his head, of his gullet, orders were being given, and the bright lights left through the broken door, taking the large black shapes and hobnailed boots with them. Now, the only illumination was the bedside candle. That was much better. It skewered his eyeballs ever so much more gently.

A dark shape moved in front of him. Leda shifted on the bed. A cool cloth dabbed his forehead, his lips, down the front of his nightshirt. He looked down and then cringed. Oh, what a mess.

"Professor." A soft sigh. "I know you, and I know Curtis. He would reach out to you in time of need. Tell me, where did he go?"

That voice. Where had he heard it before? He squinted to see the man better, but his eyes still lacked focus. Then he had it.

"Maripol. You disappeared from the face of the earth, leaving us to believe we would never see you again. How is life in the Eye?"

"The Eye, Professor? You of all people should know the Order disavows the existence of any such organization. I am a simple inspector, working on behalf of the Division of Ministerial Integrity. Back to the question. Help me find Curtis. I can help him. If he is captured by another, it will go hard."

"And it would not go hard if you capture him?" Tell me another one.

"If he has done nothing wrong, he has nothing to fear."

Professor Reuel raised the cool cloth, which had found its way to his hand. He wiped his mouth and grimaced. He really needed that water. "Why are you doing this, Maripol? Is this professional, or is it something personal, some old feud between you and he?"

"What could you mean—personal?"

"You know what I mean. Becca."

Maripol bared his teeth, lips curling to expose gleaming canines. "You insult me." And then it was gone, replaced by the former cold, aloof, urbanity, and Reuel stared at, not into, those glimmering black eyes. Had anyone ever gotten past that armor? Anyone besides Becca, that is?

As if reading his mind, Leda spoke. "Maripol, you loved Curtis as much as you did Becca. In the name of that friendship, let this thing go. Curtis has done nothing."

"Why, Head Librarian Leda. I didn't recognize you in your nightshirt. How nice to see you after all these years. This really is a reunion, isn't it?" Maripol moved to stand before Leda, took her hand in his, and kissed it with a bow. "As to my friendship with Curtis, that is moot. I serve order, that above all else."

Reuel groaned. "I tried to teach you this all those years ago, yet still, you confuse orderliness with order. Come, my boy. You were the most promising. Come out of that spider's web. Come back into the fold."

Maripol jerked upright. "Spare me your word games." He dropped Leda's hand, gloved fingers forming a fist. "Consider this: I will find Curtis. Better for him if it happens sooner than later. If you see him, tell him to contact me. Tell him to come in alive while he still can."

With a bow, he whisked from the room.

Reuel's head was throbbing. The room refused to be still, and his gorge was rising again. Careful not to move his head, he shed the filthy nightshirt and lowered himself to the pillow, inch by painstaking inch. To move at all was agony, but move too quickly and it tore at his brainstem.

A cloth draped his eyes. A moment later, Leda sat beside him again, the mattress sagging with her weight, a shift of what had to be only inches but seemed to be the giant waves of an ocean storm. The strength he had feigned during the sparring match with Maripol deserted him.

He groaned. "What—" He swallowed bile. "What did I tell them?"

She removed the cloth. There came the sound of trickling water. Then the cloth was placed back on his forehead, wet and cool. "You babbled. You told them nothing."

He hiccuped a sob. "Oh, thank Creator God. I was sure I had failed."

"You can thank Phillip. His preparations worked, just as planned." The weight on the bed disappeared, and light footsteps traced away. The chains on the door rattled into place. "Will they be back?"

Would they? Reuel was having trouble assembling his thoughts.

The swish of legs rubbing on nightshirt, then the cool cloth was renewed. Her voice, normally precise and clipped, quavered. "Do you think they'll bring us in for questioning, for torture?"

Her hand rested on his cheek. That felt good. He was a little better now. If he kept his voice low, he could speak with no more than the second or third circles of hell as the price. "I think not. Torture is a method of punishment—not used to extract information, no matter the pretense otherwise. If we passed this test, they will be convinced we harbor no useful information. No one beats the truth serum."

"No one but Phillip, apparently. Close your eyes. You need rest." She blew out the candle. The mattress rolled as she lowered herself onto the bed. He gritted his teeth until his head, his gorge, and the room resettled.

He began to drift. Some unknown time later, she said, "Your hands are cold." He woke to the realization he had laid his palm on her shoulder. Her lovely delicate shoulder. He snatched it away, paying for the movement with a renewed throbbing at the base of his skull.

"I'm terribly sorry. It must be this cold breeze." Just above his head, the drapes billowed in the shattered window frame. He pulled the blanket tighter and tucked hands in armpits.

She sniffed. "Yes, well, a mission is a mission. If you have other interests, afterward, pursue them in the appropriate manner. But first, do your research. Your knowledge in this area is lacking."

He was trying to follow this convoluted line of meaning, but it was like trying to read Sanskrit. Harder, in fact. He could read Sanskrit, a bit. "Research?"

"Romance will be in the reference section, filed under the letter *R*. I suggest you start there."

~

MONDAY MORNING, before the first hint of color showed on the horizon, Lars tapped on Leif's back door, hugging arms around himself in the chill. No light appeared inside, but Leif stepped out, a backpack slung on one shoulder.

"Morning, brother." Leif smiled as he locked the door. "Ready for the big doings?"

"I am. You ready to find yourself a new gig?"

Leif's grin widened, lighting his eyes. "You bet. I'm more eager than I've been in—oh, I don't remember how long. Ah, to be out from under the ogre's thumb!"

Lars guffawed. Who'd have thought he'd ever have a glimpse of the old, carefree Leif again? It had been years.

Perhaps Leif going freelance was a brilliant stroke. Maybe now, the family could work together in a healthy way, avoiding the tension poisoning the entire organization. Man, they needed to catch a break.

At the wagon train, they located the Northwoods freighter, full of the restaurant's finished product. The shop had worked overtime through the weekend, so many sacrifices made to produce this load. It better mollify the business agent.

He boarded the cab, not minding riding herd on the freight, though managers in other companies saw it as below their station. Northwoods invariably stacked functions, sending management as freight jockey when one of them had a meeting in Capital. Made sense. Why pay two men to do two jobs when one could do both? "I'll take first watch at the controls."

Leif stretched out on the bench for a nap. "Glad it's just two of us. Room to sleep." He was snoring in seconds, but shot up with a yell when they coupled to the southbound engine, and several times more during the trip south, but fell back to sleep each time, snores resuming within a few breaths. The sun was high in the morning sky before Leif came to full wakefulness, sitting up and stretching. "How far are we?"

"Nearly to Two Rivers." Lars handled the controls through

the downgrade into the station, squinting against the yellow glare slanting through the side window.

Leif pulled a thermos out of his backpack and poured. The rich aroma of coffee wafted about the cabin. "Think we're gonna catch the early express to Capital?"

Lars pointed at another wagon train assembling in the station yard. "Looks like it, if that's it."

"Little brother, why don't you hop out as the train slows, see if you can get us slotted. I'd love to miss the six-hour wait for the next express."

"You bet." Lars slid out from behind the controls, preparing to make his dash as Leif took over.

They were in luck. The stationmaster took his ticket and grunted. "Two minutes to spare, just closing out the manifest now." He tore a flimsy from Lars's ticket, initialed it, and slipped it into a slot second from the rear on the outbound train.

Lars moaned. He hated rear positions. The built-up play in the daisy chain slapped the rearmost cars hardest. He didn't even want to think about the downhill grades, and the ones south of Two Rivers were some of the worst. Just like the slack, the cars' side-to-side wanderings increased in intensity closer to the rear.

But if that's the price to spend the night in a real bed, he'd pay it. He accepted his ticket book back from the agent. When he sauntered up to the freighter, Leif already had her coupled to the new train. As Lars passed the rear car, he yelled a hello to the driver, who responded, "Hello, good night," his accent thick. But the car tires were squatting heavily, which was wrong. Only light loads were allowed in the rearmost positions for safety reasons. At the freighter, Lars relayed his concerns.

Leif scowled his unbelieving look but dismounted, then walked around the rear car, checking the springs. He then tapped on the window and motioned for the driver to slide it down, to a reluctant compliance. "Are you carrying a heavy load?"

"No load. Empty." Again, a thick accent muddied the reply.

Leif jammed hands on hips and widened his stance. "Your tires suggest otherwise. No way you're empty, bud."

"Yes, empty, empty." The man slid his window up, ignoring further attempts to communicate.

Leif stomped off toward the terminal building. He returned moments later with a lineman who had a quick conference with the driver before reporting, "Car's empty. No problem here."

"Empty!" Leif reddened, and spit flew with his words. "Just look at those springs. That thing ain't empty—it's overloaded."

When the lineman shrugged and walked away, Leif ran after him, shouting. "That car's overloaded, and where's our caboose?"

The man called over his shoulder. "No caboose today. Blew a tire on the trip up."

"You don't think that's a problem?" Leif yelled after him.

The man didn't respond, aside from the gesture he shot over his shoulder.

Leif picked up a horse apple and tossed it after him, his throw well short of the mark.

Lars caught up. "Now what?"

"We either take what we get or wait six hours."

Lars rubbed the back of his neck. "I guess I like this train well enough."

A man waited by their car when they returned. Leif, apparently in no mood, shouted, "What?"

Nonplussed, the man pointed at the sign on the car's side. "You are Northwoods?" His voice carried a heavy accent.

Leif jerked his thumb toward the rear. "Best get back to your car. Train's about to start, and I hope you know how to handle that thing."

The man blinked, his face scrunching. "What car? I have not this thing."

"You're not from that car back there?"

"No. I come find Northwoods. Have message for Lars or Leif."

"That's us." Stepping forward, Lars grinned to put the stranger at ease. "What can we do for you? Message from who?"

"From friend rode train one week ago," the man answered.

Lars and his brother both gasped. "Father Curtis?"

The man put a finger to his lips, then waved to the cab. "We speak inside?"

Lars ushered him up the ladder. Once the cab door closed, he asked, "What's the message?"

"Not message, exactly. Request. He asks help in recover property. Also asks you come to him, meet. I ride north with you to get for him, take you to him."

"We're headed south right now." Leif gestured the opposite way. "Won't be going back north till the end of the week."

"South where?"

"South to Capital."

The man's face brightened. "Ah, this is good. I have need travel to Capital. We ride both ways, you and I?"

Lars looked at Leif and back at the stranger with scrunched brows. "You want to ride to Capital and then back to North-woods with us?"

The man nodded with a grateful smile.

Lars ignored Leif's negative signal. "Sure."

Next to him, Leif growled and shot him a dark look.

Lars shrugged. "Any friend of Father's is a friend to us. Is he okay? We've been wondering where he got off to."

"Is safe . . . for now."

Lars was about to ask for more information. But the engine let off a blast of air horn, and the light panel lit green.

Once on cruise, Leif locked the controls. "We haven't got

your name, and what in the Hegemony is going on with Father Curtis? How do you know him?"

"Name is Phillip. Servant of Professor—ah, of a professor friend to Curtis. Curtis safe, hiding."

"Hiding?" Leif cocked his head.

"You hear of Curtis charged guilty in murder, yes?"

The world tipped, and Lars gripped the lip of the splintered old bench. "Murder of who?"

"Did not do. Is trick they use. Murder of man on train and of man killed later, not on train."

"That's a lie." Lars hooked Leif by the upper arm, dragging him forward as if presenting him for evidence. "We were with him and can prove that."

The mysterious man brought a beefy hand to unruly dark hair, but rather than smoothing it out, he only rumpled it more. "Who knows this, knows you with him?"

"I don't think anyone does." Leif raised a brow at Lars. "We didn't say anything about it."

Phillip nodded. "This is good. You say nothing, or you will be murderers too. Then you be dead."

Lars gawked at his brother. The shock chased all thoughts from his mind, but a growing acid burn churned his insides. Had he said anything? He might have, but when?

CHAPTER 20

L eif couldn't believe it. Father Curtis, a convicted
murderer? Of course, it was all garbage, more crooked
dealings from Capital, but what else was new? He
thought of their last trip with the padre, adjusting the controls
automatically, a tiny portion of his attention on the road, his
main focus on that night. Father Curtis had been strange.
Moody. Distracted. Not at all his cheerful, friendly self. Especially after that emergency stop.

What had that conductor said? Someone in the passenger
compartment injured or dying? Were those the people Father
had been accused of murdering? If so, he and Lars could testify
he'd never gone within a hundred feet of that passenger car, at
least not before the attack had already happened. But was that
a good idea? Folks who got involved where they weren't wanted
had a way of attracting strange troubles themselves. Or disappearing altogether.

He'd better warn his brother to keep mum, at least for now.
He turned to poke Lars, who was himself facing Phillip, prying
him for more information. But the car tipped forward, and the
bottom fell out. Leif's stomach moved up while the rest of him

went the opposite way. He zipped back into his seat and craned his neck out the side window.

Just inches below, a thin metal guardrail blurred past, beyond it only a sheer drop, treetops far below. This was the dreaded mile-long descent to the Kearny River, and he wasn't set up for the steep grade. Not even close.

He scanned the instrument panel, and his hands flew to correct his settings. But the car was already rocking, timbers popping, and nothing he did seemed to help.

The rear car was obviously having problems, and now their problems had become his own. He should've been paying attention. Had it been driving so erratically the entire trip? Bracing himself, he feathered the steering lever. Still, the whip-sawing grew more extreme with each oscillation.

Now, their car was being jerked left and right, feeling as if it was about to tip sideways. A giddy rush tingled through him. He clicked on another notch of brake to damp the motion, then another. It had no appreciable effect.

He slammed the brakes to full stop. "Lars! We have no caboose to alert the engineer."

Tires were hopping, and nails began popping from the ceiling planks. The cab was filling with the stinking black smoke of burning rubber. The car ahead had now been dragged into a wild left-right motion.

"Chop the coupler and pray the brakes hold!" Leif wrestled with the controls, grunting with the effort.

Lars popped the cab door open. Holding onto a steel hand-hold, he leaned down and pulled the coupler release lever. Nothing. His shoulders shuddered, his thin T-shirt flapping in the wind as he heaved harder. Again and again. "No good." He shouted over his shoulder. "Too much tension. It won't release."

He bounded back into the cab and grabbed the fire ax from its socket. One leg wrapped around the ladder, he began swinging the ax into the yoke to force the coupler open.

He was midswing when the car's front tires bounced over a pothole. The freighter launched a foot into the air. Lars lost hold of the ax, and it flew end over end. A flash of sunlight glinted on the blade as it bounced off the steel railing guarding the sheer drop to their right. Lars lurched forward to recapture the flying ax, but his balance failed. He disappeared under the front axle.

Phillip dove headlong through the door, his legs splayed in the frame. His back hunched, muscles bulged, and he began to inch backward. A hand shot into sight and latched onto the coupler's frame. Lars's bloody head followed, and both men struggled to lever themselves onto the running gear.

Then came a sickening crunch, and a shudder ran through the train. Flashing lights in front of Leif lit up in an emergency stop warning. Their tires were already locked and smoking, but now sliding tires screamed from the cars ahead. The train jerked to a stop.

A black cloud of smoke rolled past, making it impossible to see, impossible to breathe. Leif raised his shirt to cover his mouth and nose. Still, it was like trying to breathe soup. He coughed, his throat was on fire, and that cough dragged the nasty fumes deeper into his lungs, forcing a gagging, uncontrollable bout of lung-ripping convulsions.

Wheezing, he groped for the side-window catch, but the glass had already fallen. He squeezed his head through the opening, sucking in great mouthfuls of comparatively clean air, finally hanging there, limp, afraid to move lest the hoarse, barking cough begin anew.

As the air cleared, Lars hopped off his perch and pointed behind the train. "Oh, crap. Oh, crap. Come help!"

While Lars dashed out of sight, Phillip followed him, but Leif had to lock the controls first. When he rounded the corner, his brain refused to make sense of the sight rearward. Once it did, he wished it hadn't.

Bodies spread across the road like windblown leaves, interspersed with torn metal and shattered crates. Back up the hill, a freight car lay on its side. The supposedly empty rear car, the roof and walls torn open, only the front driver's cab recognizable. The running gear was a twisted mess, and the rear axle, no longer attached to the frame, rested several yards back up the hill. Something dark and smoking tangled with it.

People lay moaning and twisted, dismembered parts interspersed with quivering bodies. Lars was on the ground, applying a tourniquet to the stump of a man's missing leg. Phillip was beyond him, giving a woman CPR. Passengers had begun to drift from the train. They acted like spectators, some removing cameras from pockets and purses, standing with hands over open mouths, taking photographs.

Leif shouted at them. "Help them. Quit staring and *help* them!" Moving as if in a dream, he started capturing bystanders, leading them one by one to a victim, instructing them, then returning to seize another awestruck onlooker. He continued in a blur until, holding the last man by the sleeve, he could find no victim to assign him.

Others kept pouring from the forward cars, now including the crew. Their training showed itself. Overseers shouted orders. Emergency medical supplies were broken out of lockers and deployed to the victims.

Leif searched for a place where he might be needed. Up the road by the smoking mess of the rear axle, a man wielded a broken steel rod, poking at something. Leif strode in its direction. The unrecognizable, mangled mass resolved, becoming a small vehicle. He sprinted to it. The personal transport must have been headed in the opposite direction, running head-on into the last freight car.

Beyond the driver's side window, a man slumped, head back, unconscious. Flames crackled in the engine compartment. This car ran on gasoline, not electricity, and that gasoline was waiting to explode. He had only minutes, maybe seconds.

Hadn't the fire ax fallen near here? Yes! There, next to the guardrail. He snatched it and sprinted to the car. "Watch out," he warned as he swung the short ax at the rear passenger window, wanting to keep the driver out of its arc. On his first swing, the glass burst so suddenly he lost his grip. The ax shot into the interior and cartwheeled out of sight.

He reached in, unlocked the latch, and swung the door open. Then choked, freezing in place as he faced a kid, little more than a baby, unconscious in a car seat. The ax could have hit him. He shuddered, pushing aside that vision. Why hadn't he seen the danger sooner?

But no time for berating himself. He shot a look over his shoulder at whoever had been following him. The man still stood there, the steel rod hanging from one hand. "We have a child here!"

He fumbled through to the opposite door and unlocked it. Then he yelled at the man, who stood unmoving. "It's a child. A kid! Get him out!"

Leif sprinted around the car and opened the now unlocked rear door, intending to reach in and unlock the driver's door. On the opposite side, the man was fumbling ineffectually with the buckles securing the car seat. There was no time. Leif grabbed his belt knife and leaned across the back seat. With one fast slash, he separated the child seat from the wide straps. He pushed it toward the man. "Take the whole thing. Go."

He then unlocked the driver's door and lifted the handle. The latch released, but the jammed door failed to open. He gave it another jerk. But the car had accordioned, and that door would never open again.

A crew member arrived with a fire extinguisher and sprayed the flaming engine.

Leif stretched over the back seat to check the man's pulse.

His skin was cool and clammy, but raspy, labored breaths left his lungs.

The crewman had extinguished the fire, at least for now, and Leif, unable to do otherwise, elected to leave the man where he was in a vague fear of doing more damage if he dragged him out the other door. A pair of women were performing CPR on the baby, and the driver was still breathing when the ambulances arrived.

Leif led one EMT to the car, another to the child. He then sat on the guardrail. He should be doing something, but what? His brain seemed to have slipped out of gear, disconnected from the world, everything so vivid and yet so unreal.

Lars and Phillip joined him, also sitting, arms and mouths hanging limp. They stared as the emergency crews stabilized and removed one victim after another. Blood and hydraulic fluid mixed in greasy trickles, running from the crown of the road to the shoulder. Leif's legs began to vibrate, and he gagged at an odor—one that had surrounded him since the accident, but one he hadn't noticed until now. He pulled out a handkerchief and held it over his nose, but couldn't eliminate the smell of hot oil, raw meat, burning hair, and something worse. Something he recognized, but his mind refused to focus on. They moved further up the guardrail, finding a fresh breeze.

The road was soon cleared of wreckage as if nothing had happened, except for the blackened deformed patch on the asphalt where the car had burned. Eventually, the only ones left were the peace officers interviewing the crew while passengers filtered back to their luxury cabins.

A trooper approached, a lineman in tow. "Which position were you folks riding in?"

Leif and Lars pointed toward the Northwoods car. Leif was about to explain Phillip had been with them, but he was nowhere to be seen. Catching Lars's eye in warning, he told the officer. "The two of us."

The uniform took their statements and cleared them to go. They found the engineer inspecting their freight car.

"Darn lucky." The engineer whistled. "The coupler between you and that mess back there sheared off, or you might be down there now." He faced the forest floor far below and mocked a shiver.

"You're gonna need new tires before you leave Capital, but what you got should get you there. We'll take it nice and easy, just to be sure. Don't let her start swinging, though, or you'll have a blowout."

Grateful not to be left stranded, Leif climbed aboard.

The train started rolling, and Phillip materialized, leaping through the cab door. He settled into the middle seat, his breathing regular, no sign of exertion.

"Where did you go?" Lars beat Leif to the question.

"I wait. Better to be not noticed. Better to not show papers."

The brothers shared an arch look. Lars's eyes were wide, the whites showing bright against his soot-streaked face, skin pale where a sweaty forearm had wiped his brow clean.

And then Leif realized what had so nearly happened back there. He clamped a hand on the brawny man's shoulder. "I gotta thank you. You saved my baby brother. That was fast thinking. A miracle you got to him in time."

It must've taken some strength to reel Lars in from under the axle. He had to have been within inches of death. Dropping his grip, Leif began to shake and clamped down on a blast of erupting emotion. If he lost control now, who knew when he'd get back on top of himself.

Phillip's lips quirked a self-conscious smile. "I thank the Almighty he lives. Close thing."

Lars had grown even more pale. Now, he patted Phillip's broad shoulder with a shaking hand. "I'm gonna need a few before I can drive."

Leif nodded. "You lie back and relax, little bro. I got this. I thank the Eternal you made it. Seriously." He wiped a tear and pretended it was an itch. Again, he tamped down the sobs threatening to rip from his chest. No time for that now.

The tires, indeed unsuitable for another trip, had severe flat spots, making it almost impossible to keep on track. He maintained his place at the controls for the remainder of the trip, white knuckles on levers, the acrid stink of stress sweat filling the tight space. Lars was obviously in no condition, though, his hands were still shaking, and he looked like he was going to throw up.

Leif sighed when they arrived, for the first time allowing himself to feel the tension, the pain in his back and shoulders.

He filed into the hotel room after his companions, shoulders slumped, pack dragging, while Phillip looked like a man well rested and ready to start a new day. Their filthy, blood-stained britches and sweat-soaked shirts had nearly caused the desk clerk to deny them lodging until the manager recognized Leif.

Now, in their room, Leif dropped onto the edge of the bed beside Lars and Phillip. Hands fisted, he stared at his boots. He tried to speak, but his voice broke. "That kid. That little kid. Oh man, I hope he made it." He began shuddering. Hot tears streamed down his face. "I feel like there was something else I should've done."

He choked, failing to hold down the flood. "I keep going over it, playing it back in my head, thinking of all the things I should've seen, done differently. It took me so long to realize that was a car up there, and I never saw the kid till I broke the window."

Lars flopped face down into a pillow, shoulders jerking silently. Phillip put one hand on each of their backs, murmuring. "Is okay. Is good to feel now. You feel nothing until is safe time. This, too, is good. Feel now. Feel all."

After a time, Leif regained his composure and fumbled for a handkerchief.

Lars shot upright, his face red and twisted, eyes hot. "What was up with that? They lied. They could have killed us all. They killed all those people!"

Leif scoffed. "You couldn't tell, little bro?"

"Tell what?"

"They were northerners, illegals, packed in there like sardines. A load of them headed to some sweatshop down south. That's why the paperwork showed an empty car."

Lars palmed his face. "I've heard of people filtering down from the north, but who's heard of them hiding in freight cars?"

A sharp sound, a mangled laugh, burst from Leif's throat. "They weren't hiding. They were being smuggled. It's big business."

"Big business?" Lars lowered his hand, a brow arching toward disheveled hair. "How's that? No way could you sneak many of them through. The line cops would spot 'em. They should've spotted this load before they left Two Rivers." His eyes grew round, and he slapped the flat beige quilt. "That lineman you reported them to should've spotted them. He'll sure have some explaining to do."

Leif patted his baby brother's shoulder. Lars was still such an innocent kid. "You don't get it yet, do you? That lineman knew what was in that car. That's why he shut me down when I complained."

Lars just goggled at him.

So Leif rubbed his back again. "You best believe it, baby bro. There's a ready supply of hungry northerners, and factories and farms down south need cheap bodies. Supply meets demand, with lots of dough to be made in the middle."

"But the government—"

"Gets the biggest slice."

"But *how?*" Lars jumped off the bed and stomped to the

flyspecked window. "Even if someone is importing them, then what? They can't fade into the population."

"They don't have to. There's an arrangement. They stay in their ghettos. Everybody knows about it, and nobody says anything. Why do you think Dad tells you to avoid those areas of town? Those people grew up with no rule of law, and don't respect ours."

Lars pointed out the grimy window, indicating the city spread out below their fifth-floor view. "How can anything this big happen without someone doing something about it?"

Phillip spoke up. "Peoples want world be predictable. Powerful peoples help little peoples believe what they want believe. Everybody happy."

Leif nodded.

Lars balked, pacing the worn-out carpet from bed to the bare window and back to the saggy bed. "So, I'm just one of the happy little people? A fool believing the whole sham?" He slumped back onto the bed, hand to face. "They lie about everything, don't they?"

Poor kid. Growing pains hurt. Leif raised both hands, bloodied palms out. "World's an ugly place."

"Would be good place." Phillip shrugged. "Except full of peoples."

"He made a joke!" Lars snapped out of his glower. "Phillip isn't made of stone after all!"

Phillip scrunched his big mug into an offended expression. "I joke. I joke very good much times."

CHAPTER 21

The next morning, Leif woke having no memory of going to sleep or of waking at all during the night. His head was clear, his body surprisingly free of pain, but his shoulder screamed when he tried to roll. Not without any effect, apparently. He carefully moved the rest of his limbs, but aside from some muscle twinges, all else seemed well. Phillip was already gone. Leif ambled to the restroom to perform his morning ablutions.

The minor mystery of where Phillip had gone, at least, was solved when he returned, carrying a tray of coffee and pastry. He set his burden on the side table, white teeth flashing in Leif's direction. "Good mornings."

Lars stirred, his disheveled hair falling into his eyes. He rubbed his face, then spotting the pastries, snagged one, and took half of it in one bite.

Phillip handed Leif a coffee. "I go to meet man who waits. When is dark, I see you here, yes?"

Leif agreed, yanked the corner of Lars's sheet, and rolled his brother out of bed. "Time to go. Let's get this load off so I can find some new clients."

At the freight yard, they walked toward the tug rentals. Leif was about to enter but stopped and nodded at the ticket window. "Hey, little bro, let's check on the accident. They should have an update by now."

When they inquired, the agent closed his eyes and sighed. "Oh, terrible thing that."

Leif tried not to think of exactly how terrible, the merest thought of what he'd seen, what he'd been forced to do brought a rising bubble of breakfast to his throat. "Any word on the injured?"

The agent waved him away and reached to slide the grimy window closed. "No news will be released until notifications of families are complete."

"I understand." He tried again. "It's just we were on the scene and hoped to hear how those people were. It was terrible."

The window slid back open. "You were there? Oh, I am sorry." The agent looked around and then leaned in. "I shouldn't tell you, but between us, both of them were DOA."

Surely, he misheard. "Both?"

"Yes, the father and son whose transport struck the train."

Lars shouldered to the window. "Okay, but what about the people on the train?"

"Oh, a few were shaken up. Nothing serious, thank the Eternal."

Lars held up a palm. "That's not right. Lots of people got hurt—bad. What about them?"

The agent stiffened. "I'm afraid you are mistaken."

Leif pulled Lars away, but his brother shook free and planted himself before the window, a stubborn set to his jaw. "No mistake, mister. You got your facts wrong. I was there. Now check again. It was the midday express from Two Rivers."

"Yes, that's the one." The agent had lost his bland, officious tone and was now biting out his words. "Two fatalities in the private transport. No other injuries. Period. Now, I suggest you move along." The window slammed closed.

When Lars began to argue, Leif hooked him by the elbow and hauled him away.

Lars wrestled free and slapped at Leif's hand. "What's your problem?"

"I doubt he knows much, and he'll only tell you what he's told to say, anyway. You need to think about how easily they made the whole thing disappear. People who can do that, can do anything they want, *to* anyone they want. You want it to be us next?"

"But it's not the truth!"

Leif tsked and wagged his head. "Little bro, the truth is whatever they say it is. Let's get this job done."

Over an hour later, they'd found a tug to haul the freight car to the restaurant site. As they rounded the street corner and the building came into view, another freighter pulled away from the loading zone. A lump of hot lead burned his guts.

Lars gripped the edge of the dash, rising in his seat for a better view. "What's Artisans doing here?"

Not willing to answer the obvious, Leif swallowed hard. Maybe he was wrong. But through the sparkling new glass, a dining room full of tables and chairs was visible, the last of them being positioned by the stubby project manager.

Leif hopped from the cab and marched inside. "What is all this?"

The little man's lips uncoiled in a greasy smile. "What, this?" He spread his arms wide, inviting. "We call these tables, and these are called chairs." His pudgy hand patted the nearest. "And can you believe it? They were delivered on time."

Lars pushed past Leif, hands on hips. "We have your furniture right there on the truck, and ours is on time too."

"I'm sorry. Your services are no longer required. We'll send you the invoice for all this once we have the final tally." He waved to indicate the now-full dining room.

"You can't—"

Leif caught Lars's shoulder and edged him out of the man's face. "Sir, with this delivery, we are in full compliance with the contract terms. Let's sit down and work this out."

"Nothing to work out. You failed. We replaced you."

Lars lifted a chair. "You don't think this crap is going to last, do you? You're making a huge mistake." He tipped it on one leg and put his weight on the back. There came a sharp popping sound, and the chair collapsed into pieces. "You see? It's even worse than I thought. Let us help you haul this garbage to the curb and bring the good chairs in."

The little man vibrated in place, making a noise like a teakettle coming to steam. "Get out." He pointed at the freighter. "And get that rust bucket outta here before I have it towed."

The trip to the hotel was deathly silent. Odd that Lars wasn't venting. This white, silent Lars was worrisome.

"You gonna be okay, little brother?"

Lars made a grim nod.

"You sure? That wasn't your fault back there, not really. You were just trying to show him."

Back in the room, Lars flopped face down onto the bed to stare out the window. He flattened his mouth into a tight line and muttered, "Guess I know what I gotta do now."

AFTER LEIF LEFT to meet with potential clients, Lars took his briefcase to the lobby and made a call on the landline. "Dad, just checking in. Is the bid good as is?"

"Yep." Dad's voice sounded tinny as it echoed from the handset. "Now listen to me. If we're not the low bid, push for an immediate hold. You know how those guys at Artisans cut specs. If they're low, we're gonna challenge."

"You bet, but I have a feeling we're gonna nail this one."

He hung up, then went to the business center. There, he slid the envelope out of his inner pocket.

He spent some time using the copier, then worked on documents. He placed the papers in his briefcase and locked it before hiking back to the room. Jaw tight and steps firm, he leaned forward as if pushing against some unseen wind.

FATHER CURTIS WAS in the dreamscape again. All was as he'd last seen it. The cherubs were engaged with the false entity that still presented itself as a creature of light. The dark forms at that pyramid's base had stopped all movement as if looking on enrapt.

He considered the Sword. Using its afterimage, he again attempted to reveal the nature of things. Aided by true vision, he could now see the dark entity had begun extruding bands of darkness and was wrapping the two unwary children, those black appendages intertwining about their bodies. If they weren't warned, they would soon be ensnared.

He shouted and waved to gain their attention. He searched for a weapon, for anything. Nothing.

What route would he have to take to reach the Sword? The inky creatures were now avoiding that pyramid. His lantern had been of little use in fighting back the darkness, but the light of the Sword pierced it with ease. Even so, too much distance, too many enemies, remained between him and the Sword.

Some sects of the Order held that all human beings had an aura, visible to those who knew how to focus the inner eyes.

That sect contended the color of a person's aura indicated the purity of their heart.

He tried to see his aura, but he didn't have the trick. If he did possess such, perhaps he could use its light as a weapon. Maybe he could make the light within him grow powerful enough to beat back the darkness. If so, perhaps he could cross the plain to save those children. He couldn't witness them fall as he almost had in his first dream!

He studied the Sword again to capture its essence. The light wasn't a single color, but a combination working together in harmony, like the notes of a musical chord. In his mind, he plucked a single thread of light, of color, out of that spectrum. He held it, listened to it, tasted it. Goodness was its flavor.

He began thinking good thoughts, attempting to infuse that goodness into the core of his being, into his heart.

He imagined he could feel the energy begin to radiate from his body, creating a circle of light about himself. Confident in his new weapon, he used his mind to project that light even harder as he marched toward the dark mass below.

CHAPTER 22

The bid letting was scheduled for ten thirty a.m. at the Committee administrative headquarters. Lars delivered the bid early and went across the street to Committee Hall. He'd walked by the building several times but never set foot inside, so had pestered Leif until he agreed to play tourist.

They climbed to the spectator balcony, high above the main floor, and looked upon a massive space hundreds of feet wide, with a domed ceiling so far above that he wouldn't have been surprised to see clouds. All was richly ornamented in wood paneling and carved stone. He let out a low whistle. "I've never seen the like."

Leif snorted. "Your blood, sweat, and tears at work, brother. Enjoy it."

"I can't even calculate the value of the woodwork in this room. How can the Committee spend the citizen's money on this when people are without heat or running water?"

Leif didn't answer. Lars didn't expect him to, but, man, priorities at the central government had become skewed.

This troubling revelation aside, the Committee in session presented an interesting spectacle, a welcome diversion from his churning worry. He rubbed his aching neck, then rested a fist on his middle. Breakfast still sat like a brick in his burning belly. But even with the family's future on the line today, at the sight of the first procession he sat straighter, eyes wide, studying every marvelous detail, all else forgotten.

The Committee filed in with great pomp, each wearing a robe of office and accompanied by a dozen aides. These placed themselves behind the raised daises the Committee members would occupy.

Leif pointed. "Check out Advisor Haman in that throng."

As Lars found their overseer, standing next to one of the Committee members, a trumpet blew, and a door behind the centermost and largest dais opened. A withered old man in the finest of robes entered, led by a multitude of underlings. Two security men helped him hobble to what amounted to a throne.

This was the Architect, the man who had restored civilization after the Bad Times and later founded the Republic. A hush fell, and a bishop stepped into a position next to the throne, raising his hand in benediction. That same bishop had led the search at Grandpa's farm.

He intoned an invocation, after which a clerk opened the floor for business. A long line of suppliants entered the room, passing a phalanx of security guards. This was the last court of appeal. Appellants came here to request judgment or submit a final plea before punishment.

The pomp and surroundings might've been fascinating, but the proceedings were mind-numbing. Dry old men read dry wordy legalese from documents. Other dry old men spoke more dry legalese in response. Having lost interest in the soul-killing process, Lars straightened when one case caught his attention.

A family was losing their farm. Their local advisor had approved the construction of an industrial complex and condemned their property in order to build a new road to that site. The advisor stood waiting at his podium. Impatience twisted his features while the old couple tottered to the petitioner's circle, the woman clinging to the man for support.

"Beggin' your pardon, sirs," the old man began. "If we lose our little farm, we have nowhere to go and no way to support ourselves. We humbly beg that the road alter course a bit to allow us to remain in our home for our last years. It'd break our hearts to be tossed out, sirs."

The advisor spoke in response. "If the Committee would review attachment 14 to the file in question, they would see the planned road's course, as well as that of the road, shifted north to miss the property in question, as proposed by the petitioners. Altering construction in this way would cause the roadway to cross a stream, not once as it does under the current plan, but three times. We detail the cost of two additional bridges in the same attachment." He closed his folder with finality. "This is not an efficient or appropriate use of public monies."

The old man shuffled through the papers on his podium. "No, that can't be right." He studied the paper, squinting, hands palsied. "We asked you to move the road to the south. That'd leave it crossing the stream but once. We never said north."

The advisor sighed. "You are in error, sir. Please refer to the signatures at the bottom of attachment 14." He waited as the old man navigated to the correct page. "Is that your signature, sir?"

"Well, it appears to be, but this isn't what we told you when we met. This is wrong."

Chin high, gaze hard, the advisor addressed the Committee. "Sirs, as you are aware, this is the final appeal for this matter, and the rules are clear. No alterations can be accepted at this point. I cannot speak as to the petitioners' intentions, but the documents do not lie. This is the proposal submitted to our office. Those are their signatures. To alter the course of the road based on their signed proposal would increase the expense to the public. To ask the Committee to spend such a sum simply for their comfort is self-serving to the extreme. This would not be for the greater good!"

He then turned to the old couple. "You, sir, should be censured for requesting such a waste of public resources."

The clerk's gavel cut through the growing murmurs. "Time for oral arguments has expired. Would the Committee please vote? To entertain the appeal of the petitioners all in favor, say, aye."

The committee members sat in silence.

Lars shot to his feet, and he wasn't the only one in outrage.

The Architect had been shaking his ancient head and now struggled to his feet. His weak, thready voice barely rose to the balcony. "This is not the purpose for which we created this Republic. This is not justice. Without justice, there is no greater good!"

The bishop reached the Architect and whispered in his ear. The old man protested anew, but another hissed word in his ear took all the fight out of him. He slumped into his large chair. The bishop flicked a finger at the two security men, and they stepped forward, stood the Architect, and guided him toward the door. He turned back once, but the men raised his feet off the floor and carried him away.

The clerk continued, seemingly oblivious to the interruption. "All opposed say nay." After a round of nays, the clerk banged the gavel. "Petition denied." Another sharp rap. "This concludes business for today."

The old couple stood at the lectern, motionless, a sea of departing delegates swirling about them, the babble of voices becoming distant, then dying altogether. Eventually, the room was empty. With a gentle finger, the old man wiped a tear from the woman's creased face. Taking her about the shoulders, he led her from the room.

Lars sat back down, heat boiling from his cheeks. "That advisor cheated them out of their home."

Leif grunted. "I wouldn't be the least surprised to learn that road shifts south where the old man said he wanted it. But not till their property is in the advisor's hands. Legalized theft."

"Somebody needs to do something."

"Good luck with that."

Lars brooded until the janitorial staff threatened to chase them from the empty chamber. They walked to the administration building, still too early for the bid letting. So he led Leif down a hallway and to a café where an indoor patio faced a corridor intersection.

He ordered them both coffees and selected a seat on the patio, offering a view in all four directions. He opened his briefcase and arranged notepads and papers, getting ready for the letting. Leif started a conversation, but with his mind in chaos, Lars didn't hear his brother. He kept his gaze fixed on one corridor, his foot bouncing.

A man was approaching, and as he neared the table, Lars went into motion. He planted a foot and stood. In the process, he tangled with the officious-looking man who had been passing by, carrying a thick pile of manila envelopes.

The man went down, arms splayed. The envelopes slid in a widening pile across the polished concrete. Lars had kept his balance, and he dropped to his knees before the man recovered. With his work papers in one hand, he scooped up the dropped envelopes with the other, tidying them into a neat stack. He helped the man to his feet, then placed them in his hand.

The man scowled. "Kindly watch where you are going." Then, with a sniff and another frown, he continued on his way.

Lars let out a long-held breath. "Looks like they're bringing in the bids. Shall we?" He sketched a bow in invitation.

Leif shook his head but stood to follow.

They found seats. Aside from the clerks at the front, only a scattering of people were present. As the clock neared ten thirty, the room filled.

A smug-looking young man and his companion seated themselves two rows ahead, their expensive clothes out of place in this crowd. Lars could smell the fancy cologne even from this distance.

A man sat next to the pair and began a conversation, complaining about labor attrition. The self-satisfied man said, "Why worry about that? When you lose one, you get another."

His attitude set Lars's teeth on edge, and he craned to overhear.

"Do you have any idea how many people that would take? Where am I supposed to find them all?"

The young man laughed, elbowed his companion, and winked. "If you know the right people, you can get them by the trainload."

Leif poked Lars's ribs, then whispered, a hand shielding his mouth. "Artisans. The owner's son is the arrogant jerk on the left, the one who thinks he's so funny."

"Never met 'em before." Lars forced a tight-lipped smile. "Hope they have a really bad day." Both his feet were bouncing now, and his jaw ached from clenching. When were they going to get this bid started?

The door opened, and Advisor Haman swept in, brusque and businesslike. He opened the meeting by listing the bid packages in today's letting. The package Lars was interested in was last on the list, and he endured the next hour of monotonous proceedings with the muscles of his jaw throbbing. He rubbed them, but it didn't help. His stomach was getting worse too. Definitely should have skipped breakfast.

When the time came for the furnishings' bid, the two young men from Artisans gave each other arch looks. He stifled a snort. *Hope you choke on this.*

Just as German had predicted, the clerk picked up the first

manila envelope and, holding it face out, the certificate of qualification visible, slit the top with a letter opener. He then reached into the envelope and extracted a stack of documents. One by one, he inspected them, passing them to two other officials who repeated the perusal before pronouncing them to be in order. The clerk then handed the stack to Advisor Haman, who made a similar inspection. Satisfied, he announced the name of the bidder, Artisans Millworks, and read aloud the bid amount.

It took extreme restraint, but Lars kept his face stony, his heart pounding, a ringing starting in his ears.

Leif whispered, "That was a lot higher than our bid, wasn't it? Am I remembering right?"

Lars shushed him with a look.

The clerks repeated the process with the last envelope— *their* envelope. When the documents were passed to Haman, he inspected them with apparent boredom. Then he read the bid amount and stumbled on his words. He did a double take, eyes widening, before he recovered himself and read the numbers again.

The clerk announced the bid letting's conclusion. People stood, gathered papers, and headed for the door.

The two men from Artisans shoved their way toward the advisor where he sat, still studying the Northwoods bid proposal. The young men exchanged heated words with him.

At first, he seemed conciliatory, but his face soon contorted with ill-contained fury. He stood and jabbed a finger into the face of first one and then the other. His words carried percussive force, audible even across the room. "I do not take the orders here. I give them."

The two men spluttered, then whirled, and stomped from the room.

Leif cupped a hand to Lars's ear. "Explain to me what just happened?"

"Later."

⸌

BACK IN THE HOTEL ROOM, Leif locked the door behind them, then spun, planted hands on his hips. "Okay, what was I missing back there?"

Lars opened his briefcase and spread two copies of the bid proposal onto the faded bedspread. "See for yourself."

With a tangle of blond hair falling into his eyes, Leif leaned over them. "There are two versions here, and neither is the number from the letting."

"What else?"

He palmed the hair from his forehead. "Only one of these is valid. The signatures on the other are copies. The valid one's the number I expected. I thought I remembered right. Our bid in the letting was ten percent higher."

"Correct. What does that suggest?"

Leif wrinkled his nose and let the papers fall. "Why don't you tell me?"

"Artisans cheats at lettings. They know our bid before they submit their own."

"How?"

"Advisor Haman is corrupt. He checks our bid and gives it to them. Not always, or it would be obvious, but they get the gravy work while we survive on scraps. Until this time."

Leif's eyebrows rose to an impossible height, his eyelids stretched tight, and his unruly bangs dropped into view. "So how?"

"I gave them a fake bid twenty percent higher than our original. Then I used the blank forms to submit a new one ten percent higher than we had planned." Lars let his smile grow to a self-satisfied smirk. "I helped them fool themselves and upped our profit in the bargain. When they were done cheating, I switched the envelopes back. Remember when I knocked that pencil-necked geek down and helped him pick up those envelopes? That big stack of brown envelopes with bid stickers on them?"

Leif held up the form. "But the fake bid wasn't valid. The signatures weren't original."

"They wouldn't have thought to check that when they were doing the cheat. All they cared about was the number."

"Oh man." Leif dropped onto the edge of the bed, elbows braced on his knees, and planted his face in his hands, moaning. "You just crossed the advisor. He's going to kill us. Literally."

"Oh, come on."

"Seriously, little bro." Leif rubbed his face, pulling his eyelids down. "These guys play hardball. Oh, crap. Oh, crap. Oh, crap." He stood and began pacing. "I have a meeting with the advisor this afternoon. Before then, I have to figure out how to make this right."

Someone pounded on the door. They jumped and eyed each other.

Lars's voice cracked. "Maybe Phillip lost his key?"

Leif opened the door to two uniformed Committee guards. The biggest crossed beefy arms over his chest, filling the doorway. "Identify yourself."

"Um, I'm Leif." Leif cleared his throat and pointed at himself, then jerked his thumb to Lars. "He's my brother, Lars. We're from Northwoods."

The guard consulted a piece of paper. "The two of you will accompany me."

Leif opened his mouth but produced only a croak. He tried again. "Where are we going?"

Two more guards appeared and put him and his brother in arm holds. The lead guard said, "With me."

CHAPTER 23

Father Curtis rubbed his burning eyes. He sat back and pushed away a stack of books to clear a space on the table. The overflowing piles of texts he'd studied threatened to bury him in an avalanche. He began to fear he would dream of a barren wilderness filled with pyramidal piles of these tomes instead of rocks.

His back twinged again, and he stood and stretched, touching his toes. Hmm, late evening already by the count of his new digital watch, a gift from the professor. Still, day and night lost meaning without outside sources of reference.

He scowled at the pile of papers before him. He'd have thought he would've already digested the broad outline of the True Text—or at least what Professor Reuel had reconstructed —but the task was more monumental than he'd imagined.

He rocked his neck to stretch cramped muscles. He needed a break. The trapdoor above opened, and he jerked, hands rising as if to ward off a blow, instinct screaming "run!" until Reuel climbed down.

The professor carried a parcel to the kitchenette. Brown paper crackled as he unwrapped a string of sausages. He hung the meat on a hook, then limped to the table. "How goes the study?"

Curtis took in shelf after massive shelf of tomes. "I must admit, this is more than I bargained for."

"Hmm, yes. It is quite daunting. Have you seen enough to make your decision?"

Curtis shook his head.

"Well, there is no rush, not really." Reuel clamped a hand on Curtis's shoulder and patted him before sinking with a groan into a chair. "If you choose to join our underground, you could do so here or relocate to another cell. Somewhere far away. Somewhere you could assume a new identity without fear of being recognized."

Deep in their wrinkled pockets, his piercing blue eyes then locked on Curtis's. "Or you may relocate under a new identity and forget you ever heard of us. We would assist you in exchange for your oath of silence."

Curtis stood and walked to the far wall and back, arms crossed, hugging himself for the warmth that was so lacking here in this cold concrete cave. And what if none of those options would do? "I'm torn. Part of me wishes to go back to my old life." He held up one hand. "Oh, I know that's not an option." *At least not right now.*

He paced to the wall and back again, walking the track he'd taken so oft these last days—days? Was it merely days since he'd been a free man? Even yes, a respected man in his small world. He shrugged that off. "I'm nearly convinced of your claims, and I do wish to know the truth. But I'm also broken-hearted. How can I not be? My entire life—all I believed and all I stood for—was an ugly sham. And my people. My poor flock . . ."

"You are torn between the comfortable lie and the fearful unknown." Professor Reuel pushed his chair back from the table and stretched his legs, venous hands resting in his lap.

"It's common. Some prefer to close the door on the soul chaos and go on pretending ignorance, even to themselves. Some succeed to an extent. You're not such a man, my boy. Knowing the truth is out there, you will be unable to rest until you go to battle, dragging it kicking and screaming into the light. Your life as a priest is proof enough of that. Even when you tried, you were unable to stop challenging the Order's core precepts while you pretended, even to your own self, you were its loyal servant."

Curtis chuckled, combing his hair with his fingers. He sought some order in life, even if all he now controlled was his appearance. "I don't know, Professor. I'm lost, casting about in darkness. I have nowhere to go." He flailed a hand in the air, his steps becoming more animated, his voice rising with his increasing heartbeat.

Reuel sprang from his chair and stopped him with a palm to his chest. "You do have a place to go, my boy, as well as a purpose. I am certain of it. The Messenger knew that and used Phillip as an instrument to save you for that very reason."

Was there really a Creator God out there, one who had intent and purpose for Curtis? The thought made his heart beat more quickly again, but he tempered his initial excitement. "The Messenger. Yes, you would think such a miraculous visitation would leave no doubt, wouldn't you? What's wrong with me? What in me keeps me from accepting things?"

"You let your intellect get in your way, my boy. You always have."

"What's that supposed to mean?"

"It means you refuse to accept anything until you have dismantled it and completely understand it. But some things are beyond our comprehension. However, what we cannot comprehend, we can often apprehend, know them to be true without a complete understanding. Your refusal to accept what you cannot fully understand, comprehend, robs you of those things and impoverishes your life."

"But how can I have absolute faith unless I know a thing to be absolutely true?" Curtis blew out his frustration. Had he just put voice to the same struggle Leif had described?

"Good . . . that is good." Reuel patted Curtis's chest and stepped away. He picked up his battered old briefcase and stopped at the base of the ladder, one hand on the railing. "Faith must be a sure thing, but you won't *think* this thing into resolution. Sometimes we have to ask Creator God to open our eyes that we may see, and this seeing is not borne of the intellect." He thumped his heart. He then tapped one withered fingertip to the side of his head. "Once having seen, knowing follows."

Curtis raked through his hair again, probably mussing what he'd tried to fix, but really, what did it matter? He'd never cared about appearance before.

"For now, my boy, pray. Pray to the one true God that He would answer the questions of your heart, that He would open your eyes to His truth." Reuel gripped a rung and began to climb, knees creaking. He called over his shoulder as he ascended. "I shall return later tonight or tomorrow. Do you need anything?"

Curtis waved a negative, lost in concentration.

Soul torn, body aching, and heart leaden, he lay on the narrow cot, the bed slats pressing shoulder blades through the thin mattress. He stared at the concrete slab ceiling. Distorted candlelit shadows flickered on the pocked surface. As the abstract shapes danced, he composed a mental prayer but stopped. How did one do this? The prayers he knew so well, the ones from the Book of Worship, were prewritten, recited from rote. But now he was asking for a new thing, so where did he start?

Giving up on the stilted prayers of his calling, he simply

plead aloud, "Creator God, or Eternal One—whatever You call Yourself—everything I've lived for are lies, artificial constructs of wicked men. I need to know the truth, the truth about You. Show me You exist. I've always wanted to know You, but now You are further from me than ever. Draw near to me. Draw me nearer to You. Open my eyes that I might see Truth—that I might hold it close, preserve it, and defend it. Help me tear away this veil of lies and expose the truth of truths. Please, O Holy One, please. I need Your help. I need You."

He slept.

He felt no different the next morning. There had been no revelatory dreams. Disappointed, but not surprised, he ate a cold breakfast while standing before the newly stoked fire, staring into the bright flames as if the answers to all these mysteries might be found there.

The thought caused a pang somewhere deep in his chest. He shook himself, left some crumbs on the hearth for Dantes, and with a hot cup of tea, sat to continue his studies.

He was reading a lengthy section of verse, an authentic printed fragment, supposedly a section of the True Text. He'd learned a network of scholars searched the world for these fragments, which sometimes occurred as actual excerpts, but often as citations in historical works, in works of fiction, poetry, even in once popular songs.

Whenever a possible fragment was discovered, researchers hand copied, encoded, and sent it to central clearinghouses. Reuel had found this one himself, hence Curtis held the rare original.

Once scholars identified an excerpt as being a possible True Fragment, they archived it with others believed to be from the same portion. Then came the laborious job of stitching together texts, often with gaping holes and multiple, slightly differing versions.

He looked at the stacks of tomes. The impossible task they

faced was like a physical weight. His arms tired, and his feet dragged at the thought of bearing that burden. How many lifetimes would it take to complete this reconstruction? Was it even possible?

Reading the same verse for the third time now, he still had no memory of what it said. His mind would not focus. With a frustrated grunt, he let the volume go, scattering loose papers as it flopped to the table.

But even with the monumental impossibility of the project, the study excited him, drew his heart to it, eager for the pursuit of the truth. His intellect, though, held him back, unwilling to accept another false system.

So, how did one know what could be trusted? How did one know the truth?

A strange sensation came over him, a fuzzy warmth entering the top of his head. Then the world receded, moving with glacial slowness, the wavering candle flames frozen in place, the dust motes floating in the aura now hanging motionless. The crackling fire, the rattling of the bare steam pipes overhead, even the beating of his own heart intensified, defying logic, becoming more muffled and yet more clear.

His body seemed like it stretched miles from left hand to right, his flesh evaporating, becoming less dense and somehow ethereal. He could feel—and yet could not feel—the grain of the table under his fingers, the weight of his body on his chair, the tired muscles at the base of his skull.

The warm sensation moved down, expanding, settling, and centering in his heart. The words I love you formed, bursting from his lips. "I love you. I love you!" He cried aloud, again and again, tears streaming down his face.

He was saying these words to God, but also relaying them from God to himself. An overpowering presence surrounded him, enfolded him, and infused his soul, an indescribable love electrifying every atom of his being.

He was loved. God loved him.

And God was real. He knew this with absolute, unshakable surety, a certainty so complete he would willingly suffer and die before surrendering that truth.

Yes, God was real, but he'd gained that knowledge in such a way, it would be impossible to relate the essence of that knowing to another person. No human faculty could capably transmit the whole of this marvelous thing that had been gifted to him. He wished there were.

Sometime later, the professor cleared his throat, and Father Curtis raised his head. He'd not noticed his arrival as he wrote, scribbling as fast as his fingers would move the pencil. Each cursive line racing against the terrible apprehension that this experience, these new concepts invigorating his brain, this truth he'd gained, might again recede from his memory. Might leave him to forget, to be cast back into the darkness in which he'd once wandered, seeking without hope.

Reuel arched a bushy brow toward wispy hair. He must've seen Curtis's face wet with tears, spilling from his chin and onto the paper.

"My boy?" Reuel hovered over him, touching his brow like a mother checking a child for a fever. "Is everything well?"

"Better than I could have imagined." Curtis smiled through his tears. "I have met your Creator God. I have found Truth."

CHAPTER 24

Leif fell into step as the guards led him and Lars deep into the administration building and up multiple flights of stairs, ending at the top floor. His racing mind barely noticed the rich surroundings, such a contrast to the sterile beigeness of the public areas. Leif let his feet sink into carpet so thick, his steps were buoyant despite the weight of dread pressing on him. And the ornate woodwork . . . He almost whistled in awe as they were goose-stepped to the end of a corridor where a guard tapped on a carved wooden door. Someone said "enter," and the guards passed them into a corner office filled with oiled mahogany and plush burgundy upholstery. A wall of windows overlooked tree-covered river bluffs.

"Sit," Haman ordered.

The guards bodily deposited Leif and Lars in two armchairs facing the gleaming paneled desk.

Behind it sat the powerful man, one hand resting on their bid proposal, the other holding a finger to his lips as he studied the boat traffic, floating on a sheet of water shimmering beneath the afternoon sun. They sat in silence, Leif growing more tense by the tick of the clock. Then came another tap on the door, and Haman swiveled back to the desk. "Enter."

A man in unadorned clerical robes opened the door and slid a file folder onto Haman's desk.

Haman arched a brow. "Is that everything?"

The man nodded.

The advisor waved. "Very well. That is all."

The man departed, but the guards remained.

"I said that would be all," repeated Haman, voice growing harder.

The guards glanced at one another, again at their leader, then shuffled out of the room, clicking the door closed.

Haman flipped through the file he'd received. He let out a low, mirthless chuckle as he slapped it in front of Leif. "So that was your trick. Do you know how many laws you two broke today? Any idea what penalties you face, you and your family?"

Leif stared at the false bid proposal Lars had shown him in their room. He wheezed through dry lips. "It was my doing. Lars knew nothing."

Lars began to protest, but the advisor's sharp gesture cut him off.

The hand then pointed at Lars. "You may go." It pointed at Leif. "Stay."

Lars was frozen in place, mouth moving.

At Haman's call, a guard entered the room. When Haman indicated Lars, the guard lifted him, propelling him from the room by his shirt collar.

The advisor relaxed into his cushioned armchair and laced his fingers over his sternum, appraising Leif. "I was angry, initially. I intended to make a satisfactory example of you. But I must say I admire your ingenuity, and in truth, I'm weary of those arrogant infants from the other shop. They forget their place. Perhaps they need some real competition for a change."

He cocked an eye. "They do say competition is healthy, do they not?"

Leif cleared his throat and choked out, "Yes, yes, they do, sir."

Haman's finger traced a circle on the mahogany desktop. "So, should we agree, just between the two of us, that this escapade never happened? Never let this nasty little secret leave this room?"

Leif nodded, afraid to hope.

"Very well. You and I shall enter a new phase of relationship. You will answer to me. You will never, never—and I repeat, *never*—cross me again. Agreed?"

He managed another nod.

"I need to hear you say it, young Leif. You and I are now partners, and you will never attempt to deceive me again."

Leif croaked, "Yes, sir. I mean, no, sir. Never, sir."

"I will be your patron. As your patron, I will give you the same terms I have given your late competition. When this contract is complete, on your receipt of final payment, you will deliver to me, in person, three percent of the total proceeds in gold bullion, yes?"

Leif goggled.

"This will apply to all of our, uh, *special* contracts going forward. Are we in agreement?"

"Okay?" was all he could think to say, a sinking feeling leadening his guts.

"Well, that's settled, then. I had intended to have this conference even before you requested a meeting, so this is opportune. I have another matter to discuss. Do I have your pledge of discretion?"

The breath, which had deserted Leif, was returning. In a stronger voice, he said. "Of course, sir. Absolute discretion."

"Good, very good. I believe you will get the hang of this yet.

You know, of course, I have very grave concerns about the profitability of Northwoods?"

"Yes. I'm concerned myself, and I have a few ideas, if I may. But with this new contract—"

Lifting a finger to stop him, Haman interrupted, "Yes, I'm sure, but first this: I do not believe your father is the man to manage Northwoods, with or without this remarkable plum you landed. I'd like to consider possible replacements. A man with experience at the company. A man who knows the people and can relate well to them. You do recognize this is a problem for your father? A talented man but, my, what a terror to morale. How do you ever keep workers?"

"Uh, well . . ." Leif stuttered. "Well . . . yeah, he can be rough around the edges, but he's the brains of the operation, the heart, you might say."

"A bit rough, yes. My point, young Leif, is I'd like you to consider taking charge yourself. You're an ambitious young man, a man with passion and dreams. Your people admire you, like you even."

Leif sat, opening and closing his mouth. His mind played the scene out before his inner eye. Him, Leif, wrenching the reins of power from his dad's hand. There was a flash of pride, of triumph, but then he watched his dad's retreating back, shoulders hunched, a broken man, wounded beyond repair. It opened a tender place, long closed, somewhere deep inside.

Finally, he cleared his throat. "I don't know how I could do that to him. Besides, this contract, along with a few things I have in mind, will bring things around. We don't need to do anything so drastic."

"Hmm. Well, we shall see, shan't we?" The advisor straightened, shifting the mood, now brisk and to the point. "So, what did you have in mind when you requested this meeting?"

Leif took a deep breath to refocus. "Sir, I've been doing

market research the past months, spoken to select clients. I've verified a real need for high-end custom furniture."

As he talked, passion overcame his nervousness. He scooted to the edge of his chair, his hands building imaginary constructs. "High-end woodwork, custom-designed, hand-crafted, full-mortise and tenon construction, not that dowelled crap Artisans puts out, but heirloom pieces passed down as priceless treasures, generation to generation."

Haman turned to watch the riverboats, and Leif ground his teeth. *You're losing him, Leif. He's bored, and you have about three seconds to get him back.*

"People want that, and they're willing to pay for it. Lots of money. This is an untapped opportunity, sir."

Haman swung back at the mention of money, but he still looked unimpressed. "So why haven't you tapped it?"

"Two problems. We don't have the capital to fund the effort. A good amount would be tied up for a long period. Oh, to be sure, single one-off pieces wouldn't be a problem, but the majority of this market consists of large millwork packages for new construction projects. As you know, an entirely new class of up-and-coming industry barons is building monuments to themselves and need to furnish those mansions."

Haman gave a careless wave. "I see the difficulty. Your finances are stretched much too thin. You cannot consider such a venture." He swiveled to the river again.

A towboat hauled a barge from the dock, headed down-stream. *Your ship is sailing too, Leif. Time to reel him in, if you're going to.* "Sure, but you know our capability, our quality. If the Committee would back us, I guarantee a profitable opportunity for all."

Haman's eyes glinted at the word *profit*. That gleam disap-peared as his hooded eyes regained their bored expression. "Possibly, possibly. And the second problem?"

That was his best hook. If he couldn't get him excited about that, the next part would be impossible. But what option did he have? He wouldn't get a second chance. So how to make this irresistible? "We import all our hardwood lumber from outside the Republic. This is difficult and expensive. The work I'm proposing will require even more costly species and cuts."

Leif stood and walked to the window, blocking Haman's view of the distracting boats. "This is a problem. But what if we had a local source of cheap lumber of that same type and quality? We could log it, run it through our own sawmill, and sell it for the same price as the expensive imports, with our own real cost at"—he paused for dramatic effect, then, finger in the air, concluded—"*ten percent* of the imported product."

Haman tsked, shaking his head. "I know little about forestry, but to grow such a stand of timber would take, what? Fifty years, maybe seventy?"

"Longer." Leif smiled.

"Our economy requires resources available for immediate exploitation. We aren't in a position to invest in long-term and uncertain boondoggles." Haman began to stand, obviously ending the meeting. "I am disappointed. However, your first idea has some merit."

Leif lounged against the window, studying his fingernails. He risked interrupting the advisor. "But, sir, I do know of such a resource. One ready for immediate extraction."

Advisor Haman paused, half risen from his chair. He sat and released the padded armrests. "Kindly explain what you mean by 'ready to extract.' How might this be? I've toured the territory. There are no stands of timber in that prairie except for the river bottoms. If you are referring to them, I must disappoint you. Our foresters have done surveys. Removing anything of value from that tangled mess will cost more than it is worth."

A rush of intoxication lightening his stride, Leif paced before the desk. "No, sir, not the river bottoms. It's an out-of-the-way place called Burr Oak, not far from Northwoods." His hands animated his points. "It's but steep glacially formed hills, worthless for farming or anything else. That'd be why you never heard of them, but back in those hills, a rancher planted thousands upon thousands of acres of nut-bearing hardwoods for his livestock."

He crossed the intricately patterned rug to stand eye-to-eye with Haman, braced on the desk, elbows locked, a conqueror come to claim his prize. "He planted them over a hundred years ago. Those trees now stand, waiting for you and me to capitalize on them."

Advisor Haman stood and pushed into Leif's face. "Sit. Down."

Leif's eyes went wide, and he flinched. What had he done? What was he thinking? He fell back into his chair, hands raised in apology. "I'm sorry. Got carried away."

Haman came around the desk, arms behind his back, and loomed over Leif. "First, the Committee will never approve costs to build a new sawmill. Second, you haven't yet procured rights to log this land, correct?"

The flush of victory gave way to a cold feeling, starting at his fingertips, numbing them as it worked its way up his arm. Leif grimaced. "That could be arranged for the right price. But, as to the sawmill, ages ago, when the railroad was built, a man installed one on the edge of Northwoods. He made his fortune clearing the river bottom for new farm fields while also harvesting the timber and selling it up the rail."

Haman had turned to the window again—a bad sign. He crossed his arms. "You did not answer my question, young Leif. Do you have logging rights?"

Leif's breakfast was inching toward his throat. He could only manage a whisper. "No."

"I thought not. And is this ancient sawmill, still in existence?"

"It is."

"It's hard to believe anything that old would be usable."

"Actually." Leif fought to push himself up in his chair from where he'd collapsed. Time to make one final plea, catch his imagination, overcome at least this one objection. "It's been in continuous operation. Granted, it's just been a hobby mill lately, but it can be refurbished. We could use it long enough to prove our concept to the Committee, then build a new mill closer to the extraction site."

"Possible? Probably? You are not reassuring me."

"I'm not an engineer." Leif levered himself to the edge of the chair. Time to close, even if it was on something small, some minor commitment, a starting place. "Why don't we have an expert visit the mill and determine if it's possible?"

"You're proposing I spend time and money to evaluate a nebulous idea dependent on multiple, unproven variables. And"—Haman held up a finger—"even if the concept was viable, Committee approval would be required, a doubtful likelihood given the current fiscal mood."

Leif slumped back down.

Haman sat, rolled his chair under the desk, and picked up a sheaf of paperwork. "Let us leave off conjecture for today. Contact these prospects of yours. When I next visit North-woods, provide me the details, including estimated budgets. We may visit your Burr Oak and sawmill, then decide if we have reason to proceed on either front. Agreed?"

As if by magic, a guard appeared at Leif's elbow, ready to lead him out.

In the corridor, Lars sat in an alcove, face pale, with guards on either side. When Leif emerged, his brother jumped up. "Why did you cut me out? What are they going to do to us?"

Much as his brother had done at the bid letting, Leif quieted him with a look and a whispered, "Later."

They were escorted down the stairs and to the lobby where the guards took their leave without a word.

As they walked to their hotel, Leif filled his brother in.

Lars gaped. "No charges? How did you talk us out of that pickle?"

"I didn't, really. He was ready to teach Artisans a lesson, I guess. You and Dad better ensure the company performs, or there'll be no next time." No reason to mention the advisor's corruption, especially that promised bribe, payable in gold.

Just what was he going to do about that? Much of the business in the Republic was corrupt. No application was ever submitted to a government official without a few bills folded inside to ensure it would be processed, not tossed in the trash.

But this was something else entirely, something not only dirty and wrong, but downright dangerous. But the best thing to do with problems with no solution was hope they go away. He'd keep mum, for now.

Lars nudged him. "You all done with your other meetings? Can we get out of this place? I'm ready to be as far away from here as I can get."

"We can if Phillip's back."

Phillip was waiting. They packed and headed to the train terminal to catch a night express. In less than three hours, they were on the road northbound. But try as he might, Leif couldn't make himself believe he'd left his problems behind.

HE WAS AGAIN in the dreamscape where last he'd charged downhill toward the evil mass, projecting the light of his own goodness.

Memory dawned. When he'd hit the line of dark mist, evil beings had surrounded him, oblivious of his mental weapon, unaffected by its invisible light. He'd been overpowered, lost his bearings and volition, almost swallowed up by the mass.

But a shape moved amongst the ravenous creatures,

seeming to be made of the marvelous light, the same as emanated from the Sword, but this was no sword. This was a four-legged creature, one his fading vision interpreted as a lion. As it neared, scattering the dark forms in its advance, all had faded to black, his memory ended.

Now, he again stood safe at the pinnacle, weak, dizzy, and nauseous. Damaged but not destroyed. He cast about for some plan, some way to rescue the cherubs and his people.

He hunched around a pain in his midsection and, in so doing, noticed something at his feet. It shone with a warm internal light, not identical to but not unlike the Sword. He picked up the thing, a thick studded belt. The note of its light pulsed through his hands and into his body, its flavor that of Truth.

His soul thrilled.

For his entire life, he'd sought Truth. In his waking world, he'd been given a supernatural experience, a tantalizing taste of that Truth. Now, here in his hands, he held a belt shining with the pure light of that very same Truth.

He buckled it about his waist, and the light increased exponentially as if, by putting it on, he'd activated it. As if it knew it was about to be employed and readied itself for battle. Surely, this would drive the dark creatures back long enough for him to cross the plain and save his people.

With renewed confidence, he charged down the hill, plunging toward the rippling darkness.

CHAPTER 25

For most of the journey home, Lars and Phillip had slept as best they could, given the freight cab's tight confines, while Leif chose to manage the controls alone. He needed the time to think.

He understood what had driven Lars to take the risks. Now, the family gained a project capable of seeing them through the next fiscal year and a chance to post the profits needed to avoid the Committee auditors' wrath.

Good enough. But what of the kickback Haman demanded? Leif snorted. Why focus on that gloom when he had much more exciting things to think about? Haman had as much as promised backing for his venture, hadn't he? He just needed to meet with a few more prospects. Get commitments.

He squared his shoulders, sat straighter, already eager for his next trip south. He'd meet with more of the people on his list, and he'd bring Haman a deal he couldn't pass up.

As they neared home, he roused the other two men. Lars rose from where he'd slept on the wood-planked floor and Phillip from his spot on the narrow wood bench where he'd been leaning against the splintered wall slats. They rubbed sleep-matted eyes and hair, yawning deeply and taking in lungs full of diesel-fumed air.

Leif asked, "So when we get there, what were you going to grab for Father Curtis?"

Phillip patted his inner coat pocket. "List here. Books, personal items. Not much. All in residence."

"All in the parsonage?" Lars rose from the floor and plopped on the bench. "But won't someone ask questions if we march in there taking stuff?"

"Who is we? This thing I do, not we. I do quietly, at night. No one sees." Phillip smiled his confidence, the early morning sun gleaming on white teeth.

Lars clamped a hand on Phillip's brawny shoulder, the other man's bulk making Leif's baby brother look like a kid. "You saved my life, and you're nuts if you think I won't be helping you. Besides, you don't know how to sneak in there. *I* do."

Leif choked back a laugh. "Do you? Seems I remember Father Curtis catching you last time. What a fiasco that was."

"Yeah." Cringing, Lars ducked his head and palmed the back of his neck. "It was wrong, but maybe there was a reason. Now we know how to help Father Curtis."

Phillip's wide eyes scrunched, but he made no comment.

"So we need to lie low until dark, right? Leif, what are the chances we can hole up at your place?"

"Diana and the kids are gone to her mom's. So sure."

"Good, it's all planned, then." Lars nodded. "Lunch and a nap at Leif's."

Their boot steps soon boomed hollow on the dining room floor as Leif led the other two into his house. "Shoes off here." He pointed at their feet. "Diana hates shoes in the house."

Familiar with the routine, Lars was already pulling his own off.

How strangely silent. Leif always came home to a

madhouse, but now the place lay as lifeless and quiet as a mausoleum. He rubbed his eyes clear of the morbid image. What was wrong with him today? Lifeless and quiet as an empty library. Yeah, much better.

"Come on upstairs. You guys can take over the twins' beds." Leif headed up first, opened the closets, and laid fresh sheets and blankets over the comforters, a fast and easy way to offer them clean linens without changing the beds.

He left the guys, headed to his bedroom, and shut himself in. Though normally unable to nap during the day, with his limbs, his brain now fatigue sluggish, he was ready to sleep through anything.

He sank into the soft bedding, the sensation as if his body, still vibrating with the remembered song of the road, was floating. He couldn't feel the linens against his skin, his weight against the mattress, only the light breeze flowing through the parted curtains.

Then Phillip was shaking him, the light outside having changed into red-gold-tinged afternoon. They ate a hasty meal, speaking of the upcoming mission. Phillip went over the plans one more time, ensuring each knew their role.

Leif shouldered his backpack and stopped at the garage door to face the empty house. It was haunting, the old place dark and lifeless, the only sounds the echoes from the garage where Lars and Phillip were hooking the canoe to his bike.

Something about standing here, alone in his home, absent the life, the love that usually lighted it, gave him a bad feeling. Like the one you get when you wake from a nightmare, not remembering what the dream had been, but the unremembered trauma still coloring the waking hours, the real world overlaid with the taint of the night vision.

He shook himself as if he could rid his head of cobwebs and closed the door, turning his back on the house.

"Lars? You ready?"

Lars mounted his bike and gave Leif a carefree grin.

Phillip straddled Diana's pink one, an uncertain look on his face. Maybe Phillip's trepidation was about the mission, but more likely about riding a pink bike with a yellow basket.

Leif stopped, one hand on the handlebars. The hollow ache in the pit of his stomach grew as he studied his brother. So young. So certain nothing could go wrong. "Sure you want to do this? I have a bad feeling."

"Just like stealing candy from, well, from the candy bowl."

"Yeah. But don't forget, last time you stole from this candy bowl, you got caught."

A SWELLING JOY built in Reuel's heart as Curtis again described his experience. It was as if the light of the sun, long excluded from this hidden place, now bathed them both in a warm yellow glow, banishing the shadows from even the depths of this stony abode.

His long-held suspicion had been confirmed. Creator God had glorious plans for this man. Reuel had cared deeply for Curtis, had protected him, but despite his efforts, events had thrown Curtis into this present danger. Now, the work of One greater than himself was becoming evident.

He sat, grasped Curtis's elbow, and shook it in his excitement. "My boy! The hand of Creator God is in this, is on you. You have experienced not one but two miraculous acts—first Phillip's otherworldly visitor, and now a true epiphany. Most of us serve Creator God our entire lives without a single gift of this kind. I believe He must mean to use you in a great and powerful way. We must pray diligently for guidance, for all of our decisions to be in alignment with His perfect plan."

Curtis patted Reuel's hand, then turned his chair to him, his eyes still shining. "I have no idea what His plan involves."

Curtis reached out and grasped Reuel's shoulder, locking eyes with him, gaze intense. "But the one thing I do have is an absolute surety it's His intention I do this work, here, with you. I've only just learned He isn't who I thought He was. I desperately want to learn about Him, get to know Him, and serve Him. I know of no better place than right here to do so."

"I cannot tell you what joy this brings me, my boy." Reuel smiled, then sat up. A new resolution straightened his frame. "If that is your decision, then I am bound by oath to dispatch some responsibilities. First, I must advise the nature of our work and its inherent dangers, much of which you are already familiar with. Then I must administer your oath and tell you a history, a true one. One you will learn nowhere else, the same history my father passed to me."

He completed the first, filling in what Curtis hadn't already gleaned. He then administered Father Curtis's oath, hugged and kissed him on both cheeks as his welcome to the Seekers. They then took comfortable seats at the fire, a pitcher of grape juice at hand, and Reuel began his story.

"When the Order introduced their rationalized religion, this new faith system was widely accepted, celebrated even. But a remnant of believers in the old religions, including the True Faith, the followers of Creator God, rejected the Writings and resisted being absorbed into the Order's religion.

"Now mind you, the Order had already amassed worldwide power and deployed this against the resistance. Books were burned. Churches, temples, and even homes raided and razed. Resistors went into hiding only to be rooted out, their entire families dragged into the streets, tried, and executed to the celebration of their communities, family, and friends."

The tale transported Reuel to that pivotal day his father had taken him hiking in the woods, stopping by the waterfall, Reuel's favorite place as a young child. With their packs, including electronics, remaining in camp, the white noise of the water interfering with the ever-present surveillance, his father had pulled young Reuel close and initiated him into the family secrets.

He could still smell the mint on his breath, the clean smell of sweat and aftershave enveloping him in the comfort only a loving father could provide. He whispered, "Oh the things they lost, that we've all lost to those monsters." He lowered his head and swallowed to ease the tightness of his throat.

In a stronger voice, he continued. "The Order and their willing sycophants had a bilious hatred, especially for the followers of the one True Faith."

Curtis leaned in. "Why especially them?"

Reuel turned his gaze to the floor and exhaled the pent breath. "Because only this remnant held to a doctrine that disavowed relativistic thinking, rejected compromise, stood on fundamental principles. They were stalwart in their belief there is only one truth, one God, one way only."

He turned to watch the fire, attempting to bring back the memory of that day in the woods, his shocked thrill at the revelations, to feel again the nearness of his father. But against his will, his mind skipped forward to the time, not even a month later when his parents were imprisoned for subversive activity.

He remembered, too, the vow. Would he see the promise he had made to himself, to his God, fulfilled in his lifetime? He glanced at the volumes on the shelves. So little recovered and he had, who knows, how little time left?

He shook himself. "At any rate, it was a pogrom. In a previous age of communication by letter, such a purge would have been much less thorough. But in that age of instant global communications, the Order could monitor all transmissions, destroy all electronic copies of the True Text with the simple push of a button. The remnant resorted to hiding written copies however they could. A group formed, devoting themselves to doing exactly that. They called themselves the

Keepers of the Truth, hearkening back to another group of the same name. Legend says that ancient sect guarded the True Text for millennia, against pogrom and tyrant, to ensure mankind would never be without Truth. At least until now."

"And because of them . . ." Curtis gestured to the fragments. Books and books of them, piled on the table, filling the shelves, a stack of them next to his rocker.

Reuel hoisted his juice cup. "Ah, sadly, no. They were systematically hunted, their archives destroyed." He gestured to the fragments as Curtis had. "We are forced to this extreme because, as of this date, we have never found a living Keeper, nor any of their hidden texts."

He paused, lubricating his parched throat with a long cool drink of the tart juice. One foot kept the chair in motion, the rocker creaking like his old bones. "This is our history—mine, and Phillip's, as well. We are descendants of those few Keepers who survived, though absent our legacy. What I shall share is the Truth our forebears sacrificed so much—many even their lives—to protect."

He shifted position. Even the cushion beneath him couldn't soften the wooden rocker's harsh grip on his seat, which no longer had the padding of youth and muscle.

"It grows late." Unable to sit any longer, he pushed to his feet, gripping the rocker's arms as his hips adjusted to carrying his slight weight. "When we again meet here, I will tell you more. For now, consider what I have said."

CHAPTER 26

"See you at the river landing." Lars waved in farewell to his brother, then pedaled the short four-block trip to the lake, rehearsing the plan again in his mind. Having convinced Phillip to allow him to recover Father Curtis's possessions, he shivered as the first niggling of self-doubt began creeping up his spine.

Phillip had refused to make a written record, instead insisting the list be memorized. Lars now pedaled, repeating the mnemonic song he and Phillip had created, fearful the list would disappear at the wrong moment.

They pulled up onto the sandy lakefront beach, vacant at this hour, and slipped the bikes into empty racks at the locked concession booth.

Over the sound of the waves lapping the shore, Lars whispered, "Wait here." He slipped off toward the church. This too, Phillip had resisted, but Lars could make up excuses for anyone discovering him at the rectory. An unknown stranger couldn't.

He sauntered down a sidewalk bordering the park, paying little attention to kids playing basketball on the far side of the tree-filled expanse, the growing dusk, the low-hanging limbs masking them from view. Only the impact of the ball on the ground, the flittering shapes, the scuffing shoes proved their continued presence.

He strolled past a block of residences, keeping beneath the silver maples lining the street, allowing himself to be swallowed in their deepening shadows, then onto the church grounds.

While maintaining a casual pace, he scanned the buildings for lights. Abreast of the rectory, he glanced around once more, then melted into the low evergreens. He crawled beneath thick foliage, the sharp scent of juniper sap warming his breaths. In the dark, he could still make out the indigo berries where they hung, could see in his mind's eye the dusky surface. How long ago had it been since he'd harvested these very bushes?

Grandpa swore by their oils as a remedy for arthritis. He made a tincture and distributed it among other older parishioners. Lars couldn't testify as to the effectiveness, but the old folks sure seemed happy to get it.

He crept to a recessed basement window, shooing a rabbit from the leafy nest it'd snuggled into there. Careful to be silent, he brushed aside the crackling leaves and held his breath before lifting the lever, then breathed again. The latch he'd jiggered years ago had never been repaired! He slithered snakelike through the opening and landed, hands first, on the kitchenette counter.

The butter and garlic odor of the basement kitchen brought back memories of so many evenings spent here, making popcorn and pizza, playing board games in this youth clubhouse under Father Curtis's supervision.

Out of habit, Lars slipped a hand into the reward bucket. This lure had been the impetus for his original nighttime incursions into this room. He popped a chocolate in his mouth, removed his shoes, and padded to the stairs.

On the main floor, he passed through the study and bedroom, identifying and collecting items while murmuring the mnemonic song. After double- and triple-checking the inventory, he arranged it in the backpack, cushioning it with an extra pillowcase from the closet.

As he snugged the straps about his shoulders, he sighted a framed picture of Father Curtis as a boy. Father Curtis had shown him this memento before, explaining it was his only photo of his family. Toddler Curtis posed with an older girl and two adults.

Other than that one brief mention, Father Curtis never spoke of his childhood or his family. Why was that? Lars wrapped the photo in another pillowcase. Not wanting to deal with the pack fastenings yet again, he slipped it into a jacket pocket.

He retraced his steps out of the window and into the junipers. In full dark now, he stepped into the shadows, moving more quickly toward the park than when he'd come.

ACROSS THE STREET, a man was frying eggs when a shrill beeping emanated from his pocket. He extracted an electronic tablet, and after glancing at it, he sidled to a window overlooking the church property. He studied the darkness before he pushed a button and held the tablet to his head.

"Package is on the move." He listened and then answered, "No, never got eyes on them. But the signal is clear, headed north, out of range within fifteen at current speed." He listened again. "Roger, will keep eyes on. You'll notify chase team?"

Another pause.

"Roger. Out."

LARS SCANNED the empty river landing, gaze darting in all directions. What had happened to Leif? He wasn't here, only the fluttering shadows of tree limbs on the dark rippling waters. Lars and Phillip stood astride their bikes, searching the empty gravel boat ramp, while Lars worked to tamp down his rising alarm.

The moon was a mere slit, enough to cast glimmers on the river, but not enough to pierce the deeper tree shadows. Out of one, a form emerged. Lars jumped before it came into focus as a man carrying a canoe on his head.

Leif called, "Anyone gonna give me a hand?"

When Lars kicked down the bike stand and jumped to help, Leif pointed. "Lars, if you go straight into the brush I came out of, you'll see where I hid my bike. Take the other two over there, will you?"

As Lars wheeled past, Phillip snagged a strap and slipped the pack from his shoulder. "I check items before we go."

Bikes hidden, he returned to the landing. Phillip was squatting next to the open pack, items strewn on the ground, and he was now tucking everything back away.

Leif stood at one end of the canoe, and Lars ran to the other. Together, they lifted it, balanced it on their heads, and portaged it to the boat ramp. Phillip had suggested this mode of transportation. "Is seventy mile to Two Rivers by road. Only forty-five mile by river, less. River run diagonal. We are there by morning. Safer. Trains observed. River patrol easy to dodge. Float down in dark. Paddle home in day. If tomorrow you find patrol, no Phillip, no bag, no problem."

Setting down his end of the canoe, Leif squared his shoulders. "Last chance. We don't need to take this risk, little bro. Not just to see Father Curtis. He can send you a letter if he has something to say."

"He asked us to come." Lars set his jaw. "It's important."

Leif scoffed. "What's he got to say that's important enough to risk your life?"

"How would I know?" Lars raised his arms to the sky. "That's what we've gotta find out."

"Bro." Leif stepped forward and put one hand on Lars's shoulder. "Listen to me. It's not worth it."

He shook off the hand. "No one said you have to go. I can do it without you." He edged the canoe into the current, and Phillip, having watched their exchange, stepped into the prow.

Lars turned his back on Leif and began to push the canoe free.

At the last moment, Leif grabbed the gunwale and stepped in, leaving the rear position for Lars.

Leif grunted as he settled into the rocking canoe. "If you're determined to get yourself into trouble, I'd better be there to get you out."

They pushed off and steered into the center current, gliding so silently on the glassy water that, for a moment, Lars was floating, free from the bounds of gravity, drifting in some black expanse. He lost all sense of up and down and had to grip the edge of his seat to be certain it was still there.

The narrow sliver of moon reappeared from behind the clouds, and he regained his sense of space, reorienting. A sigh escaped. High in the sky, more puffy clouds crawled across the face of the moon, their cotton-candy gray becoming luminous as the bright crescent backlit them. The stars reflected like white points of fire on the inky river, the light rippling with the water's movement.

No wind stirred, except that of their passage, and the night sounds drifted from the impenetrable darkness on either bank, the trilling of insects, the animal calls seemingly amplified in this unfamiliar setting. The night sky provided just enough illumination to navigate around sandbars. The canoe made barely a sound as it ghosted along. Aided by silent paddling, they moved downriver and kept to the center channel for better speed.

Now, did Lars imagine a glimpse of twinkling lights around the next bend? He shifted, tilting the boat as he pressed for a better view. It might be road traffic, but it also might be . . . He tapped Leif and nodded in the direction, willing his brother to hear his thoughts.

Soon, a patrol boat emerged from behind a muffling stand of trees, still a mile distant. Red and blue running lights glimmered. The bright white searchlight, currently stationary, pointed to lead the way.

Seeing Phillip and Leif had done so, Lars shipped his paddle and rested it on the gunwale. Water dripped from their oars. That and the distant roar of the approaching motor launch created the only sound. Phillip jabbed a finger toward a tree on the right bank. Partially undermined, it had fallen and now grew sideways over the river, hanging low and dipping branches, like long bony hands, into the water, swaying with the tug of the current.

They steered toward the bank, drew under the tree, and reached up to grab the limbs, using them to haul the canoe into position. They then sat, still holding on, steadying against the light current.

They waited, breath suspended and muscles tense. To be discovered here, like this, with their unexplainable cargo . . . Lars stifled a shiver. What had made him insist on accompanying Phillip to Two Rivers? Why had they taken such a risk?

He wanted to see Father Curtis, of course. That and the trip sounded like an adventure when in the safety of Leif's house. But he should've thought this through. What would happen to the family business if both he and Leif were arrested for smuggling? Nothing good to be sure.

Beyond the branches, the boat prowled closer. The bottom dropped out of Lars's stomach. How stupid. They'd hidden in a tree, the branches of which were the only moving things on the riverbank. It was bound to attract attention.

The lights made agonizing headway. It almost seemed the boat would pass without incident, but as the launch neared, an overzealous trooper swung the searchlight from side to side, sweeping both banks. The spotlight stopped on their hiding place.

CHAPTER 27

L ars's breath stuck in his throat, adrenaline causing his blood to rush in his ears with a low throbbing roar. But no alarm was raised. Was the foliage dense enough, close enough in color to the green canoe to camouflage their position?

The light swung forward, and the boat motored on, disappearing upriver.

They waited, not daring to move, their heavy breathing turning to whispered sighs, the branches continuing to sway back and forth, the current swirling about as if chuckling at some secret joke. Once they could no longer see the searchers, they slipped out from under the boughs and back to the deep waters, again accelerating with the aid of the deceptively swift current.

Then Phillip, from his position in the canoe's front, burst into motion, paddle churning the water, causing the craft to wheel left. Taken unawares, neither Lars nor Leif steered, but remained frozen.

A shape coalesced out of the gloom, closing fast, arms reaching out to grab Lars by the head. No, not arms—branches, the ends of which were broken into sharp stabbing points that seemed to leap toward him, threatening to impale him.

Phillip's evasive action had turned the canoe sideways, and now the current drove them toward the snag, a tree submerged in the river's center.

"Row!" Lars shouted, oblivious to the noise, and began stroking, digging deep and leaning into his oar. Dark stories spoke of folks meeting their fate, tangled in underwater roots of such.

Phillip had already been paddling to clear the tree, and now Leif lent his strong arms to the effort. Branches under the waterline screeched against the hull, but they scraped by the obstacle and were again slicing through clear water. Lars searched the interior, expecting the gushing fountain of a hull breach, but found no damage.

"Wow," he whispered. "That was close." The near miss strangely thrilled him. But did the escape or the danger itself evince such a heady joy? He shivered. Sometimes he worried even himself.

They continued with no other incident, not another soul on water or land for the remainder of the trip. As they floated along, paddling in an easy, steady rhythm, Phillip audibly counted bridges. When they came to a particularly wide concrete overpass, he spoke in a low voice. "Stream to right. Go up two hundred yards. Dock there."

Up the tributary, they found a moldering dock, more a pallet on posts driven into the stream bed than a proper dock, but Phillip grasped a post and tied the canoe, assisting the brothers off before disembarking himself.

Earlier, Phillip promised they'd meet Father Curtis at a remote safe house, not where he was living, but one in the wilds outside of Two Rivers. Father Curtis was to make his appearance by three a.m. every night until they arrived, and they'd made good time, landing well before one.

Phillip led them away from the dock, through a tall patch of cattails. As they walked, the cattails turned to reeds, then to tall grasses. Ahead, a line of bluffs blocked the stars, and closer, a darker tree line cast shadows too deep for the eye to penetrate.

They moved through the grasses toward the woods. Even in this near absolute darkness, Phillip traversed an invisible trail as surely as if it were daylight. A hulking shape materialized, set back in the first outgrowth of trees, and Phillip veered toward the structure.

After a squeak of hinges, he disappeared inside. A light flared as he lit a hooded lantern and used it to hurry them indoors. "Sit here." He gestured to a table before the single window. He then extinguished the lamp. "You are now quiet and keep watch."

His silent shadow slid toward the door.

Lars stiffened, pivoted on his hard wooden chair, and whispered, "Where are you going?"

"I watch in forest. You watch here." With that, he vanished.

They sat in the stuffy cabin, making no sound, straining to hear what was going on outside. Lars's sense of smell heightened in the darkness, and the odor of mildew and mice accosted him.

Was that a movement near the path? He couldn't be sure. He squinted to focus but made out nothing.

Then Phillip was beside him, gliding into the cabin. He scooped the dark lantern from the table and tugged at Lars's pack, whispering in his ear. "Give, now."

Lars twisted his arms out of the straps and handed it over.

Phillip took it to the moldy bed, where he spread a blanket over his head before lighting the lantern. With the blanket muffling the light, he dug through the pack. Scuffling noises and grunts drifted from the makeshift tent as he appeared to inspect each item, holding something in his palm that emitted a green blinking light.

Lars inched closer, ducked under the blanket, then leaned over Phillip's shoulder for a better look. Whatever Phillip held in his palm began blinking rapidly, the green light having become red.

Phillip froze. He then moved the object away from Lars. The red light disappeared, replaced with the green. As he moved it back toward Lars, the red reappeared.

Phillip groaned. "What is this thing you take but not put in pack?"

Lars slipped a hand into his jacket for the pillowcase-wrapped photo. He held it toward Phillip. "Sorry. I forgot. Is something wrong?"

Phillip snatched the picture and opened the back of the frame, then used a folding knife to pry at something Lars couldn't make out.

Phillip pointed over his shoulder. "Need breadboard."

Leif, still seated at the table, relayed the scarred board to Lars, who passed it on to Phillip. Phillip placed something on it and then wrapped the package with the pillowcase, binding it tightly.

"Follow very quiet," he warned before heading off into the deep woods. Under the trees, in the impenetrable dark, he had them reach forward, each touching the shoulder of the man ahead. And again, Phillip displayed an uncanny ability to see the path. Meanwhile, Lars shuffled in absolute darkness, afraid to trip on uneven ground. Phillip navigated them through the woods with a sure hand, and the path remained level and smooth.

Stars began breaking through the curtain of trees, and then the line of the bluff tops loomed. They stopped deep in a thicket of sumac trees, and Phillip whispered, "Stay. I return." He hefted the backpack and slipped away, as silent as mist on a moonless night.

Lars waited alongside his brother and tipped his face toward the star field, the gnarled branches and conical fruits visible only as crisp black shapes against the comparatively bright sky. The closely intertwined trees with their palm-like leaves offered an excellent hiding place.

He pressed against a gnarled trunk and slid to the ground. The unreality somehow masked the fright that should've overwhelmed him. The delicious heaviness of his limbs, now unwinding as he rested, was a soporific. He was ready to lie down in the deep leafy litter and nap. Strangely, as he reclined his head against the trunk, the sight of those ripe sumac cones made him want to pick some.

Grandpa loved his sumac lemonade.

A BLACK BOAT had pulled to the riverbank and now blocked the stream Phillip and the brothers had turned into.

A lone man wrapped in black stood motionless in a stand of willows, watching. He checked a tablet and touched the side of his head with a forefinger. "Yellow 3, package is now stationary. Any contact?" He waited and repeated, "Any contact?" He tapped on the tablet before speaking again. "Yellow Actual, this is Yellow 2. Have lost contact with Yellow 3. Please advise."

After a moment, he spoke again. "At last check, package was stationary. Let me reconfirm." He worked the tablet and then spoke, his voice showing the first signs of animation. "Package on the move. Back on the river and a hundred meters downstream of my position. Still no contact with Yellow 3. Please advise."

A second later: "Roger. Package is moving south. Will follow from a distance and report."

The man sprinted to his inflatable, untied the bowline,

stepped in, and pushed off in one smooth motion. As the craft reached the depths of the river, bubbles surfaced in his wake, issuing from a slice inches below the waterline.

Phillip lay in the tall grass at the river's edge until the boat disappeared. When he stood, he folded a knife and slipped it into an inner pocket before melting into the darkness, moving in the opposite direction.

FATHER CURTIS PICKED his way along the steep path from the bluff to the floodplain.

On this, his third night making this trek, he knew the route and had little trouble following it, but a weight pressed upon him at every thought of Phillip. How could he have been so selfish to have asked for his belongings? Material possessions weren't worth the risk to anyone. He could never forgive himself if his friend had come to harm.

This experience, this wait for a missing friend more than any of the other dangers, drove home the reality of this deadly world he'd been dragged into. He had resisted admitting to himself the real threat to his life and to those who associated with him. He fisted his hands and thudded one against his chest as if he could dislodge the hot constriction in his throat. He'd never make that mistake again.

Walking through the broken rock, he swallowed hard. "Creator God, bring peril on me if peril there must be, but spare Phillip," he whispered as he neared the bottom of the descent. He started and almost lost his footing as hands appeared from behind a head-high scrub cedar and clamped onto his arm and mouth.

Strong arms hauled him off the trail and into the dense growth. A face appeared and whispered, "Is me, Father. Is okay."

The hand withdrew, and Curtis whispered back, "Phillip, praise Creator God. I've been so worried about you."

"Is good, but mans hunt us. We go quick, quiet. Wait here. I bring friends. Then we go."

Curtis began a question, but the muscled hand covered his mouth again.

"Talk later. Now must escape. Wait. Be silent." Phillip evaporated into the shadows, leaving no sound of his passage.

Curtis hunched among the cedars, ignoring the sharp sticks poking his backside. He peered into the dark, willing his heart to stop racing.

Minutes later, movement rustled down the slope. Then dark figures appeared on the path.

Phillip reached to hoist Curtis to his feet, and they were off, climbing back up the bluff in a tight single file. With each step, compared to Phillip, Curtis sounded like a water buffalo crashing through the brush. He'd thought he moved without noise in the field, but he was quite loud, as were the other two, at least against the measure of Phillip's flowing stride. The man glided through the dark. This skill Curtis should possess. He'd ask for lessons when time allowed.

Phillip led them up the steep path, weaving between the last of the short, tough scrub cedar and onto the open grassland atop the bluff.

They passed under an overpass, through a cut in a chain-link fence, and to the rear of a warehouse complex. They ducked behind piles of rusted pipes until they were opposite a grease-stained walk door in one of the metal buildings.

Phillip sat on his haunches, silent, and watched the surroundings. Apparently satisfied, he signaled the others to follow and dashed across the open space to the door.

Inside, he pulled out a penlight and used the dim beam to thread between racks of steel tubing and to a corner office. There, he signaled the others to sit in the ripped chairs and to remain silent. They waited while he peered through the cracked door. Then he perched on the desk's corner, still keeping one eye through the narrow window. "Think all clear. Okay you talk now, but quiet."

Curtis had exchanged handclasps with the boys. Now able to speak, he posed his first question. "What happened out there? Who was hunting you?"

Phillip pursed his lips. "Order, maybe. Men in black. No ID."

The brothers shared a confused look. Then Lars asked, "How would you know if they carried ID?"

"Was man on ground. I searched."

"On the ground? How did he get there?"

Phillip shrugged and mimed hitting himself on the head. "Small tap. Easy. He sleep."

"What were they after?" Lars shot from his chair. "How did they find us?"

"My fault." Phillip grimaced. "Trackers."

Curtis's head snapped up. "Will they follow us here?"

"No problem." Phillip shook his head. "Float to Capital. Books in safe place for now, hidden. I check later, make certain, then bring."

Lars and Leif shared another look that seemed to ask, "What is this guy?"

Curtis suspected he knew the answer. Keeping his voice subdued, he asked Phillip, "Would you mind removing your shirt?"

Phillip's eyes narrowed. "Why ask you this?"

"Humor me."

Phillip tensed, then relaxed. His shoulders sloping and lips down turning, he inched down the neckline of his T-shirt.

Lars gaped as the shirt revealed a stylized-eye tattoo above Phillip's heart.

Phillip kept his head ducked, eyes to the ground, and

replaced his shirt collar. A single tear trickled down his cheek. "Am no more of the Eye."

Even having suspected this, Curtis stiffened. Goose bumps tingled across his nape. "No one has ever left the service of the Eye—alive, anyway. You and I both know this."

"Is true. Is reason I hide like you. Hide from same peoples."

"No one leaves the Eye," Curtis repeated. "*Ever.*"

"Never." Phillip raised his gaze to Curtis's, his voice drifting to a near whisper. "Until now."

After an uncomfortable silence, Phillip stood. "I go now, get backpack. I return. This place safe. No peoples come this day. Rest is okay, but watch." He offered a hand to Curtis. "You trust me, my friend? Or you come guard. Be sure I do not betray?"

A hot flush stung Curtis's face. He owed this young man his life many times over. How could he have allowed distrust to temper his thinking? He gripped the proffered hand, then placed his palm on Phillip's neck. "Of course. I'm sorry. It was . . . a shock."

"Shock, yes. All peoples know Eye is not friend, is thing to be feared. This is truth. But I am not for you to fear, my friend. You know this, yes?"

"Yes, of course, and I do count you as my friend. A very good friend. Again, I'm sorry."

When he'd gone, Leif hoisted his pack and took a step toward the door. "Come on, before he comes back."

Lars snagged the strap of Leif's pack. "Hold on. He saved my life, or did you forget?"

"Doesn't mean he won't turn us in, does it? How do we know we can trust this guy? And what's the deal with that tattoo?"

Curtis motioned Leif back to his chair. "Phillip has saved my life more than once. I do trust him, though it jarred me to see the Eye."

"What's the Eye?"

Must they get into this right now? They had more important things to discuss. But, yes, their widened eyes and set jaws
suggested they wouldn't leave this alone.

"The Eye of the Eternal is a clandestine sect of the Order, a
covert brotherhood—secret soldiers. The unseen hand, the
whispers in the shadows, the knife in the dark. It doesn't offi-
cially exist, but everyone in the Order has seen things."

"Wait." Leif shot to his feet. "Are you saying Phillip is an
assassin? I told you we should leave while we could."

"Relax. Phillip is no threat to you. As to what he once was?
Who can say? It's always this way with the Eye. No one knows
what they do. The bishops deny the Eye even exists, and there's
no proof otherwise."

Lars said, "But now there's that tattoo. That's proof."

Leif jumped up again, pointing at Curtis. "Yeah. We should
ask Phillip some questions. Get some answers for once."

From the doorway, Phillip said, "Some answers deadly. Best
remain questions."

Lars jerked, color rising to his cheeks. He cringed and
rubbed the back of his neck. It'd been his job to keep watch.

Phillip swung the backpack toward Father Curtis. "All is
safe. No more trackers. Boys have long trip, must go now, or not
home in daylight."

Chagrined, Curtis grasped the boys' shoulders. "We've had
so little time. I needed to tell you so much, and I don't know
where to start."

Phillip held the open door, motioning for them to go. "No
moon tonight. No time. Brothers must go. Now."

"Please, a moment." Tightening his grip on the boys, Curtis
gusted out his breath. "There's no way to say what I have to tell
you in a short time, but I'll do my best. Dear boys, dear friends,
know this—the Writings are not holy writ as I once believed. I
know this is shocking, but the good news is there is a God in
heaven. He is real, of a certainty. You won't find Him in the

Writings, but you can find Him if you try. Pray, ask Him to show Himself to you. I can't tell you how He'll do this, but He is faithful. If you earnestly seek Him, He'll honor your desire."

He then moved both hands to Leif's shoulders, meeting the older boy's eyes. "Leif, you I pray for. I sense a dark road ahead for you. You'll be lost if you embark upon that journey without the light. Turn back. Please, Leif, turn to the light."

Leif's cheeks reddened, and he broke eye contact.

Curtis then grasped Lars's hands, smiling now at this boy after his own heart. His soul ached. To have to part again so soon was unbearable. "Lars, you I pray for. I feel compelled to tell you not to trust what you think to be good—or in your own wisdom." His throat clogged. He cleared it, pushing on as fast as he could. "Pray to Creator God, ask Him to guide you in what is right." Where these words had come from, he didn't know, but he felt their rightness and thought a quick prayer of gratitude for them. The wetness of tears cooled his heated cheeks, surprising himself as much as it must discomfit the others.

Curtis began to turn away, but Lars caught him in a tight hug before dropping back and dabbing his eyes with a shirtsleeve.

"Please. Must go." Phillip gestured to the door with increased urgency.

So Curtis kissed each boy on the forehead before allowing Phillip to escort them away. Once they were gone, he sank back into the ripped chair, springs creaking beneath his weight, shoulders caving around his hollowed chest, a heaviness settling into it, into his limbs. He'd been away from his people for what? Less than two weeks? It felt like months.

He gasped, struggling against the tightness grasping his heart, overcome by the need to mourn. To grieve the life he'd lost. The people. It had always been about the people. Now, once again separated from these two, the closest thing to sons he'd ever had, he bowed under the full force of that blow.

He wept, wordless cries welling up, spilling forth, sounding like the utterances of a stranger.

Drained, he stood and donned his widow's cloak, picked up his cane, and left the building. Outside the door, he caught himself and stooped to put a particularly sharp pebble in his left shoe.

CHAPTER 28

Phillip had been right in insisting they start home as early as they had. Leif gulped in air, his energy waning. Yet he tipped his oar into the water again and again, his arms burning, numb, growing weaker with every stroke.

Rowing downstream had been a breeze, and Leif, never having canoed a river, had expected the return trip to be just as simple. Once upon that wider ribbon of water, they steered toward the river's center, the deep main channel where they'd maintained their position for the trip downstream.

But, with both rowing strenuously, they scarcely progressed. Even when keeping to the slower waters near the bank, they made little better than a walking pace. Dawn brightened to full daylight, and then afternoon stretched on, the sinking certainty they weren't going to make it growing mile by laborious mile. They'd planned to take turns rowing and resting, but if one of them stopped paddling, they lost all forward motion. The inability to rest was the worst part, your arms giving out and knowing if you took a break, for even one stroke, it would cost many more to make up the lost ground. It was the worst kind of torture.

He remembered the old legend of Sisyphus, rolling that

boulder up the hill. This must be how he'd felt. If this wasn't something close to that mythological hell, he didn't want to see what was.

At least it'd been a dry summer, keeping the river low and slow. Had it been at normal levels, they may not have gotten home at all. As it was, they arrived just prior to full dark, arms too limp to carry the canoe, couldn't even lift it off the ground. They settled on pulling it clear of the water and leaving it there, staggering on stiff legs to the bicycles.

They pedaled up to his garage minutes after dark and nearly fell getting free of the bikes, letting them clatter to the grass. Someone had pinned a note to the door. He groaned. "Now what?" He peeled it off to read by the light of a match Lars lit for the purpose.

Leif groaned again. "The folks know the Northwoods freight car's back in the yard and want us to come over—also, do I know where you've gotten off to? You didn't come home last night."

Lars yawned. "Sounds like Mom."

They stowed the bikes and walked the two blocks to their childhood house, neither wanting to endure another minute on anything resembling a canoe seat, or a bike seat, for that matter.

When they entered, the cheerful glow of kerosene lanterns greeted them. Supper was cooking, the roast chicken and potatoes steaming a bouquet that caused Leif to become dizzy. The exertion of the last twenty-four hours had burned more calories than he'd gained from the hard rations they chewed as they rowed.

He paused over the pan, savoring the floral aroma of herb-roasted meat. "Wow, what are we celebrating?"

Mom looked up from the stove. "Just in time. You must have smelled the food." She stopped short on seeing them, sniffed, and scowled at their filthy clothes. "You can't sit at my table in that state. Go clean up. Lars, loan Leif some clean clothes. What in Hegemony have you two been doing, anyway?"

"Oh, we just went canoeing for a bit." Lars lowered his head and avoided her gaze.

"Canoeing?" She sniffed again, then narrowed her eyes. "Well, hurry up, or the food will be cold."

They did hurry, hunger and Mom's home cooking a motivator. Once seated, they said grace and dug in.

Mom smiled, a brightness in her eyes. "We have news. A messenger brought a purchase order today. It seems the two of you landed the job."

Dad sat at the head of the table, Leif and his brother flanking him as always. He reached out, clapping their shoulders. "We're gonna save this company yet." Almost unrecognizable, he exuded a palpable cheer as he jostled, then released them. "Now, if we could get electricity. Why don't you ask your new best friend Haman for that, next time?"

He laughed at his joke and stabbed a portion of chicken.

Mom picked up her coffee and coiled both hands around it, holding the steaming cup before her face. Her astute blue eyes peered over the rim. "There was an attachment written by Advisor Haman himself. He agreed to a ten percent premium above our original bid. His note mentioned a special arrangement with you, Leif. What was that about?"

His blood pressure dropped, and a ringing started in his ears. "Well, uh, I had a chance to speak to him alone after the letting. I pointed out construction was running ahead of schedule. I convinced him we needed extra money to cover the expedited timeframe."

She sat her cup on the table, one brow rising. "That's unheard of. Imagine, getting a contract *above* your bid price."

Dad harrumphed and adopted a grumpy expression, but he couldn't hide his cheer. He cuffed Leif's arm. "We do make a good team when we work together, don't we?"

Lars glowed at Leif from across the table and winked, a forkful of mashed potatoes en route to his mouth.

As Leif ate, not tasting the food, he sensed a golden bubble surrounding them, the light unnaturally bright, his spirit expanding. When had Dad last shown him such approval? He couldn't remember. It felt good—really good. Even as part of him remained guarded, afraid to trust the good luck.

That glow stayed with him for his trip home. Tiny droplets of fall mist fell on his head, and he raised his face to the dark sky, laughing like a fool, mouth open to catch the raindrops. The mist solidified into a pelting rain. He didn't care. He whistled while he walked, raising arms to embrace the cold torrent, swelling with a buoyancy, an almost physical sensation, just as his full belly was swelling with the feast.

Feeling as if his head were miles removed from his feet, he opened his kitchen door.

Diana sat in the glow of a single tall candle, a lacy nightgown flowing to the floor, a wineglass in her fingers, a half-empty bottle on the table. Her lips, luscious and glistening, turned up at the corners, and she batted her long eyelashes.

"Um, hey," was all he could get out, the connection between brain and body having gone fuzzy with overload.

She giggled. "Is that all you have to say? I've been waiting for you here all evening, and all you've got is, hey? Come here, my love, and have a glass with me."

He stood frozen. "Where are the kids?"

"At Mom's still." She pouted her lips. "We haven't been nice to each other lately. I thought we needed a quiet, romantic evening to make up."

He brightened. "Oh, I like the sound of that." What a turn of his luck—first his dad, then his work, now his wife. Everything was going to be all right. Better than all right. He even stopped worrying about how he'd deal with Haman's payoff.

He was pouring himself a glass of wine, face split in a goofy grin, when the walk door to the garage banged in the rising breeze.

"Forgot to latch the door." He held up a finger. "Wait right here!" He dashed through the garage and latched the outer door. Flashes of lightning were making fiery webs across the sky. "Storms getting worse."

A lightning bolt split the night, illuminating the garage as if it were daylight.

His joy evaporated, draining like water from his being. It first left his head and then vanished bit by bit, lower and lower, vacating his heart, his gut, his bowels. His legs, so recently springy, were now heavy and aching. His body had been filled to bursting with an internal light. Now it was gray and lifeless, the flesh of a dead man.

At the base of the stairs, there were wet outlines where boots had rested, dripping moisture onto the floor.

A man's boots.

Not his.

CHAPTER 29

At home—yes, Curtis now considered this cloister such—he joined the professor who was at the table, hunched over his work. Home, but more than that. Phillip and the professor had become his new family.

His recent grief subsided in the recognition of how blessed he was to have the love of Creator God and the fellowship of these two remarkable men. He'd never again wallow in self-pity.

He unpacked his things, sorting books and belongings on the table. When he came to the package wrapped in a pillowcase, he frowned, unsure of the contents, then unwrapped it, and revealed the picture.

He gasped. He'd forgotten to ask for this, his only memento of his family. He blessed Phillip for correcting the oversight. He'd have to thank the man again.

He owed him for so much already, even before this. How could he ever repay him? He winced over how he'd humiliated the young man, making him show that tattoo. Really! It was obvious he hated it. Besides, he needed no more proof of Phillip's fidelity, had no right to entertain even momentary distrust.

Professor Reuel sat staring at the photo, his expression strange.

Curtis looked from the old man to the picture and back. "What's wrong?"

Reuel turned away, eyes again hooded, and adopted a neutral expression. Then, as if he reconsidered, he widened his lips into a sad smile and whispered. "They were such a lovely couple, and your sister, ah, what a little spitfire she was!"

Curtis fell against the straight back of the old wooden chair, his mouth working to form words. "You . . . knew my parents? Why have you never mentioned this?"

"Oh, my boy, until this week you were unaware of the Seekers. I had no choice but to avoid the subject."

"The Seekers? What has that to do with my parents?"

The professor sat, lips pursed, eyes averted.

Had Curtis heard him right? His grip loosened. The photo slipped free to clatter onto the table, forgotten. "Are you telling me they were Seekers?" His voice went up an octave, his throat closing until he squeaked. "Are you?"

Reuel squared his shoulders, his gaze agleam. "My boy, they were the best of us, and they gave the greatest sacrifice of all. They were exemplary people of faith and heroic defenders of their brethren."

Curtis stood and spun, wandering around the windowless room, weaving among the towering shelves, peering into the deeper darkness beyond as if in search of something. "But . . ."

So many questions to ask, but it all coalesced into one, didn't it?

He then planted fists on the table before Reuel. "How can that be? Why didn't I know?" Would the secrets never end?

Reuel pressed against the back of his chair, distancing himself.

Curtis lifted his face to the heavens, as if seeking an answer there, but found only the shadowed concrete ceiling, the rattling pipes overhead. He sagged.

But Reuel lurched forward to snag his arm, pulling him close, pain twisting his wizened face. "When your parents died, you were too young to broach the subject. Children are not initiated into the secrets until they are of age, and not then unless they have shown an inclination to pursue the truth."

When Curtis remained towering above him, Reuel motioned to the nearby chair. Its wooden legs squealed against the floor as Curtis dragged it out. He dropped into it and stared at that old photo where it lay on the ink-blotched table, overshadowed by the great stacks of tomes, of the fragments.

All Reuel's secrets—all these unrelated fragments, unconnected lives—became shattered pieces of glass fitting one to another in some great mosaic, the greater picture unfathomable other than to him who created its design. A design Curtis was beginning to sense, even if he could not see the whole.

And that great unseen designer had fit Curtis into his own preordained place in this grander whole. A place that, try as he might, he could not escape.

"Your grandmother knew. She intended to raise you in your parents' absence, to prepare you, and to tell you when the time was right."

Reuel rested an icy hand on Curtis's arm, so shrunken with age that he could barely feel the weight of it. "When she passed and your aunt shuffled you off to religious training, you were still too young. It was for me to inform you when you came of age. As you now know, I instead chose to protect you from the secret, to offer you a normal life. You and your family had already sacrificed so much." He squeezed Curtis's arm, the cold of that hand penetrating his sleeve. "But Creator God wanted you, and His purposes will not be denied, not by any man."

Sacrificed . . . What did it mean? Curtis squirmed and

jerked his arm free from the shivers spreading up it. But the chill remained, penetrated, coiled around his gut. Perhaps it came, not from the professor's touch, but his words. "So tell me. Was the story of how they died a lie too?"

"No, at least not insomuch as the facts made public were true. Some facts were omitted." Reuel sank back, brought a hand to his eyes, and rubbed them. He spoke with them closed, as if viewing the past instead of their long room. "As was reported, they were killed in a tenement by a warlord's soldiers. This much is true. It was not, however, a robbery gone wrong. Your parents were on a mission, far from this place, in a small city on the southern shore of Mare Nostrum. They learned they'd been betrayed and fled, taking the team with them."

A shudder went through the older man, and while waiting for him to compose himself, Curtis studied that picture, beginning to see something new in those familiar faces.

"They were hiding in that tenement safe house, along with several other families, when the soldiers came. Your parents blocked the apartment door with their own strength. This gave two other families time to escape through a secret way. Your sister was sent with the others but broke free. She ran back to your mother just as the door was breached. All three died in the gunfire." Choking breaths racked the professor before he reopened his eyes. "I am truly sorry, my boy, and I am so sorry this was kept from you."

Curtis put palm to forehead, pressing his temple to put down the dizziness. "How many more secrets are there? What else will I learn by accident? What else?"

"I am only aware of one other secret of note, and it's not mine to tell. There are many minor secrets, but these involve the work and are open to you as needed. I hold nothing more back relating to you or your life."

For some reason, Curtis believed him, even after all the subterfuge, all the deception. He still loved the old man. "This other secret . . ." He removed palm from forehead, the dizzy spell passing. "It's about Phillip?"

"I am not at liberty to say."

"I've seen the tattoo." He watched Reuel closely. Could he penetrate the bland exterior, see the truth behind those deep-set eyes. "Is that it?"

Reuel's chin crept up, his soft gaze assessing. "Have you spoken to Phillip of this?"

"Yes, he says he has broken from the Eye and is in hiding."

The old man sighed and nodded. "If he has divulged this much, then I am at liberty to do so as well."

Was that transparency, at last, in those eyes? Could it ever be, coming from that old spy? "What's the story?"

"Well, much like you, he lost his family, his entire family, as a young child. You were lucky. Your grandmother took you in. He was made a ward of the Order. From a young age, he was trained as one of the Eye."

"How in Hegemony did he break free? Or even have the independence to think of it?" Curtis thought of the rumors he'd heard. "I can only imagine the level of brainwashing he experienced in his formative years."

"Indeed. As to the details, only he can share that story, if he chooses. Suffice it to say that, when he did defect, he was sent to me for safekeeping, for protection, but instead, it seems I am protected by him." He raised an age-crooked finger. "But rest assured, his fellowship with you is genuine, and he would risk his life to protect you, has done so."

"And did again last night."

"There, you see? It is as I said."

A wash of daylight flooded the room through the opening trapdoor, and Phillip descended the ladder.

Curtis rose to meet him. "I am sorry. You didn't deserve that. Earlier, about your tattoo."

When he held out his hand to shake Phillip's, Phillip took

the hand and pulled Curtis into a bear hug, squeezing the breath out of him. "My brother. No apology. My brother."

Then Phillip walked to the professor and rested a hand on his shoulder. "News from our friend."

"Oh?" Reuel cocked his head, a new gleam coming into his eyes.

"I travel to Nob. Is possible portion of True Text is found. Must be protected, smuggled to safe place, quickly."

Pushing against the table, the professor struggled to rise. "I shall prepare to depart with you."

Phillip's hand shot out and caught Reuel's arm. "No. I move fast, hard. Too dangerous. You stay."

Although Reuel protested, it sounded weak. He must know a man of his years would be of little help in the field.

Curtis gripped the old man's other arm. "We have our job to do, and it's here."

Reuel slumped, palm passing over his brow. Then his shoulders squared, and he nodded as if to some unheard question. "Indeed, we do. If you must leave, Phillip, please let me finish my tale in your hearing. A retelling on the eve of a mission of such importance seems appropriate. This will not take long."

Phillip pulled a chair from the table and spun it around, straddling it, arms crossed on its back.

Dantes leapt into Curtis's lap, and he stroked the cat's head, the soft purrs vibrating through his fingers.

Professor Reuel first said a quick prayer. He asked Creator God to protect Phillip in his coming trial and for success should it be His will to bless them with such.

Then he took a deep breath, and his voice took on a sonorous timber, an unusual gravity. As he began speaking, the aspect of his telling transformed the space. The dusty old room became a cathedral, the worktable an altar, and the candlelight illumed a deeper, more liquid glow.

"This thing I tell you I received as a true telling from my father, as he did from his own, upon pain of death. Know these things I say are true. The first man and woman were friends to Creator God. They walked with Him in a perfect paradise, unimaginable to us in this dark, corrupt world."

He grabbed Curtis's hand from across the table, shaking it with surprising vigor. "Think of it, my boy! No pain, no suffering. Not even death. This hopeless confusion, this distance, this isolation we now feel did not exist. He walked with us and loved us as friends. We didn't search in the dark for Truth, for Truth was with us, at our fingertips for the knowing, for the asking."

Curtis now recaptured that feeling, that treasured memory, his overwhelming joy in the presence, in the awesome love of God. His heart leapt at the thought of enjoying the friendship of that awesome and loving Being, forever and always. What wouldn't he do to claim that . . . well, that paradise?

Professor Reuel let go of Curtis's hand and sank back into his chair, the burning intensity leaving his eyes, his gaze now overshadowed and distant, his arms falling listless. "But something happened. That relationship was broken, that paradise lost. We now wander aimlessly in this dark world, alone. Hopeless. Creation, once bright and perfect, now a realm of shadow and pain."

A stab of loss struck Curtis as if he had been there to watch mankind blown as though by some mighty wind from the presence of God. As if he had himself been torn from that loving embrace. He couldn't stop the cry of pain blossoming from the very center of his being.

Dantes, frightened by the outcry, fled across the room and disappeared through his hole. Curtis reached toward Reuel, pleading. "How do we fix it?"

Professor Reuel's voice had thickened, and he now stopped to regain his composure. "My boy. My son. I do not know."

Curtis stood, his chair skittering across the concrete. "No! There has to be a way."

Reuel's old eyes had gone watery and dull. Next to him sat Phillip, hand on the old man's shoulder as if holding him upright. Reuel's voice gained strength. "I say I do not know. But this I do know. This I do believe." He stood, his voice now booming, echoing through the windowless chamber. "Creator God made a promise. He has made a secret way back to Him, back to paradise. A way to restore this world to its original perfect state." He lowered himself back into his chair and passed a hand over his eyes.

"What is that way, you ask? It is that very lost knowledge we seek to recreate, here in this sanctuary." He waved toward the piles of books. "Somewhere out there is the answer. If we don't find it, don't recover the secret, the world will remain broken, and all of us with it."

Curtis considered the stacks of volumes. How much time had he spent in them? He'd barely sampled the smallest percentage of the collection, but enough to understand it would take years to grasp the whole of the project.

But to recreate the True Text? How many lifetimes would that take?

It was impossible. Hopeless.

He hunched into himself, drowning in the smothering despair this revelation cast upon his soul, dousing the fire so recently kindled there. "We'll never put the True Text back together again. Never find the secret."

Reuel shot forward. Doubled fists pounded onto the table. The flames quivered atop the candelabra while the blow echoed from bare concrete walls. "We must! You do not understand the gravity of the situation."

He pinned Curtis with a glare. "You, my boy, are an eternal being. We all are. When this mortal coil"—he thumped his chest—"breathes its last, our souls live on. Forever. Lacking the secret, without which we cannot find our way back to Creator God, we will spend all of eternity in a torment to which no torture in this world can compare."

He rose, panting as if in pain, and pointed at Curtis's chest. "If we do not find it, you will be better off—never—to—have—existed!" He fell back, hands trembling. "As will be all of this broken creation."

Phillip held Reuel with an arm around his shoulders as he sat, head down, chest heaving. Finally, his breathing settled, and he raised his head, eyes hooded no longer, their ice blue locking onto Curtis's.

"So you see, my boy. We must not fail."

MARIPOL CONCEALED HIS CONCERN. The possibility a mere emotion, such as mortal terror, might affect his demeanor, this he had purged from his being long ago.

He navigated the secret ways to the bishop's private office, marching to his doom with jaw set and head held high. Once at the hidden door, he checked a display that would alert him if the bishop had other visitors.

There was no such signal, so he rapped on the frame. A catch clicked, and the panel opened to reveal a sitting room, plush silk rugs covering the floor, jet-black wainscot topped with brocade wall tapestries, gilt needlework glinting in candlelight.

In a silk evening robe, lush fur at the collar, the bishop sat at an ornate black desk. Lind, the Bloody Inquisitor, sat across from him.

So, here they were, his judge and his executioner. At least he wouldn't wait long for his sentence. Perhaps, with luck, his death would be equally swift.

The bishop wrote for some minutes before looking up, indicating with an open hand that he could sit.

Maripol stayed standing, at full attention. He would finish as he had started, a worthy soldier for his god.

Fingers laced, the bishop sat back, inspecting.

A buzzing began in Maripol's ears, but he claimed victory over the urge to rub away the nasty vibration, even when it seemed about to bore into his brain. The room blurred, his vision swam, and he began losing his equilibrium. His senses told him he was falling.

He ignored them, instead focusing on keeping muscles locked, unmoving, trusting bone and tendon. He was not going to as much as sway. He would not show weakness, would not give them the satisfaction, especially here at the last.

He thought of a bloody silver pin, pressed into his hands by his dying father. He thought of the vow he had made, to his father and to himself.

Without a tremble, without so much as a tic, he stood solid, drawing on the iron of that vow. He would die as he had lived. Unwavering. Unflinching.

The bishop sat up, sealed the document with his signet ring, and slid it toward Lind before rising to depart to an inner chamber. The door closed silently. There it was, then. His sentence delivered.

Lind picked up the envelope and rapped it once on the polished dark wood desktop. He lifted an eyebrow. "Well, your recent performance has been, shall we say, subpar?"

Maripol nodded once, focus straight ahead. "Pardon, your grace." He made no excuse, nor would he. Correct execution was its own witness, failure, its own testimony.

"Pardon, you say? Hmm, we shall see. For now, be grateful for reprieve. You may even *earn* pardon, should your performance please us in another matter."

"Another matter?" He almost let his surprise show. "But the priest?"

"A diversion. We now seek a greater prize. You are to depart forthwith, with all haste." Lind handed Maripol the envelope. "You have unfinished business in Nob."

THE END.

For now.

~

To continue the story visit jawebbauthor.com/free where you'll find all our free ebooks and audiobooks, including the opening chapters of Inheritance: Book 2 of the Seekers Series

ACKNOWLEDGMENTS

This book would not exist if not for the many people who played a part:

My precious wife, who lovingly and patiently supported my writing obsession.

My daughter Erin and my friends David and Debbie Olson, who were alpha readers of the very ugly first draft of this novel. They told me it was "really good." Not true, but it motivated me to keep working. So thank you.

Deirdre Erin Lockhart, my mentor, editor, and trusted friend, without who's tireless effort and extraordinary dedication to this project, this book would not have succeeded.

Stefan Rudnicki, audiobook narrator and honored friend, who saw the potential in this book and was a great encouragement when encouragement was most needed.

Thank you to the team of volunteers who poured through early drafts, both the Beta reader team, and the Arc reader team. Your efforts contributed greatly to the quality of this novel and I'd like to thank each of you personally. Those team members are- Carley A., Erin B., Judith B., Curtis D., Birgit, Patrick T. Crown, Serenity H., Debbie H., Robert J., Tina L,. Miranda S.

To you, and to all the others who have made this novel possible but were not listed here- Thank You!

J. A. Webb

Printed in the USA
CPSIA information can be obtained
at www.ICGtesting.com
CBHW030438241124
17753CB00001B/5

9 781965 915011